NIGHTLY OWL
Fatal Raven

Nightly Owl, Fatal Raven

Jessica McHugh

Nightly Owl, Fatal Raven © 2018
by Jessica McHugh

Published by Raw Dog Screaming Press
Bowie, MD

First Edition

Cover Image: Jennifer Barnes
Book Design: Kevin Kusisto

Printed in the United States of America

ISBN: 978-1-947879-03-4

Library of Congress Control Number: 2018931200

www.RawDogScreaming.com

For Dave, who needs no revision.

Chapter One

The ocean urged her to stop treading. The Capesman sang of glorious surrender. The deadly fathoms seized her, submerged her, and thinned her breath to a distant memory. Still, the woman battled on.

Spent years seemed like fragments of someone else's life. Time had been a precious thing once, fragile as moonlight on ocean skin. She saw it now and her reflection therein, but it did not shine as it once had. The years had changed everything about her. They'd stolen memory, heart, and hope, and her identity lost further worth as seawater glutted her lungs.

The moon rippled above, in another world, and the deeper she sank, the more that realm of earth and oxygen became a stranger. Impossible black clouds billowed in the water. They surrounded and swallowed her, snuffing the light, stealing her senses, and attempting to steal the fight from her body. She'd come so far and gotten what she needed from the sea floor, but she couldn't make it back to the surface.

In the terror of surrender, with the opposing collapse and stretch of death striking every organ, calmness flowered in her brain. She'd failed, but at least it was over. She had only to walk the Capesman's pier, and she'd be free.

Fingers closed around her neck and yanked her out of the glaring darkness, through the watery realm, and back into the world she'd accepted never knowing again. The hand threw her aside like a mildewed towel, and her face struck slick wood with a cheek-splintering crack.

Someone slapped her back, and she jolted forward with sputtering lurches. Boggy vomit drenched her clothes and sloshed across the floor of the boat as oxygen burned through her lungs. Her breath was strained, webbed, and her pulse weak, but she was alive—which meant she had to fight again. She opened her mouth to insult the Malay guard, but his iron grip wanted a part in the argument too. It tightened around her throat, crushing her words to a strangled squeak as he lifted her into the air.

She tensed her neck to fight the strangulation, and her feet kicked weakly for the floor. The hooded man drew her close and exhaled reeking breath. His eyes blazed yellow with glassy black pupils reflecting her haggard face. Jewels of water clung to her shaved blond hair, and her eye patch, askew on her face, revealed the flatland of flesh encasing her gouged left eye.

The guard hocked and spat. A glob of phlegm clung to the tip of her nose, stretching and swaying before succumbing to gravity. He released her neck, and she crashed to the vessel's floor, her stomach reeling. She threw herself against the port side and curled her body over the edge as acidic sickness surged up her throat again. Once she was empty, belching only bitter air, the guard pulled her backward and pinned her to the floor with his boot.

"What were you thinking?" he growled. "Did you really think you could escape?"

His heel ground into her sternum and his toes into her clavicle, but she refused to wince. The corners of her mouth curled upward instead until she wore a face-spanning grin. The guard mimicked her for a few seconds before cocking back his foot and swinging it at her head. His boot nailed her cheek and bounced her skull against the vessel floor. The taste of copper and bone flooded her senses, and the cool breeze delivered her an image of her face slathered in a greasy, crimson mask.

"Answer me!"

She glared up at him, spat a frothy dart of blood, and hissed. "I'll speak no more but 'vengeance rot you all.'"

He shook his head and knelt beside her. "Such a pity. Such a waste. You were such a pretty girl once."

He dabbed a fingertip in her blood and traced the branching veins tattooed on her forearms, over her chest, and up her neck. He licked his lips as he painted her, a low hum burbling from his throat to his belly. She wasn't sure which guard it was—they dressed alike in shadowy shrouds that erased their features—but when he licked his lips and grunted, she surmised it was Camden. Every guard in Malay Prison wanted to reduce her to a twitching pile of pulp—she wanted it as much the other way—but Camden's violence was most lustful of the lot; the kind of fuck who'd use coagulated blood as lubricant.

His cheek lowered to hers, tacking momentarily before his tongue snaked her earlobe. "Still, wretched as you are," he started, "I'd give anything to crush you from crown to cunt."

His hand drifted south, and her knee crooked sharply.

She slammed it into his crotch, and he yowled, gasping for breath as he collapsed on top of her. She wriggled beneath him, trying to slip from his heft, but his meaty claw gripped her nearest piercing. He tugged, and her tragus flesh tore easy, spilling blood down her neck. She gritted her teeth through the pain and punched Guard Camden over and over until his face felt like a wet sack of broken glass. She wrenched herself free and stood shakily, first watching Camden's scarlet-speckled eyes roll back in his head, then observing the boat's position, swaying less than a yard from the island shore of Malay Prison.

A knot of guards clambered toward the vessel, armed to the nines and bloodlust raging. It would be useless to resist them, pointless to run, and suicide to swim, so she collapsed beside Camden who gripped his bruised manhood in unconsciousness. She held up her hands in forfeit, but her good eye remained defiantly peeled. She wanted them to know that her surrender didn't mean the game was over. They had the upper hand this time, but they wouldn't have it forever. Especially since she'd gotten exactly what she needed from the sea, still hidden inside her.

She knew the bludgeon was coming before it was raised. It had her name written all over it—so bold that after striking her skull, it could've imprinted a mirror image of "SHAL" on her forehead.

Chapter Two

How much time had Shal lost in Malay? Five years? Six? Those wasted years of her twenties should have been glorious times of discovery and ascension, not warped into languishing hours of needless rehabilitation. She'd fought the forces that tried to tame her, but her rebel message to the men of Malay was not accepted with quiet judgment. The prison was so fierce the walls had scalding iron fists, and though the guards were mere puppets of Malay's ferocity, they were puppets whose strings strangled both prisoner and faith.

The penitentiary was built upon an island two thousand miles off the coast of Cartesia's Cascade Quadrant. It was nearly the size of the massive quadrant itself, but Shal found it suffocatingly small. No wall felt stationary; they closed in on her by the second, making it difficult for her to breathe. But she never showed it. The more it hurt, the higher her chin lifted, and the prouder she stomped through the densely populated prison. As social as she was, there were still some cons Shal didn't know. Every other week, a new shipment of prisoners arrived, but barely half survived the first six months and at least three died the first night—most by their own design. Death was the only gift one received in Malay.

Besides the considerable number of cells, there was also a mess hall that left much to be desired. There was hardly enough food to go around, and many of the weaker prisoners went without eating for days at a time because of bullies stealing their portions. But forgoing a meal or two was sometimes better considering Warden Grejous's fondness for lacing their lunches. Tranquilizers, mostly, but once in a while, he threw in one of Doc's special mixtures to make the cons violently ill, just for the fun of it. Despite the dangers of the mess hall, there were far more harrowing places within the prison.

It was home for the worst of the worst, though the occasional petty thieves or vandals popped up in the Malay community and were punished just as harshly. Because of the severity of the convicts' crimes and their penchant for rebellion, violations had extreme repercussions. Even minor infractions such as falling out of line during work detail earned convicts a trip to the control room. Outsiders were encouraged to think of it as therapy and rehabilitation. In reality, it was a torture chamber filled with devices fashioned to break the will, and frequently the bones, of whomever defied the Warden and his cronies.

Each machine was associated with an infraction. Cursing at a guard or sleeping through work call earned a stint in the slicer. A prisoner would be strapped into the glorified throne affixed with bladed mechanical arms that swung around the con and slashed his or her exposed skin. It was the least torturous of the control room devices, so a stretch in the slicer lasted longest. The jumper, a five by seven iron box with a scalding floor, ceiling, and walls was a more exhausting punishment, usually incurred by those caught brawling or attempting escape. But the juicer was most loathed by the prisoners of Malay. Though it left no scars, the flexible shaft repeatedly shoved down a con's gullet to induce vomiting left most prisoners as useless as the filth they disgorged. It was typically associated with assault and sexual infractions, but the guards reserved the right to assign it to anyone they deemed deserving. An uncovered sneeze had once earned Shal ten minutes of repeated retching in the fucker.

The control room operated in the bowels of Malay, but the tormented screams charged up the levels to Shal's cell, where she felt each scream as a stitch in her former fractures. The Doc was an expert at disinfection and setting broken bones, but it wasn't a painless process. Within an hour of damage, the Doc would screw a metal splint to the bone, slather his special antibiotic salve to the injuries, and send the con back out into the yard to continue work. Though the salve prevented infection, it burned like hell when it mixed with sweat, to the point of chemically cauterizing one's wounds. Shal had collapsed from the blistering pain the first time and earned a stint in the slicer for breaking formation. The raw flesh of her right leg still sizzled as the guards strapped her into the chair, but she remembered the Doc's grimace most of all. As he switched on the machine, his lips peeled back from his yellowed teeth when he spoke in convivial, melodic rasps, "I wager this will take your mind off the pain in your leg."

He performed these procedures with such lightning speed, Shal thought the Doc could reattach a con's head and have her moving stones in the yard before the blood cooled.

The Doc wasn't famous only for his barbaric remedies. He also operated the ominous dream machine. It was hard to get a sense of the device's function because those who'd experienced it rarely returned to the community with their sanity—if they returned at all. It allegedly allowed the patient to journey into his or her mind, even relive select periods of time. But because it invaded the deepest recesses, some cons were left trapped in their memories, unable to return. Shal wished the concept of getting trapped in the past didn't sound so appealing, but as the holes in her memory widened with every year, she found the prospect of sensory recovery more than a little intriguing. She could swear she had happiness in the past, when she was young, with her father. She couldn't even remember his face now.

Malay Prison was a temporal vacuum sucking up youth and hope and stalling every impulse to be a normal woman—even if "normal" meant wasting away in a garbage quadrant like Diem. But the prison couldn't dampen her greatest ambition. It reinforced the fact that a fuckload of men in Cartesia needed killing, and nothing save the Capesman himself would stop Shal from carrying out that task. Her hope for a good or easy life was dead, but she believed wholeheartedly she would breathe free air again. It would drive and strengthen her. It would propel her through the quadrants, all the way to Skylark Tower in Grace City, where the bastards bathed in electric light and stolen joy. As wholesome as free air would be, nothing could nourish her more than spilling the blood of Cartesia leader, Chancellor Doa. But until that day came, her nightly dreams ushered his happy slaughter and Shal woke smiling.

She smiled now too. She'd been forced back into Malay, but it was no failure. She would try again, and not by sea.

Chapter Three

"Good to be home?"

Shal lifted her aching head to Warden Grejous. His pockmarked face twisted into a vicious grin, and he exhaled the stench of rust and rotted meat. His fingers resembled overcooked sausages tipped with burnt coconut shavings, but filth emanated more from the man's attitude than his appearance, his wiry frame packaged in a crisp, pinstriped suit with polished wingtips. Ty Grejous glared at Shal with contempt as Guards Garber and Bagsa tightened the ropes lashing her to the chair.

He circled her, humming slightly and swinging his cane as if considering a game they might play, then spoke in an affable but glass-gargled voice. "You're looking a little water-logged, my dear."

"Almost drowning will do that to a person. I guess I should thank the Capesman for releasing me, whenever we meet."

"I'm sure you will soon enough," he said. "You didn't really think you could escape, did you?"

She stared into his cold eyes but didn't answer.

"Speak up!" he barked.

Grejous whipped his cane across Shal's face. She barely flinched at the copper tip's strike, but a low growl rumbled in her throat when it sent her eye patch flying.

"So sorry." Vicious insincerity powered his every movement from the way he plucked her eye patch from the floor and positioned it over her eye, to the hostile manner of snapping it back onto her face.

Oh, the things she longed to do to him. She'd dreamt up such delicious agonies for Warden Grejous, but those violent fantasies paled in comparison to the ones she'd concocted for Chancellor Doa.

Ty wheezed. "You know the chancellor will get that patch one day. It'll be the star of the his collection."

Shal's face screwed into a knot as she answered. "Not today."

The warden snorted and leaned against the opposing wall. He rapped his fingers on the glossy oak cabinet containing the chancellor's beloved "Con Collection." During her first year in Malay, Shal had formed a strong bond with a formidable woman named Preya, a twice-convicted murderess with a penchant for playing Liar's Dice. When Preya disappeared after a heated altercation with Grejous and Doa, Shal assumed the worst. During her own quarrel with the Warden a month later, she accused him of having a less-than-wholesome relationship with the chancellor, and in his rage, Grejous threw Shal against the cabinet. The doors flew open and confirmed Shal's suspicions about Preya—other rumors too. Until then, most stories about the Con Collection had been regarded as myth, but when Shal saw Preya's beloved hand-carved dice beside the trademarks of other convicts who'd fallen in Malay, she shuddered at the terrible truth.

She doubted Chancellor Doa liked his hired dog slobbering over his trinkets, but what his boss didn't know wouldn't hurt him. Grejous ran his fingers across the lustrous oak, and his lips quivered as if tickled as he opened the cabinet. He exhaled in delight at Preya's dice, at the false teeth, locks of hair, and shining Sheriff's badge, then eased it closed.

"They were all strong, and they all broke eventually," he said, flattening his palm against the door. "They broke in pain, in shame." He wet his lips, and his tongue left brown slime between cracks of dry skin. "You will be no different."

Shal threw back her head, and a magnificent chortle blasted from her throat.

"I didn't think it was possible for you to get dumber. Doa will never break me, Grejous, and a whiny little lapdog like you, flicking the chancellor's shit off your dick, won't even come close."

Grejous howled and chopped at her clavicle with his cane. Pain slammed through Shal's body like fire through a cotton dam, but she gritted her teeth and blinked back rising tears. He crouched in front of her, but she refused to look at him. She looked into her own eyes instead, reflected in the warden's burnished wingtips. Patches of dried blood made an optical illusion of her face, creating caverns and ravines in her cheeks and chin, and her eye patch was the murkiest pit of all.

He grunted, spraying her forehead with flecks of snot. "You think you're special? You think you have a better chance of survival over the rest of these dregs? Think again, bitch. Every prisoner who contributed a piece to that collection said the same shit, and where are they now?" He pushed himself up with his cane, his knees cracking, and glared down at her. "I've heard it all before. I've laughed at it all before."

She rolled her eye. "Sorry to bore you."

"Oh, you're no bore, my dear. Neither your refusal, your torture, nor your eventual destruction will give me cause to yawn."

The Warden opened the door to his office, and two guards marched in. They untied Shal and lifted her up. "Take her to her cell. I want her well rested for her visit to the control room." He floated his reeking rictus inches from her face and growled. "It's going be a doozy, too. A real treat. Now," he said, curling a finger under her chin, "get this pathetic slag out of my sight."

The guards hauled Shal from the Warden's office with an abrupt tug that wrenched her neck muscles. They bashed her against the scabrous walls of the corridor leading back to the cells, purposefully she assumed, and spat their own barbs as they towed her. The usual shit—her mission's futility, her poisonous cunt, what little time she had left to live—had become no more offensive than a gnat fart after so many years. She instead focused on the sound of someone playing "There's No Place like Home" on a harmonica, then thought if the convict had smuggled in the instrument the way she assumed, he shouldn't put it in his mouth.

The guards unlocked the gate to the containment area and pushed Shal inside. She massaged her aching neck as she strode deeper into the Malay morass, passing underneath the first block bridge where a convict was being loaded into his cell. Shal surmised he'd recently arrived because he walked timidly into his pen like he couldn't believe his fate. The guards helped him accept it with a violent shove however. He collapsed to the floor but quickly jumped to his feet, ready for a brawl. The guards laughed, and his body roiled as if his brawny muscles might burst from his sienna skin. Shal took stock as she strolled past him. He looked a hard man, for sure, but when the bars slammed home, his eyes wore a blend of grief and fury—an air Shal knew all too well.

She passed seven blocks and ascended two flights of spiraling stairs before reaching her cell. It had been ransacked in her absence, and her hidden stashes had been pilfered, but her self-made work-in-progress copy of *The Complete Works of William Shakespeare* remained perched on the tiny shelf above her bed. Her fellow convicts knew well enough to leave that treasure alone. She wished she had the original with her—to glide her fingers over the soft, delicate pages, to hold it to her lips and breathe deep—but after millennia of hiding and smuggling and passing the tome from person to person and back and forth across the quadrants, carrying it with her became too risky. Selfish, too. Few pieces of rift gold remained in the hands of the common man. If Shal lost the antiquity or, worse, saw it destroyed by the likes of Warden Grejous, she would never forgive herself. But after years of nightly reads and recitations, she knew each word of each play as readily as her own name. The verses consoled and strengthened her now in Malay, but Shal more adored the relic beauty of the thing, how something so delicate could permeate every sense and remind her that even something this fragile could survive. It survived still, she believed, and waited for her in freedom.

From the neighboring cell, Morchai pressed his face against the bars and smiled, but Shal couldn't muster a response. The cell sensors detected her, opened and closed the door with shuddering clangs, and Shal's cage slammed closed once again. It wasn't long before the walls followed suit. Sweat beaded on her forehead, and her heart raced. She quickly grabbed her copy of Shakespeare, held it to her heart and imagined it was the original. Her lips inhaled, traveled, and memorized even more of the material as her fingers slid over its makeshift cover. They glided as effortlessly as they had on the original skin of her father's book, and though she had to imagine the sensation of tracing the playwright's embossed name, Shal's pulse slowed to a serene thud.

The book had come from a place beyond Cartesia. Before the slabs of ruined land were divided into Quadrants, before the Council assumed full control, before beasts like the bonecrunchers emerged from the secret chasms of the Earth and the good citizens retreated underground, back when Cartesia was a better place.

By the Capesman's cock, it *had* to have been better than this.

While the Last War and tectonic shift bent the laws of morality in conjunction to human survival, it was God's death that catalyzed the ghastly bedlam of the modern age. God's death opened the rift, a strange gash into the realms beyond Cartesia—notably the one called "Earth."

Shal doubted she would've been religious before God's death made His existence evident. Nor would she have recognized the validity of the foreign stories the rift bestowed on Cartesia—if God hadn't been at the heart of nearly every one, from Jesus to Eurydice. If that common thread hadn't been evidence enough, she would've lied and prayed her ass off to live in the holy days before her birth. Some still worshipped the old God millennia after His death, but it was as one worshipped a deceased pet—more in monument than faith.

Shal's world had its deliverer and its version of Heaven, but the Capesman and the Crossroads didn't inspire the hope or scorn that William Shakespeare credited God in his plays. The bard wrote much about bloodshed, betrayal, and war as well, but Shal thought he would have shredded his pen before imagining a place like Cartesia. While William Shakespeare spoke at length of slaughter, he spoke as equally of love. Cartesia had no such balance. Even the rotten, blood drenched love of his *Macbeth* was a romance in comparison.

Few vestiges, intangible or otherwise, had survived the effects the Last War. Even the word "war" itself had sloughed its old meaning and assumed connotations as normal and involuntary as breath. The concept of love—when compared to that expressed by Shakespeare—had been twisted and pitted into something quite different. Alliance was more important than romance, and because of the world's rampant infertility, those looking to procreate had to couple by any means necessary, without a hint of love between them. Sex was survival, but survival wasn't only about reproduction. Sometimes it was the only way to live through a scrap with Council soldiers. And sometimes two people, strangers, perhaps even begrudging allies just needed the reminder that they weren't alone. That the entire world wasn't cold and hard and powered by hate.

Except most of it was.

Shal had heard many tales of life before the world changed, in her father's beautiful whispers at her bedside. He would spin such glory at night, coaxing her into dreams of peaceful lands, of a life without famine or the threat of death at every turn. But Shal had known little else, and even in her dreams found naught but desolation and the fear that the one person who spoke of peace would be torn away. It was the only dream Shal had that came true.

She did not dream much after that. The trauma plagued her in waking, too, stealing what good thoughts lay dormant in her brain until she was certain no notion of kindness or peace remained.

"Psst!" Morchai called from his cell. "Hey, you all right, Shal?"

She sighed at her book and inhaled the musty pages. "Yes. I'm okay."

"Go to the control room?"

"Not yet, and I don't want to think about it. How many shipments have there been?"

"One biggie," Morchai said. "They're taking on a lot of cons lately."

"Any prospective allies?"

"One in particular stood out. Quiet guy but seriously pissed. Name's Torgal."

She sat up and balanced Shakespeare on her knees. "What's he in for?"

"Broke into a butcher shop, robbed the place," he said. "Killed the butcher too, but he claims it was accidental."

Shal danced her fingertips over the first page of *Titus Andronicus*. "Is that all?"

"We can't all chainsaw the shit outta Senators, Shal."

"More's the pity."

Shal sighed with the flush of memory. For one of the worst days of her life, her heart still throbbed with pride when she thought back on it. The acerbic stench of Senator Danzig's blood, the feel of it slapping her hot across the face as she tore the whirring blade through his sloppy excuse for a human frame. The more the chainsaw chewed him, the less light in his beady eyes, duller and duller until they were useless obsidian rattling in his skull. It was glorious.

Morchai toed his cell bars, the repetitive, hollow dings like an ellipses leading to the topic Shal dreaded.

"Raoul's been a wreck," he said. "Been wondering why you took off without him. Without us. I was curious myself."

"Doa killed my mother, just like I said he would. What would you have done?"

"I wouldn't have given two shits about someone who gouged out my eye," he said. "She tried to kill you, Shal. Her own daughter. You shouldn't have cared whether the bitch lived or died."

Shal's fingers ventured through the pages, into Act Two, Scene Three, where she walked back into her mother's house. The smell of gin, of filth and fear. The anger and the emptiness.

A barren detested vale, you see it is;
The trees, though summer, yet forlorn and lean,
O'ercome with moss and baleful mistletoe:
Here never shines the sun; here nothing breeds,
Unless the nightly owl or fatal raven.

Memory summoned blood to her lips and a twitchy itch to the steppe of flesh beneath the patch. She wanted to think she was better than her mother, but Shal's life was just as desolate—in and out of Malay. She found some consolation in knowing she had more strength in prison than the chancellor's wife had anywhere, but there was little to celebrate in being as hard and brutal as the Shakespearean Queen of the Goths. Like Tamora,

Shal was a fiercely protective and brutal leader, but she feared sharing the woman's depravity as well.

She grunted, shaking away the bloody memory as she set the book aside. The ancient mattress whined as Shal slid to the floor, and planting her against Morchai's shared cell wall, she exhaled a response she often struggled to believe. Today, however, even with a head full of seawater, it was easy to believe.

"I made a vow to protect the weak, Morchai."

"Your mother nearly killed you. How does that make her weak?"

Shal scratched the itch under her eye patch. "If she were strong, she would've succeeded."

Morchai grunted. "If you'd died out there, she would've. It wasn't worth the risk, Shal."

"Maybe not, but getting the root was definitely worth the risk."

A puff of joyful air pelted Morchai's side of the wall. "Bless the Capesman—you got it?"

Her stomach was slightly cramped, and she massaged it lightly. "Yup, still got it. I haven't had the chance to unpack." As she dropped her weight onto the bed, Morchai spoke again, slow and tentative.

"That's great, Shal. But we have a problem."

She groaned and rolled from the mattress to the floor, where she pumped out ten pushups in just over five seconds.

"What else is new?" she said.

"It's Xula."

Shal paused, her body in plank formation. "What about her?"

"Right after you took off, she started rambling like mad about Raoul and you and the Capesman. She kept saying he was coming for her."

"Xula's been crazy for ages." She twitched her nose. "I guess we all have. But she's a special case. Not that I blame her for it," she said and resumed her pushups. "Besides, I thought she didn't believe in the Capesman."

"Well, something must've changed her mind."

"Fear of death," Shal said. "Nothing mad about that."

"Why start fearing now? She's been a vigilante for years."

"You don't have to tell me, Morchai. She's served in the Tamora since the beginning, and she'll serve for years to come."

"No she won't. That's what I'm trying to tell you." Morchai drummed his fingers against the wall. It could be done with or without Shal hearing the thuds, but he did it loud enough for her to catch, to stop her reps and pay attention. His voice was soft and somber when he at last spoke again. "Xula's dead, Shal. She hung herself the day you left."

Despite Shal's long history with Xula on the battlefield, she didn't know much about the woman. Xula was a resilient soldier, but she struck Shal as flighty, impulsive, and—especially following the death of her lover, Helena—quite mad.

But insanity came in varying shades from con to con, and many donned their first lunacies long before incarceration. There was always some man, some Council scum, who pillaged bodies like bank vaults. Thuggish as the dogs were, they knew well enough the most obvious treasure wasn't the most valuable. On the hierarchy of what you could steal from a woman, the cunt was merely one door to her keep, which contained all the intangible assets making her who she was. Strength, empathy, defiance, confidence—these were the plums of war, and Chancellor Doa's allies feasted on them in and outside of Malay, smacking their lips, sucking their fingers, and making it all too easy for hate to bloom in the salted earth of a warrior's soul.

Male soldiers weren't immune either, and often easier to tame through the shock of violation. It was a glaring truth the underground taught their children from birth. The Chancellor and his cronies didn't go for the fuck. They went for the fracture. They went for the moment their victim's eyes filled with the big question: "Do I really need to be here anymore?"

Shal had asked herself dozens of times, but she always had a quick answer. Yes. She needed to keep going. For her sister. For revenge.

For others, the answer got farther and farther away until one day, it did not come at all. Shal could only make assumptions about what drove Xula over the edge, but angry as she was losing one of her best soldiers, the rage quickly gave way to jealousy. Xula was free of Cartesia. She never again had to feel her soul splinter and wilt or convince herself she had a good answer to that big question. Shal hated that she'd seen this coming for years, since she and Xula were as free as people like them could be.

She never worried about Morchai, though. He was stand-up guy, a shark in a world of jellyfish. In his life before Malay, Morchai dabbled in murder-for-hire, but he was a con man at heart. The ruse that earned him an all-expenses-paid trip to Malay Prison was a fraud involving an orphanage and the disappearance of 1.2 million dollars. The Welton Crest Home for Orphans received a donation from Senator Crest who had lived there as an orphan himself. Morchai infiltrated the orphanage in the guise of a parentless youth, and before the day was through, succeeded in stealing every penny of the monetary gift.

Shal, an avid fan of pilfering from politicians, admired him for the stunt, and they became fast allies in the days of open war.

"Xula will be missed," she said, deadpan.

"That's all?"

"With as many corpses as the Capesman collects each day, being missed by the living means a whole hell of a lot," she said. "Separations become reasons. Her death is our motivation to live. Though, it would be stronger if she hadn't done the deed herself."

Shal pushed up from the floor, wiped her sweaty forehead on her sleeve, and flopped back onto the bed. The deteriorating mattress stabbed her spine in a way she'd taught herself to see as normal, comforting—but never homey.

She laid the book of Shakespeare open on her face and breathed in the antiquity. She'd just drifted off into an agitated half sleep when the alarm sounded. Moans from her blockmates followed the first clang, and the bridges filled with armed guards. Shal didn't bother to stand when her cell door squealed open. Let the guards exert the energy; she figured she'd need as much of hers as she could muster. Her will, as well as her pain threshold, would soon be put to the ultimate test.

Chapter Four

Gray slop crushed Guard Toye's mustache. He tugged Shal from her cell and shoved his sneer at her. "Don't scratch or bite, little girl. You don't have a chainsaw to help you now."

Bile jumped up Shal's throat. She didn't have a problem disgorging her revulsion in his face. In fact, it might improve the scent of the rancid mush in his facial hair. But she pinched her lips and allowed him to swing her around, slamming her against the wall between the cells.

"You're wasting your time, Wind-Up Toye," Morchai said. "She's not going to tell you anything."

"We don't care if she talks," he growled. "The sound of breaking bones makes a prettier song anyway."

Flecks of saliva spattered Shal's cheeks; at least, she hoped it was saliva and not his mustache slop.

"I've done every machine and walked away with a smile," she said.

"Not this one," he said with a sneer. "We've got something special for you. Something new. Think of it like christening a ship in the old days. You're a champagne bottle, baby, and we're gonna smash you to bits."

Guard Toye yanked her from the wall and shoved her ahead of him. Shal wasn't afraid she'd die today—they liked torturing her too much for that—but trepidation accompanied the mystery of the new machine. It increased as Toye dragged her down rickety staircases, through the rank winding tunnels of Malay, and closer to the agonized screams ringing from the control room. When Toye pushed open the door, Shal recoiled at the putrid stench of blood and vomit. He shoved her as hard as he could, sending her flying and skidding across the floor.

She slammed into the craggy wet wall beside the equally disgusting feet of Rashus, chief of the control room. He had a fleshy pumpkin of a face, and his head wobbled on his brawny shoulders when he waddled. His flabby chest was bare, and his stomach hung sloppily over his broad belt, but he removed the bullwhip wound around his body with surprising grace.

Rashus lifted Shal to her feet with a guffaw that sounded choked by phlegmy pudding. "We're going to have a bloody good time today. New machine, new results. Maybe even a new Shal when we're done. What do you say to that?"

Shal's gaze shot to the ceiling so she wouldn't have to look at his gourd-like visage. Her mind ventured elsewhere, where comfort and understanding could be inhaled over the stink of the juicer.

"Then I must go and meet with danger there," she said, "or it will seek me in another place and find me worse provided."

He scoffed, "Whatever," grabbed her arm, and dragged her to the newest torture device.

The aptly named "Knocker" resembled a sadistic throne fused with an ancient rowing machine. Shal was shoved onto the concrete plank seat and forced to sit with her right leg extended and left leg crooked to the side. The guards secured her arms and legs, strapped her body to the chair's elevated back, and stepped aside to watch the show.

Rashus placed what resembled an odd metallic tent over Shal's right knee. He jiggled then locked the base into the concrete divots beside her knee and turned two screws on either side, holding her leg firmly in place. Pain prickled through her as the metal constricted her knee, but Shal assumed the worst was yet to come. Rashus attached a formidable hammer to the apex of the device, and his face strained as he cocked it. With the mallet locked in place, he flicked a tiny switch on the side of the tent, and the Knocker ticked like a metronome counting down to pain.

With each staccato beat, another bead of sweat pearled on Shal's forehead. She stared at the Knocker, which flinched with threats for over a minute. Figuring it was broken, Shal searched her mind for the perfect remark to mock Rashus's failure.

Then the hammer swung.

The mallet soared at Shal's kneecap with lightning force and dislocated the bone with a scraping slam. Shal's knee surged with burning pain, and she howled as her leg swelled and purpled like an ambitious plum.

Rashus knelt beside her and leaned his bulbous head against her trembling body. He exhaled, his voice sweetly brutal when he whispered, "Shal, I have to know if the Knocker is effective, so you need to be honest with me. Tell me, love. Does it hurt?"

Shal's teeth were clenched, and she frothed as she growled. "Yes."

"Do you think some cons would rather die than suffer this pain?"

"Yes."

Guard Toye bent over her. "Are you going to try to escape again?"

Shal sucked back her bubbling drool, her lips trembling as she forced them into a grin, and said, "Yes."

Rashus grunted as he unscrewed the Knocker from her dislocated patella. The guards began loosening the rest of Shal's bonds, but Rashus halted them. "Leave her tethered," he said. "Let her figure out how to stop the pain herself. Then take her to the yard."

The guards released Shal's arms and snickered as she fought to free herself. She screamed, the acute pain juddering through her muscles as she tugged on her restraints and twisted her right leg back and forth. With a growl, she slammed her knee against the concrete table. The blow whacked her kneecap back into place, and she sighed in immense, almost orgasmic relief. The delicious feeling was short-lived, but relief remained on Shal's face as the guards tore her free of the contraption and dragged her from the control room.

The rats scuttled through Malay, listening and watching. A crumb on the prison floor didn't last long with the filthy scavengers around. Neither did a corpse. They were always first on the scene when a convict died. By the time someone discovered the body, the rats had already devoured significant amounts of skin—usually the face—and Shal figured their particular appetites were no coincidence. Warden Grejous made no illusions about how much he hated dealing with the aftermath of a dead body. Too much paperwork, too many questions. He preferred to let the rats finish the job than deal with things like respect for the deceased, particularly when he had none for the living. The less recognizable a dead con was, the less follow-up required. Let the Capesman deal with the details.

Shal stomped and kicked as many rats as she could when they dared to scamper around her feet. They weren't the most dangerous of the Warden's allies, but she'd take what slaughter she could get. She squished an especially large rodent under her left heel before the guards shoved her face-first into the door leading to the yard. Her skull bounced off the iron slab, and she stumbled backward, dazed for the moments before the door opened and sunlight stabbed her pupils.

They hurled Shal blind into the dirt, and their cackles remained hanging in the island swelter after they disappeared inside.

No one came to Shal's aid, nor did she expect it. Breaking the line or rhythm of work was strictly forbidden and earned a guaranteed trip to the control room. Even a glance in Shal's direction might earn them a strict reprimanding.

Still aching from the Knocker, Shal refused to spread her suffering. She stood as steadily as possible, her nose in the air and chest broadened by defiance. She tried not to limp, but each step to the stone circle sent excruciating bullets through her bloodstream.

Before she reached it, Guard Gaia pressed his whip against Shal's chest. "Not yas. Not today."

He gestured to the line of swiftly marching convicts spiraling down the staircase into the rock pit. They emerged from the bottom and deposited the large stones into a pile where other prisoners broke the rocks with cumbersome mallets. It was a task with all rhyme and no reason.

"I'm pretty sure Grejous would rather me work as a fanner today. My leg's got a boo-boo," she said. "Wouldn't want to break the Warden's favorite con, would you?"

"Hurt leg, huh? Must be why the Warden wants yas to march." He shoved Shal, and her weight slammed down on her weak knee.

She forced herself into a shuddering semblance of standing and worked herself into the line of stonemovers, gradually adopting the painful pace. She chose the lightest-looking stone at the bottom of the stairs, but it was still damn heavy, and her knee throbbed as she started up. To keep her mind off the agony as she trudged the incline, the craggy chunk of rock testing her arms, she silently sped through the Prince's final soliloquy from Scene Four of *Hamlet*.

"O from this time forth, my thoughts be bloody or nothing worth."

Shal repeated the verses as she climbed into daylight and her line weaved across the yard to the circle of stonebreakers. She deposited her rocks in the pile, each dropoff falling between the rhythmic mallets slams.

The yard teemed with convicts performing these repetitive tasks. Beyond Shal's chore, prisoners gathered dust from the stonebreakers and deposited it into barrels. After the barrels were full, the lids were nailed into place, and the barrel-rollers moved the vessels to the edge of the work pen where they were piled. The convicts weren't given an explanation for their odd tasks, and those daring enough to question it were issued swift and bloody answers.

Shal passed Raoul as she limped in after work. He was on his way to the yard, bringing up the rear of his block's line, when he nodded to her. He was silent, but she heard his salutation loud and clear in her mind.

Telepathy was something of an enigma in Cartesia, and because those with the ability often chose to keep it secret, its genetic penetrance was largely unknown. For instance, Shal, a child of non-telepath parents, possessed the skill, but she hadn't known she had the ability until a more practiced telepath reached out to her at age ten.

Raoul didn't have the luxury of hiding his talent. He'd been forced to communicate solely through telepathy since the day the Council removed his tongue. But for many months after Shal arrived at Malay, his mind was silent too. Their bond was slow to build, and though he and Shal eventually formed a generous discourse, Raoul never explained how his mutilation came about. He was a secretive person, often taken with periods of extreme elusiveness, which Shal, plagued with bouts of amnesia, couldn't judge him for.

But there were times of itchy torture when she sat in her cell and wondered what crime had shipped Raoul to Malay. He was in the prison before Shal but acted standoffish with most cons, and though he was fairly well behaved, rumor had it he'd earned a hell of a stretch in segregation for chomping two fingers off a guard's hand. Shal's curiosity about Raoul was a dangerous but enchanting ember, and the constricting hollow of her prison cell gave way to fiery assumptions. Could he have been one of the King's Men? Or an underground refugee?

Shal had eventually worked up the sand to break her silence with the silent man. His eye was bulged with bruises when she sat opposite him at lunch, and though his gaze momentarily flicked up to her, he quickly focused on his plate of gray sludge.

"What's your story?" she'd asked.

He'd glanced from side to side, and then, opening his mouth, Raoul waggled his stumpy tongue at Shal before heaping gruel into the bare pink bowl of his mouth.

"Interesting... Is that why you gnawed off Flayer's fingers?"

It was a casual question. It was peaceful. Still, Raoul's eyes had flared intensely before his voice thundered a chuckle through Shal's mind.

"No," he'd said. "I didn't have anything better to do."

He was a funny fucker, all things considered, but she'd learned nothing of his history except that he kept it close. Shal respected his secrecy, however. As long as he despised the Council and fought like he had nothing to lose, Shal knew all she needed about Raoul.

The day she realized she favored him over her other allies, she was glad to be standing beside the Ides4 block, since it had the biggest bathroom. When she caught herself fantasizing about the plucky, tongueless man, her stomach lurched with acerbic bursts. She had to push by a gouged, knobby con to get to the toilet, but she got there, curled over the frigid bowl, and vomited up the caustic flavor of affection.

Once she was empty, a small face had ducked under the stall. "You okay, Shal?" Shal spat into the bowl and nodded. "Fine, Kid. Pudding must be off today." The Kid shook her head with a sigh. "The best stuff is either sour or dosed." Meeting Shal outside the stall, the little girl had handed her a wad of toilet paper to wipe the drool from her chin. "Saw you talking—well, *communicating*—with that Raoul guy. I take it he's sympathetic to the cause?"

Shal nodded. "Seems to be. The Council nixed his tongue, so I'd say he has more than a few issues with them."

"Tongue or no tongue, the guy's pretty hot."

Shal had squinted doubtfully. At eleven years old, Sabina was the youngest prisoner in Malay. Known inside as "the Kid," she had been convicted and confined to the prison a year earlier for killing two Council's soldiers: a feat that earned eternal reverence from Shal and her allies. According to the Kid, the night after she and her mother took up residence in an abandoned house in the Diem Quadrant, the building was raided by a group of squaddies looking for spoils and sport. Sabina and her mother fought back the best they could.

"We'd been holding a pistol with one bullet," Sabina had explained, "but Mama made me promise not to use it until it was absolutely necessary. I don't know if it was necessary—the soldier had already snapped her neck by the time I got my finger on the trigger—but I sure as shit enjoyed firing it."

The Kid had described shooting the Council solider at close range the way she might've described a new toy. With the exuberant poetry of retribution, she illustrated the scene for Shal and her cohorts with wild gestures and gory imagery. But like most tales of incarceration, the end was sadly predictable.

The soldiers had pursued Sabina through the house for nearly an hour before capturing her, but the tiny girl fought back. She stabbed a blade of wood through the closest man's throat and laughed as his blood gurgled and spurted from the gaping wound. The men clapped the Kid in irons and whisked her to Malay, where she wore the dead soldier's blood for the next week in segregation.

Resilient as Sabina was, she was just a baby, and Shal despised that she'd been thrust into this kind of maturity. Referring to Raoul as "hot" was jarring for the girl's age, but more so for her environment. "Hot" implied sexual attraction, even romance, and such feelings weren't encouraged in Malay Prison. Outside, either. Only now, in the underground, were the people of Cartesia learning to love again, to trust and let blossom that endangered shade of humanity.

Distasteful as it seemed to Shal, she admired the child for reclaiming her right to feel. She'd had it once herself, she thought, when she was young and angry and wanted to burn her emblem into the world—even if "the world" meant one lonely boy.

She'd lost that boy long ago—his memory, too—and parts of her rejoiced, but the Kid's joviality about Raoul's allure restored a sliver of Shal's own. As she watched him navigate the blocks, her stomach no longer churned or coated her throat in scorching bile at thoughts of his body against hers.

After the first time Shal and Raoul had sex, they cursed themselves for not doing it sooner. At least once a week, Shal and Raoul found a way to be alone, even for a quickie under a table in the lounge. He satisfied Shal in all ways possible for her, but there were times she wished he still had his tongue.

Sleeping with another con revealed an invisible world. Shal discovered consensual sex in Malay was more frequent than imagined. The prisoners did their best to hide their trysts, of course, and they suffered deplorable penalties if discovered. A visit to the control room was the least disturbing. While the bulk of Shal's violation by the guards occurred within the first month of her imprisonment, before they realized she'd fight them tooth and nail, there were some who loved the challenge. They found honor in earning contusions and pulped noses from warriors like Shal and Raoul—as long as they could shove them into cages once their revolting joy was done. On the outside, they'd be dead men, and they knew it. What monsters like Toye and Rashus and Camden didn't know was that Shal had every intention of killing them while they were still inside Malay Prison.

Chapter Five

Over the next few days, Shal watched the new con Torgal during work detail, meals, and the meager leisure time she was afforded until finally introducing herself to the burley young man.

"Be bright and jovial among your guests tonight," Shal said as she approached his lunch table.

The cons beside Torgal quickly transferred their trays to other tables, and Torgal directed his eyes at his bowl of colorless gruel.

"You look nervous," Shal said as her shadow stretched over him. "Am I making you nervous?"

He shook his head, but he wouldn't meet her gaze. It climbed as high as her neck, then shot back down to her right leg, which she favored as she sat beside him.

"What happened to you?" he asked.

"Grejous, Rashus, the world. Does it matter?"

Torgal's face pinched. "It should."

Guard Meister paused in his stroll through the lunchroom. He peered suspiciously at the pair until Torgal lowered his head in silent apology. Once the guard continued on his way, Torgal whispered, "How do you put up with it?"

"No one copes with this shit the same way, and I would never suggest someone function as I do."

Torgal's expression pleaded her on, and she sighed.

"I find it easier to make a sieve of my heart. To keep the mesh tight and restrict what touches me so deep."

"Does anything touch you?" Torgal asked.

Shal smiled. "I suppose not."

"Then why bother fighting the Council? I assume you're here because you want to recruit me, but why would you want to fight for a world that has no love for you?"

"Because I lied," she said. "As evasive as love is above ground, trust is a rarer commodity. The promise of food, shelter, protection—anyone left to die in

29

the quadrants would be tempted to turn traitor for those luxuries. In here, it's worse. You have no idea how many cons believe Grejous's promises of release."

Torgal lowered his head.

"Has he made you such a promise, friend?"

"If you don't trust me, why call me 'friend?'" he asked.

She pushed up from the table, groaning when her aching knee brushed the bench. "Friend is one syllable. Enemy is three. I don't have time for more enemies."

Morchai whistled from the bridge, and Shal acknowledged him with a nod.

"If you insist on being the latter, I will not fight to convert you. Nor will I seek to save you when all this comes crashing down," she said. "Morchai will speak with you further and relay to me your decision."

She turned, and Torgal latched onto her arm—an unwise move. Shal spun around and shoved the con to the floor. Guards snickered, and cons crept closer to witness the burgeoning brawl, but it ended with Torgal's immediate surrender. Shal waited for the onlookers to dissipate and then crouched beside him.

"You can't do your time to get released, Torgal. I don't know what you've been told about this place, I don't know where you come from, but this—beating, dosings, torture—this is your life now. It will be your death, too."

"But I'm innocent. It was an accident," he said.

"You're already in hell. What does innocence matter?"

Shal offered the man her hand. He hesitated at first, examining it like she might've poisoned her fingertips or hid a dagger up her sleeve. He clapped his hand to Shal's, she pulled him to his feet and slapped his back.

"Want some advice? Lose the 'accident' bullshit," she said. "Even if it's true, you'll get on a lot better if people think you're capable of murder. Even easier if you throw around the word 'pre-meditated.'"

"I don't want to get on with these people. Whatever you're planning, I can't risk getting involved," Torgal said. "I have to get back home."

Shal's chortle was acrid and dry—a reaction as bitter as the truth. "Do you really think Grejous will let you return to the life you knew? A con is a con forever, Torgal. At the very least, he'd cast you out as a rogue, marked and doomed to exile. There is no absolution for you or anyone else. Whatever you called home, it's razed, burned, gone."

"My family is my home."

"Like I said…"

The hall quaked with a flush of guards. Hoods obstructed several faces, but Shal knew Toye took the lead. He stroked the length of his bludgeon, his lips wet with anticipation. Torgal and numerous cons retreated from the coming storm, but Shal leaned back on her hands, kicked her feet up on the table, and grinned with cavalier cool.

"And here come those clamorous harbingers of blood and death," Shal said as the guards reached the table. "Time for my mani-pedi already? Or is my massage today? It's so hard to remember after all of those bashes to the brain."

A guard snorted and clapped his bludgeon to his palm. "Smart-mouthed bitch."

"Better than your breed, doll," she said. "What does Grejous have in store this time? Another easy stretch in the Knocker?"

"It ain't Grejous who wants you," Toye said.

"So who?"

"Maybe the Capesman. Maybe cuz of what I'm gonna do to you."

Shal's throaty laugh sprayed Toye's boots with spittle. He shot out, grabbed the back of Shal's head, and forced her face down to the table. He ground his truncheon into her cheekbone and he snarled into her ear.

"You don't think I could kill you?"

"Too many of your higher-ups want that honor, Toye old boy," she hissed. "Wherever you take me, I wager you have direct orders to deliver me in one piece."

The guards exchanged glances then bowed their heads.

"That's what I thought," she said. "You have no more power than the rats, Toye. But if the rats fuck up, Grejous will have them killed. Not you, though. You fuck up, you get demoted to a Council soldier. And I think you know what the big boys like to do to their soldiers."

Guard Toye yanked Shal's head from the table and slammed her face against it again. Her skull bounced off the stone and she wilted to the floor while Toye and his cronies roared with laughter.

Shal's brain swam with blood and gruel, and her face felt like raw egg, viscous and sticking to the cold floor as she tried to stand. She spat blood, and her arms shuddered as she pushed herself to her feet. Tonguing her swollen lip, Shal stared at Toye's many swirling faces to force focus back to her eye. The room had just stopped spinning when he gripped her by the arm and flung her into the guards' hungry hands.

"Enter!"

Guard Toye opened the doors to Warden Grejous' office, and he shoved Shal inside.

Her legs buckled, and she crashed to the floor.

"Stand up," Grejous barked. He crossed around his desk and leaned on the edge. "I said stand up, or else."

Shal wiped blood from her mouth and sat back on her heels, but she didn't rise. When the warden strode toward her, she hocked a scarlet wad of phlegm at his wingtips.

"Your boy-Toye threatened me with the Capesman, and now you're singing that old tune? Come on, Grejee. You sure as shit aren't sending me to the pier any time soon."

The shadows shifted, and a low cackle vibrated from a dark corner of the room. A grin greased the warden's face as a man stepped out from the shadow, dressed in his finest threads and black hair slicked back with a substance smelling of burnt flowers and oil. He bent down beside Shal and attempted to caress her face, but her earnest attempt to bite off his fingers sent him into an amused retreat.

"Same old Shal," said Chancellor Rojer Doa. "Is that any way to treat your father, little girl?"

"You're not my father," she said. "You're my mother's last mistake."

"Then you must've been her first. I have to say, she never did anything so well as trying to end you. In fact, she came closer than any of my associates," he said. "A dear woman she was. A great loss."

Shal gritted her teeth. "Dear enough to die at her husband's hand?"

His smile twisted up one side of his face. "You have no proof of that."

"I don't need proof. I warned her about you years ago. I told her it would happen."

"And she didn't listen, did she? She never did," he said.

"Except when you broke her down. She listened to every disparaging remark."

"Done to death by slanderous tongue?" he replied playfully. "*Much Ado About Nothing*, right? You're not the only one with a taste for rift gold. Do you even know any literature outside of that raggedy tome of yours?" Doa's chuckle was like a snake hissing underwater. "You should come to Skylark sometime.

We have quite a library. The only library left in the world."

Her brain boiled with rage at his audacity at letting Shakespeare's beautiful words touch so vile a tongue. The only thing to quell her rage was knowing Doa was wrong; Skylark didn't have the *only* library in the world.

"Even if it wasn't you," Shal said, "I'm sure you weren't too broken up over her death. No doubt you found a way to channel your grief into some pretty, young boy."

Grejous leapt to the chancellor's defense and chopped at Shal's shoulder with his cane.

She collapsed to the floor again and grunted as she pushed herself back to her knees. "I'm sorry," she wheezed. "I didn't mean to imply you'd try to fuck someone who isn't related to you."

The cane flew again, this time bashing her chin and throwing her onto her right side. She moaned and writhed as Chancellor Doa crouched next to her.

"Still obsessed with that, are you?"

Shal spat crimson. "She was your daughter, Doa. Your own flesh and blood."

"She was fertile."

"And now she's dead," Shal said.

He nodded, a simpering smile spreading his cheeks. "My poor, naïve child. What a cynic you are. Besides, it proved more sensible in the end to sell her."

"You're a piece of shit, Rojer."

He stood up, his arms open as if boasting a golden physique. "I'm a man of the world.. I do what I must to survive. Certainly you can understand that."

Grejous chortled. "You give the bitch too much credit, Chancellor. You can't expect a mangy gutter-rat to grasp the common sense of kings."

"There was only one King," Shal said with a grunt.

"A usurper. A fool," Grejous replied. "Certainly not anyone to be emulated."

Rojer patted his cohort's shoulder. "Would you be so kind as to leave us alone? I give you my word I will return her in one piece."

"As you wish, sir."

The Warden nodded to the guards. Toye removed a choke chain from his robe, looped it around Shal's neck, and handed the leash to Chancellor Doa. Rojer chuckled as he tugged and tightened the chain on Shal's throat. She gagged and coughed, and the Council dogs laughed as she struggled to breathe. The cackling continued as Grejous led his men out of the room. Once Shal and her stepfather were alone, he circled her like prey.

"I have to admit, you look better than I expected, Shal. I instructed Grejous to go easy on you, but I didn't think he'd actually listen."

"I know what you mean," she said dryly. "I'm always surprised when people listen to your bullshit orders."

Doa jerked the chain harder and constricted her throat. Thin breath shot from her lungs and didn't come again until he slackened the leash. Shal fell forward onto the floor, coughing and sputtering.

"Like training a dog," he said whimsically. "Except dogs learn faster than you."

"Maybe it's *you*. You've never known how to handle a bitch."

He snickered as he began methodically wrapping the excess chain around his arm. When it was nearly taut, he yanked. She tried digging her fingers underneath the chain, but he kept it tight as he dragged her across the floor. He wrapped the more of the links around his arm and lifted her up. She gurgled as she clawed at her neck, her face turning from red to purple, and her lips turning pale blue. She weakly pounded her fists against his chest and belly as he guffawed. Her vision spotted red and black, and with one last burst of strength, reached down and dug her fingernails into his crotch.

Doa howled and dropped her to the floor, where she pulled the chain from her neck and breathed painful, webby breath. Blood dripped cold down her neck, and her chest felt sunken and tight, but there was sweetness in watching the chancellor massage his aching groin. She hoped she hurt him enough to save at least one woman or man from his lusty wrath.

He moaned as he stood behind Grejous's desk. "You've clearly forgotten everything I taught you about handling a man."

Shal's voice was strained when she growled, "Suck my dick, you heinous fuck."

His outrage turned to amusement. "You're too bitter, even for me. I could never understand Danzig's affection for you. Even after I gave him Kati," he said, shaking his head. "Another loss. She fetched a good price."

"You mourn the loss of your daughter's dowry over her life. You're a horrific shit-tent."

"Of course I mourn her life. What kind of monster do you think I am?"

"There's no point in subdividing species of demons, Doa. You're equally repugnant."

She snorted out a clot of blood. When Doa stepped forward, she shot out a little more, nailing his shoe with a wet scab.

He snarled in retreat and wiped the offending booger from his shoe.

"Why do we keep doing this, Rojer?" She snorted again, spraying the carpet with blood. "You could commission my death with a word."

"Because you're my property, Shal. You can't fetch me as handsome a price as Kati, but quite a few of my colleagues would still pay a pretty penny for your distinctive charms. They love a challenge." Doa squeezed his crotch before advancing. "But first, I need you to promise you won't try to escape again."

She snorted. "You've got to be kidding."

"I could have the guards beat your legs to pulp. That would also prevent escape."

"Who'll buy a girl with pulp for legs, Doa?" she said. "Then again, your friends are so despicable they might just get off on it."

He sighed. "I can't believe you're all I have left to barter with."

She rubbed her raw neck and grunted. "Whose fault is that?"

His eyes crinkled as his smile bled to a rictus. "Yours, sweetheart. You killed her, not me."

"Danzig killed her."

"Because you startled him," Doa said.

"I was there to kill you." Shal rose to her feet and huffed at the chancellor. "And I don't regret it. He deserved to die with the rest of your Council dogs. I wish Kati hadn't been there, but I'm sure the Capesman took her to a better place, far away from people who'll harm her."

"Better place? Heaven doesn't exist anymore, dear."

"The Crossroads lead somewhere. Even you have to admit that," Shal said. "For all we know, she found the great rift, found God, found the other world. Even if the Crossroads lead six feet under, it's better than here. Beetles and bonecrunchers are more cordial company than murderous savages like you."

"Me a murderer?" Rojer Doa puffed out his chest and looked down on her with an icy glare. "I've never killed anyone in all my life."

"Just because your hands are clean doesn't mean your soul is. You can deny it all you want, but I know the truth. And when you stand before the Capesman, he will see the sins on your soul as clearly as I. You're guiltier than half the people in Malay, you sick fuck."

Shal cocked her head and spit a large wad of bloody phlegm onto the chancellor's face. He winced as he cleaned his face with a silk handkerchief and no reproach.

"I'll forgive that," he said and added sternly, "Not again."

"I don't care about your forgiveness. I only care about repaying every blow you've dealt me, Doa. You've killed everyone I love."

"It doesn't matter who you loved, Shal. What matters is who loved you, and you have few to claim that honor. Certainly not your mother, the one person who was *obligated* to love you." He clucked as he swung his head mockingly. "Like you said, you warned her. You pleaded with her. You pointed out all my evils, and she still chose me. She defended me at every turn, and because you couldn't cut through her to get to me, she cut through you. She gouged out your eye, and you still feel some sort of sad devotion to her, some need to avenge her. She never would've done the same for you."

"I don't stand up for people because they would stand up for me. I stand up for them because they're too scared to do it themselves, and because I have less to lose," Shal said. "Also, I stand because I want to watch you fall."

He snorted and twiddled his fingers at her. "So dramatic, Shal. That attitude landed you here in the first place and has done you no favors since."

"It was my *attitude*?" She tongued her teeth as she sneered at Rojer Doa. "Gee, I could've sworn it was because I reduced your dear Senator Danzig to dog meat."

"I was willing to overlook it if you relinquished this vendetta against me, but you had to be difficult. You had to fight back. That's why I had to tack on the extra murder charge."

"Of course you did. After all, the person who really killed Kati was already dead, right? Now, you're the only one left to pay—for Kati's death, for my mother's death, and for my father's."

"I'll give you your mother and father, but I had no part in my daughter's death," Doa said.

"You didn't strangle the life out of her, but you allowed Danzig the opportunity to kill her, to torture her, to spend what innocence she had left."

"I never claimed to be a model parent," he said, opening his arms as if exhibiting a waistcoat of rift gold. "I'm the Chancellor of Cartesia, and I do have greater priorities."

"Corruption," Shal growled.

He tilted his head with a soft smile. "Order."

"There's little difference when it comes to you, Doa."

"If you despise my world so much, why the escape attempts? Why go back to a world that reveres me?"

"Because I revere you too. Your head especially, how it'll glitter as it rots in the sun. Your wilted turnip of a cock squashed under my boot.

"My heart flutters at your favoritism. Now, if you'll excuse me, this little visit was just a detour. I have far more important business today."

She clenched her teeth and lunged at him with a shriek. Chancellor Doa laughed as he pulled the chain taut, whipped Shal around, and slammed her against the desk. He bent himself over her and hissed in her ear.

"Do you want to know why I killed her? Your dear, sweet mother who worshipped me?"

Shal choked on blood and saliva, and bile joined the mix when her stepfather's tongue slid over the open wounds on her neck.

Releasing the chain, he backed away. "Because I was done with her. Just as I'm done with you."

Chancellor Rojer Doa marched from the warden's office and slammed the door behind him. Once he was gone, Shal melted to the floor, pressed her hands to her face, and wept. It had been ages since her tears came from pity instead of pain, since she'd cried for herself and all the horrible thoughts careening through her mind. She cried also for the thoughts she'd lost, like gaping wounds in her brain that refused to heal. Her mind swarmed with faded memories and seethed in the accompanying anger. She thought of her real father, whose face had all but disappeared from her mind. She thought of her mother, when the woman was sweet and loving, when she wouldn't have dreamed of plunging a blade into her daughter's face. She thought of Kati, her dear stepsister with whom she had shared a short lifetime of happy days before finding the ravaged girl beneath Senator Danzig's fleshy body.

Searching for memories struck Shal's head with acrid suffering. Trauma and sorrow had erased so much of her memory, and perhaps it was a good thing, but she couldn't stop wondering: what, in all those festered wounds, had she forgotten?

Chapter Six

Guard Harris stood outside Shal's cell, rapping his bludgeon on the bars.

"You're pulling infirmary duty with Myrrah today," he announced. "Get your ass in gear."

She flopped her arm over her face and grunted. "Let Myrrah handle Rashus's cock warts for once."

He spun his bludgeon and shrugged. "Yeah, you probably couldnta save the bitch anyway. Better off dead, I say."

"Save who?"

He snorted like an ailing sow and said, "The Kid."

Shal sprang up and threw herself against the bars, which opened torturously slow. She squeezed herself out as soon as possible, slipping around Harris and down the corridor. A few guards tried to grab her as she passed, but she dodged each one.

She had to slow at the stairwell and saunter in. It reeked overwhelmingly of piss today, and Guard Camden was already primed to pummel her at the bottom. He held his bludgeon in a batter's stance that could've knocked Shal's head clean off her shoulders if she'd been full speed.

"Just on my way to infirmary duty," she said, her hands in the air.

He grunted, nostrils flared and pointed the bludgeon down the stairs.

Shal walked speedily down the steps, around the prison core and down the corridor to the infirmary. Some cons called it the red room, due to its floor to ceiling paint job. The joke was that the deep cranberry color would hide the blood, but it actually made days-old human juice more apparent, and the paint did nothing for the stench.

"Sabina, where are you?"

A hand slowly lifted into the air and pointed to the neighboring bunk.

Shal dashed past the man to Sabina's bedside and clutched her hand. The sunburned girl was spread out, her bruised limbs splayed and jaw swollen. She looked so small, so helpless, but Shal knew she wasn't. If the Kid were helpless, the guards would've done worse.

"She's sedated," said Trey, the con in the neighboring bed. "Maybe you shoulda come sooner."

Shal had never liked Trey. He wasn't a Council man, per se, but he shared too many interests with the Malay guards to be on Shal's side. As much as she needed soldiers, she refused to build an army of coldblooded killers and perverts. If she and the underground were to remake the world, she wanted to start with as few soulless cunts as possible.

She made no secret of her feelings about Trey, so he despised her just as vocally. His derisions whistled through his broken sneer, which became emptier by the month.

"What happened to her?" Shal said.

"Broke line to help Allacha. Bitch got heatstroke, and the boys started beatin' her. The Kid jumped Daylock, bit his left ear offs what I heard."

Shal grinned. "That's my girl."

"Lotta good it did her. Daylock feels pain like a tree stump. It might ring through him, leave a scar and shit, but lopping off a tiny hunk ain't gonna do the trick. Just gonna piss him off more. And boy, did he let her have it after that. Beat her, stabbed her, fucked—"

"That's enough," Shal hissed.

"What I heard, cons could hear her bones snapping from the pits. Like wet celery, and she just wailed on, on, on."

Shal snatched a bedpan from the side table and slammed it upside his head. It clanged his skull and spilled rank, fermented urine, which Trey spat out as he struggled to regain his meager senses.

He wiped his face with his arm. "It's your fault anyway. Youngest con alone, and you sayin' your gonna save the world? World starts with the youngest, Shal. You shoulda been on that girl like Council on rift gold. Never left her side, no matter how many stretches in Control you got."

"If she was my responsibility, she was yours, too. Everyone's," Shal said.

He wheezed and dabbed blood from his plump bottom lip. "Not me. I was one of those voted her dead the first night. A kid's got no place in Malay."

"The innocent have no place in Malay," Shal said. "And with the little we've got to rebuild, we can't afford to lose any children, especially not one like her."

Sabina moaned, and her fingers flicked Shal's palm.

"Shal?" It didn't sound like Sabina. The little girl's voice was a strained croak, and pooling blood obstructed her tongue.

Shal grabbed a roll of gauze and called for Myrrah.

"Shal, can you see me?" Sabina asked.

She pressed a hunk of gauze to the Kid's mouth and soaked up the blood. "I'm here, Kid. Shal's here. You're going to be all right."

The Kid shook her head and said faintly, "It was gonna happen anyway. You knew that. Everybody knew that. It's a miracle I made it this long."

"It's not a miracle if you earned it, Kid. And you'll keep on earning it."

Sabina coughed and sputtered crimson dots across the blanket. Shal sopped up the fluid trickling down the young girl's cheeks. The Kid's eyelids fluttered closed and her head fell to one side, but she continued breathing, slow but steady.

The red room doors swung open, and Myrrah hobbled in, pulling a gurney behind her. The body on the stretcher was limp and tinged blue. If it weren't for the numbers tattooed on her arm, Shal wouldn't have known it was Allacha at all.

Myrrah no longer regarded the dead body as the decorated warrior, proved by how casually she propelled the gurney across the room, letting it crash into an empty bed.

"Myrrah, get the hell over here," Shal cried. "I need your help."

The plump, ancient woman hobbled to Sabina's bed, pulled out a tiny stool, and stood upon it to examine the girl.

She shook her head. "Not good."

"I know it's not good. But you're the best healer we've got. So heal her," Shal said.

Myrrah sighed as she withdrew a jar of salve from one of her pockets and unscrewed the lid. She held it under the Kid's nose and said, "Breathe deep, girl, and dream of a good death."

Shal knocked the jar away and screeched. "No. There has to be another way."

The woman hopped from the stool and retrieved the jar. She cradled and inspected it closely, then kissed the tiny crack. She closed and shook the jar at Shal, her face gnarled like a raven's claw. "Shame on you. Don't you know how precious this is?"

"I'm sorry," Shal said. "But I can't let it end like this. There has to be another way."

Myrrah's head snapped around, beckoning Shal closer. "Sabina smells of death, girl. Any healer worth her salt would know she's done. Even a novice like you."

Shal shook her head. "There's too much stink these days to differentiate."

"Lying to yourself won't save the babe. Nothing will save the babe." Myrrah held up the jar. "You want her out of pain, send her out of the world. One whiff's all it took for me to know she was near death. One whiff's all it'll take to bring her all the way. She would thank you for it if she could."

The Kid whinnied like a deflating foal. "I can," she said. "I can smell the death, and I can thank you, too." Her eyelids fluttered, and her gaze rolled about the room as she moaned. "Doc said the Capesman's coming for me, Shal. That's why he let me lay out in the yard so long. Let me bake, he said, make me warm, make me tender."

"If the Capesman were here, you'd see him. He's not coming, Kid. Not yet."

Sabina croaked, and her clotted throat cleared. It was the first time the little girl sounded like herself. "What about the God man?" she asked. "My mama used to talk about God. He was the one who took dead people before the Capesman, before the Crossroads, before the Council."

Shal dabbed the dribbling blood from the girl's chin. "What about him?"

"Do you know the stories? I want to sleep, but I need a story first. Can you tell me a story to help me sleep?"

Myrrah touched Shal's shoulder and nodded. The healer's fingers radiated heat through Shal's body, and though it intensified her agony for a moment, serenity washed over her as she held Sabina's hand and began to speak.

"There was once a mysterious being named God who ruled over all of Cartesia from his home in Heaven—a place as mysterious as the man himself. No one saw God face to face. No one spoke to him directly. But despite having little evidence of his existence, the people of the world believed in him, loved him, and worshiped him for giving humankind this land, for it was once lush and peaceful and all things were possible.

Everything began falling apart when a man of no prior consequence passed away. In the kingdom of Heaven, he begged and pleaded with God to return him to the living world. He tried bargaining, reasoning, and he even tried bribery, but nothing would convince God to let him go. Finally, the man made his ultimate plea. He told God the people of Cartesia, devout or not, despised him for taking away their loved ones. They hated him for letting good people die and letting horrible people live to inflict further pain. The man promised that if God resurrected him, he would convince the world to love God again, in ways we lowly people could understand, for God was divine and too far above us to grasp.

This truth wounded God. Because with all his boundless power, all his knowledge and grace, at his core, God longed most for unconditional love. After much deliberation, he agreed to the man's plan, but he neglected to tell the man that, although he would be returned to the living realm, he would be neither alive, nor dead. Neither human, nor spirit. The man would henceforth traverse the world as 'the Capesman,' God's mouthpiece and herald of the dead.

God was clever and easily outwitted the man."

Shal bopped the Kid's nose, and the girl wheezed a clotted giggle. "Or so he thought," Shal continued. "With all of God's expertise, all his wisdom, he didn't foresee that adhering to a mortal's deal proved his all-mighty existence fallible and therefore, needless. That was the day the Capesman killed God. And in that great disturbance, something happened to Cartesia."

"The rift," Sabina whispered.

"Yes. The rift appeared, and the people of Cartesia learned they were not alone in the universe. From that hole in our world came objects from another place, another version of us, another version of God, perhaps. We collected as much rift gold as possible, books and weapons and technology, but groups of men collected more than the others. These are the men who would later spawn the Council and lord those transcendental gifts over us all. Following the rift came horrible earthquakes, floods, and the world fell to chaos and war. Never before had Cartesians united to pray for God's mercy.

But God could not hear their cries. He disappeared along with his kingdom of Heaven and every soul within it. Only the Capesman remained with his own kingdom to tend. Where the rift sewed itself shut, there the Capesman resides invisible to us until..."

The Kid moaned and Shal squeezed the girl's tiny hand.

"But some people don't believe in the Capesman at all," Shal said.

"Do you believe?" the Kid asked.

"I do. Though, like many others, I believe the original Capesman, whoever that god-killing grifter was, has long since passed through the Crossroads. He has handed his name and occupation to another human desperate for life, and he to another, and he to another, and so on. It is said the current Capesman shares the memories of all others as well as his own."

Sabina's body writhed on the bed, and she gritted her bloody teeth. "Did your mama tell you that?"

"My father. My real father. It's one of the few things I remember about him. Those stories. His voice, how it sounded not quite human in the dark."

The Kid sniffled, and a tear rolled down her cheek. "It sounds scary," she said.

"It was sometimes." Shal wiped away the tear and combed back the girl's wispy hair with her fingertips. "But there was comfort in it too. Even when my room was dim and cold and my father spoke like a snake in waiting, those nights taught me that the people I should fear most, the real monsters in this world, do not skulk in shadows; they stay awash in light. Evil is a gaudy fuck that lives to be seen. Of all the memories I've lost, I could never forget that."

"Why don't you remember him?"

Shal cleaned the Kid's chin of fresh blood and shook her head. "I'm afraid the brain isn't as showy as evil, and trauma is evil's greatest friend. Until recently, I was content to keep those memories as far as possible, but..." She swallowed hard. "It's not important, Kid."

"But it is, Shal. You can't forget who you are, where you came from."

"Where we come from means nothing if we have nowhere to go."

The Kid's chin quivered as her lips curled up her ashy cheeks. "But I do have somewhere to go. And I'm sorry for it. I wanted to be a part of the new world. I wanted to stand beside you."

"You will, Kid."

Sabina's eyelids fell and rose slowly, and she spoke in a voice both strained and resolute.

"Maybe you're right," she said. "This isn't the only world available to us. We might meet again someday, beyond the Crossroads, through the rift." She coughed, and flecks of blood jumped from her throat.

Shal dabbed Sabina's lips, but the girl turned away.

"Where do you think it goes?" she said. "Do the Crossroads lead to a new Heaven? A new Cartesia? Do they lead to Earth? Do you ever think you might walk through the red door and meet that Shakespeare guy you like so much?"

Shal chuckled, but it was sad and low, and a broken breath left her lips trembling. "I doubt it. But it's a nice dream."

The Kid turned her head to Shal again and said, "Dreams were all I ever had. When hope dies—hell, when it never takes root in the first place—dreams keep on going, don't they? Good or bad, they never stop whirling through your brain. You can't control when they'll show up, and you can't control how they'll make you feel. I could cry all day from real life and wake from a beautiful dream smiling."

"They're like that when you're young," Shal said, petting the girl's hair. "Enjoy it, Kid. Dreams are rarer, thinner, and less inspiring when you're older."

Sabina's face spread with a grin, and she blinked tears down her cheeks. "I guess it's a good thing I'll never be older." Her hand wavered as she reached out and touched Shal's face. "You see? This one's the most beautiful dream of all."

Her hand dropped, her eyes fell closed, and Sabina the Kid exhaled a ragged breath. After that, the only movement came from the blood still rolling down her cheeks.

Shal grabbed her by the shoulders and cried as she shook the Kid's limp body.

Myrrah pressed her emaciated claw to Shal's back, and sadness like lightning cracked through her flesh.

She pulled back from the Kid, flew across the room to kick a cart against the wall, and held it pinned there until she bashed it off its wheels.

Myrrah crossed her arms over her chest and sneered. "Sure, it's fine to destroy equipment when you only pull infirmary once a month."

Shal apologized as she caught her breath. Sitting at Sabina's bedside again, she folded her body over Sabina's and rested her head on the girl's chest. No breath, no pulse. She'd heard this dead hollow countless times without it hollowing her own breast, but those corpses were war-made and war-resigned the moment they gripped weaponry. Sabina was a part of the war, too, like any who opposed the Council, but she'd never set foot on a battlefield, never stood allied with her ilk in a marching blaze of glory. Shal was both angered and grateful for that.

She sat up and dried her face. "What'll happen to her?" she whispered.

"You know what'll happen," Myrrah said. "Rats gotta eat."

"No. I won't let them throw her in the pit."

"Far worse has already afflicted the girl, Shal. She's gone now, safe with the Capesman. She wouldn't care what happens to her meat." Myrrah issued a dismissive wave. "But fight for the baby's corpse if you want. The rats will have a hell of a feast tonight."

Shal could've scooped up the Kid's body and made a break for it, but she wouldn't have gotten far. Eventually, the guards would've taken Sabina from her, fed the rats anyway, and subjected Shal to a punishment that might land her in Sabina's infirmary deathbed.

She cradled the girl's face, closed her eyes, and though she could not remember where first she heard it, her soul sang the Kid farewell.

O'er deserts of desperation
And chilling drifts of despair,

A man stands at the Crossroads
Waiting to usher you there.

Through rivers of ruined redemption
And blessings broken in bond
A man stands at the Crossroads,
Waiting to take you beyond.

With horn in hand, he calls you
To drink with those fallen before
A man stands at the Crossroads
To open the amaranthine door.

From the herald's wearied eye
Breaks a new sunset and dawn.
The Capesman stands at the Crossroads
To carry us all ever on.

The guards would come soon to admire their handiwork, and Shal refused to watch them gloat. Shal trudged back to the lounge, her head hanging and bloodstained clothes stiffening as they dried.

The Kid was right. Shal couldn't let herself forget the past. And she couldn't allow the missing bits to corrode what remained. Before she could lead the impetus of a new Cartesia, Shal needed to repair what was broken in her. She had to fill the empty spaces.

Chapter Seven

"Are you all right?"

Raoul was on the opposite end of the block, but his voice rang clear as a bell in Shal's mind.

"Fine," she said.

He had a gliding gait, like he was pushing the ground away as he approached, and with a smirking head tilt, his mind bonded with hers. "You can't lie to a telepath, Shal."

"Some day I'll figure it out." She leaned against the railing, and Raoul slid in next to her with a scoff.

"Unlikely. Especially if you go through with this new plan of yours."

"I don't have a—" She glanced at Raoul, and his eyebrows knitted with doubt. "Okay, I admit I'm considering it. I know what they say, but the dream machine might be my only chance to retrieve my lost memories. I can't fix the world while I'm broken."

"Sabina was going to buy it eventually. Don't punish yourself like this."

"This is for me, not her."

"Then why now? When we're so close to the end, why throw yourself to the wolves on the same day they kill the Kid?"

Shal glared at him and hissed, "The end? There is no end, Raoul, not until we're dead. And even then, who knows where the Capesman takes us?" Her gaze darted from side to side at the nearby guards and lowered her voice. "I need to know what I've lost. Call me an idiot if you want."

"'Idiot' is sugarcoating it. 'Selfish' is better," he said. "You wanna torture yourself, that's fine, but it should wait until you fulfill your promises to the Tamora—and to me. You don't get to quit because you feel guilty."

"I'm not quitting."

"You blame yourself for losing at sea, you blame yourself for the Kid, maybe even for Xula. Is it your fault I lost my tongue, too?"

Shal raked her top lip with her bottom teeth and shrugged. "See, I wouldn't

46

know that, Raoul, because I don't have my fucking memories."

He put a few inches of space between them and swept his gaze across the expanse of the Malay mess hall. "I can try again. If I can read your superficial thoughts, I can go deeper."

"If it hasn't worked yet, it'll never work. But the dream machine might." She squeezed her face into a knot as she grunted. "I know you're scared. I am, too. But if you've trusted me this long please believe you can trust me now."

Raoul backed away, but his voice turned intimate. He caressed her with tone and cadence, like a consoling arm around the waist, or the hot stamp of lips upon the cheek. "You're the strongest person I know, but the machine is stronger. It fights with weaponry beyond our understanding, beyond physical warfare," he said. "Brains are delicate things, Shal. When the battle is mental, muscle is as good as butcher's stock. It'll hang and rot while the machine destroys your mind."

Shal nodded sadly. She stretched out her legs behind her, folded her arms on the railing, and rested her head atop her wrist. "Sometimes I can't remember her, Raoul. What she looked like, how she sounded. Sometimes when I think back on nights with Kati, it's like she's been snatched out of the scene. And then there's maddening panic in me that she really was snatched, long ago, that she's been dead for most of my life, and killing those Council cunts was for nothing."

"Killing Council is never for nothing," Raoul said.

"Even if I can't remember it?" she asked. "Killing Danzig for Kati was one of the most glorious things I've ever seen, ever done, and each day the blood fades in my mind, the chainsaw music softens, and my vengeance slips further away."

"But you have new vengeance to enact, Shal. Doa is out there now, begging for it. Don't you want to live long enough and be sane enough to deliver it?"

"Yes. But I also want my father back. One good memory of his face, of a goodnight kiss," she said. "I need more than shadows."

"There has to be a better way."

She sighed, and then spoke in a melodic tone, hoping it could comfort Raoul as much as he'd done for her.

> *"Canst thou not minister to a mind diseas'd,*
> *Pluck from the memory a rooted sorrow,*
> *Raze out the written troubles of the brain,*

And with some sweet oblivious antidote
Cleanse the stuff'd bosom of that perilous stuff
Which weighs upon the heart?"

Raoul applauded slowly, sarcastically. "That's beautiful. And I assume it means you're going anyway."

She didn't need to respond, and Raoul ventured no more pleas. But as she turned away from him, his hand clamped to hers, and he pulled her closer.

"Come back with your mind intact, General. This world needs you." Raoul glided his thumb over her tattooed skin. "I need you."

He leaned in to kiss her, but the gesture fell upon Shal like the individuality of one snowflake melting into the next. Just another puddle.

She retracted her hand, turned on her heel, and hissed at him: "Need me less."

As she stomped away, Raoul wished she would run back for the kiss she shunned, that she would throw her arms around him and say, "Of course I won't take the risk. I want my army. I want my revenge. I want—I need—you."

But he saw her mind too freely to think it could happen.

Shal didn't once contemplate turning around, and her voice thundered unwavering through Raoul's mind when she approached Guard Neyet and said, "Take me to the Doc."

Enthusiastic guards joined Neyet as he escorted Shal to the Doc's office, whooping and taking bets on how much brain they'd get to scrape from the dream machine this time.

She directed her gaze ahead as she marched, refusing to give the guards the satisfaction of acknowledging their presence. This wasn't about them. For once, it wasn't even about Doa. It was about Shal—her retribution, her restoration.

The Doc was widely regarded as the most vicious of Malay's men, particularly because of his kind eyes and the gentle manner with which he ripped cons apart. He'd stitch them back together too, offering questions of concern that became more specious with each tug and tear.

Shal knew this game of his, and still, when he offered her his hand upon entering the lab, she gave it to him. He led her in like a damsel to a dinner table. This particular dinner spread, however, consisted of energetic multiple-neck flasks churning multi-colored steams and reagents.

When the Doc bared his corncob teeth in a simpering smile, Shal released his hand. His hair was snow white and pulled back from his plump face in a tiny bun, with a few wiry hairs protruding from the top. He smoothed his hair repeatedly, even obsessively, but the chapped escapees never returned to the fold.

Shal hoped it annoyed the fuck out of him.

The Doc clapped his hands, snatched up his clipboard, and scanned the attached paperwork with squinted eyes.

"What's that?" she asked.

"Your file. I must admit, going by your history, you should've been sent here ages ago. Insubordination, mutiny, murder." He tsk-tsked as he shook his head. "I could've used someone like you during my last trials. Soldiers make the best lab rats."

"No one sent me," she said. "I've come to test out your little dream machine and report back to the populace. I wanted to show them once and for all how full of shit you are."

The Doc's thin lips lengthened on one side of his face. "Full of shit, am I?"

He beckoned for Shal to follow him through the room to a matte black door on the other side. The Doc opened it, wheezed a giggle, and pushed Shal into the balmy darkness.

The room illuminated then and became a beast hugging her close with iron jaws primed to swallow her whole. The walls were festooned in barbaric contraptions—scythes constructed from soldered knives, leather straps and clamps and thorny iron helmets that left no room for struggle—that drew Shal like mental meat hooks to the lustrous wooden chair at the center.

"Isn't it lovely?" the Doc purred. "I made it myself."

Shal cocked her head at the chair. It didn't have bladed arms like the slicer, and from what she could see, no deadly pendulums hung overhead. At worst, the dream machine might give her a splinter, and the wood was buffed too well for that.

"It's just a chair," she said.

The Doc furrowed his brow and pouted his bottom lip, wounded by her apathy.

"Perhaps to someone with no vision," he murmured. "Go on. Sit down."

Shal lowered herself into it slowly, but the moment her full weight pressed the seat, the unassuming chair sprang to life. Steel belts popped out from hidden slats in the arms and legs and secured her while the Doc approached, a metallic eyedropper in hand.

"What is that?" Shal demanded.

"You were right, my dear. It is just a chair. This," he said, holding the eyedropper aloft, "is the real machine. This serum acts as a crowbar for the mind. It dives into your deepest, most clandestine lockboxes. Don't bother fighting; the dream machine has every key. All I have to do..." The Doc forced Shal's eye open with a brutal tug. "...is squeeze a drop of this into your eye, and you'll get every dream, every thought, every nightmare. Everything that oughta stay buried will get shoveled on out."

The liquid dream machine swelled from the dropper tip, a milky pearl roiling with silver flecks like shrapnel. The drop stretched and fell into Shal's eye like a bomb of fire and ice cooking the organ like porridge that boiled into her sinuses. It filled those chambers and hit her brain with a painful clang that hammered then sharpened her senses.

The wall opposite her dissolved into an expanse of space so vast and dark it had no cause or dimension until a little blond girl appeared. She blinked at Shal, and a cold blast of wind froze Shal's pain.

Her body was lighter after that, like her bones were bamboo, and she floated out of the Doc's chair as the girl advanced. The young face glowed as if backlit—a lustrous orb that revealed a staggering truth to Shal.

She knew this girl. Long ago, she was this girl.

Shal's shackles vanished along with the chair, and she now floated opposite this younger version of herself. It was a Shal who'd yet to shave her hair, yet to tattoo her veins, yet to lose her eye.

The woman stared at herself, breath escaping in wisps of flowering heat as she said, "By the pricking of my thumbs..."

The girl giggled. "...Something wicked this way comes."

Chapter Eight

"Shal."

A gentle voice called to her. "Come here, Shal, and see how pretty you look."

Depth perception returned with a dizzying bang that shuddered Shal's brain. She stumbled, disoriented, as a man led her by the hand to a mirror.

Shal and the little girl were one again. She gazed upon a long ago reflection like rift gold just out of reach. Even if she could touch it, hold onto and drag it back with her to the real world, she'd have to let go of the man's hand, and no one save the Capesman himself could've forced her to let go then.

Her newly plaited hair was uneven, one braid thicker and looser, with blond hair protruding in spikes. She preferred the sloppier one and favored it by tilting that side of her head higher in its maker's presence.

Shal's father knelt beside her, twin faces cocked in the mirror, and kissed her cheek.

"O beauty," he said, "till now I never knew thee."

Shal shook her head bashfully and pulled him away from the mirror. They walked hand in hand down the hall to the kitchen where her mother stood, her back hunched.

"Luai."

Shal's mother flinched, then hunched deeper.

"Luai, doesn't she look beautiful?"

"Yes. Very," she muttered without turning. "Are you leaving now?"

Shal's father looked down on her with creased, watery eyes. He sat her in the corner of the room, laid *The Complete Works of William Shakespeare* in her lap, and said, "Wait here."

She only now realized how sad he was. At that age, she assumed that expression was *his* normal, *his* happiness. What an idiot she'd been. She wanted to throw her arms around him, that bulky body that held her gently as a silk hammock, and confess her sins—the greatest being how easily she'd forgotten him—but she couldn't move her arms, and she couldn't speak except to say, "Okay, Daddy."

Being set aside with Shakespeare was such a common occurrence Shal had built a ritual around it—the corner, the book, and the waiting. But during the ritualistic caressing and inhaling, Shal listened to the voices nearby as she hadn't listened the first time.

Her father said, "Please, Luai," with his hands on his wife's shoulders.

She shook him off and slipped to the other side of the counter. "Don't do that, Marius. I didn't ask you here. I don't want you here."

"It's tradition," he said. "I thought it would be nice to do it one more time. I wish you could enjoy it, for Shal's sake."

"Do you know what I wish, Marius? I wish I hadn't wasted the past fifteen years. I wish you weren't so selfish."

"Me, selfish? I did all of this for you. For Shal!"

"Give me a break," she said. "You've only ever thought of yourself. If you really cared, you wouldn't have risked our safety to prove you're better than Rojer." Lowering her voice, Luai leaned across the counter. "Which, by the way, you are not."

His throat rumbled. "This isn't about my pride. It's about our future, about finding our way back to what humanity was before the world got so fucked up," Marius replied. "I thought if I could defeat him politically, there'd be less bloodshed."

Luai threw her hands in the air. "But you didn't, so let there be blood! It won't be on my hands, I'll tell you that right now, Marius."

"No, of course not. Why break a perfectly good streak of shirking responsibility?"

She roared in anger. It was what Shal associated as her *mother's* normal, her *mother's* happiness.

Marius scrunched his face and pointed at her. "You're no victim, Luai. You're no martyr. You," he said, wagging his finger, "are the cruelest of opportunists."

"As it pertains to ambition and power? Yes, I suppose I am," she replied. "I'd rather be wife to a Chancellor over a renegade. I'd rather mother the free world than—" She narrowed her eyes at Shal and hissed. "She's ungrateful, and she hates me."

"I doubt she does," Marius said. "But if so, I wouldn't blame her."

"Fine. Take her when you leave. Hide underground like the rat king you are and raise her to be a young corpse."

"I'm not leaving, Luai. You're pushing me away." Marius lowered his head with a heavy exhalation. He slammed his fist on the counter and spun around to face Shal, who gazed up at him over the cracked book spine. He sighed. "You know I can't take her with me. The future of the underground is still so delicate, so dangerous, and

I can't bring her into the field. Council threats aside, my army is built from every manner of soldier, every human opposing Doa from righteous to..." He shook his head. "I can't trust them enough to put Shal's life in their hands."

"Oh yes, let's replace Rojer with people you can't trust," Luai said. "Like it or not, Marius, *this* is how you survive. This is how your daughter gets food and clean water and that rift gold she's tearing to pieces. The Council pays for it all and has been for centuries. Your tales of William Shakespeare, your legends about magical roots in the sea, God, the Capesman, all of it—it's a waste of time. It's a waste of life. And now that you're banished—" She clapped her hand to her mouth and squeezed her eyes shut.

Shal thought her mother might be crying until a soprano cackle bounced from her throat.

"I don't even know why I'm talking to you about this," Luai said. "You're not even Diem trash, that's how low you are. You're not Quadrant. You're not underground. You're nothing to Cartesia. You're nothing to me. All these years and a child together, and you still couldn't commit."

Marius stood tall, his chin jutted. "I have been committed to my daughter since the day she was born. She's precious, Luai."

"She's not precious until she bleeds, Marius. *If* she bleeds." Luai shook her head. "Actually, I don't know what I was thinking offering her to you. Rojer would be pissed to lose her before we know if she's fertile. Besides, I know he's excited to introduce Shal to his daughter, Kati. A Chancellor's child could be a wonderful influence on her. She can teach her to be polite, abide the law, and support her new father—her *only* father—in all things."

In all the arguments her parents had, Shal had never seen her father fly at her mother the way he did then. He dashed around the counter, grabbed her as she fled, and shoved her face-first against the cupboards.

Luai growled her laughter. "Look at you, Marius. Look at what you're doing in front of your child. Is this how you want her to grow up? How you want her to remember you?"

He released Luai's neck and backed away, panting.

The book of Shakespeare sat open on Shal's lap with as wide a maw of pages as the one on the little girl's face.

Her father ran to her, knelt at her feet, and pressed his forehead to hers if as trying to transmit the history of Him to the future of Her.

Obviously, it hadn't worked.

"You can't erase me from her life, Luai," Marius said.

"Why not? The rest of the world is doing it. You're banished on pain of death, your name included. Why should I exert any effort to ensure Shal remembers you?"

"That doesn't mean she won't."

Luai grabbed the back of his shirt and tugged until he stood to face her. She was the one who pushed this time, the one who pinned him to the stone island.

"Yes, it does," she said in cruel confidence. "Even if pieces of you linger, I'll make sure she knows the kind of men you were: a slapdash renegade who abandoned us. I'll tell her you died the worst of dregs."

"No. Please don't do this."

"I begged you not to challenge Rojer. You didn't listen to me, and now you're blaming me for your failure? You seem to think I owe you something, but there's no ring on this finger, Marius. We don't have a happy home born of love or trust. I owe you nothing."

"Doa won't give you want you want. He's worse, colder, than I ever was. He won't marry you."

"He's already asked, and I've accepted," she said, beaming. "If you don't believe me, I can call my fiancé."

Marius stepped toward Shal, and Luai reached into a drawer and removed a two-way radio. "One of ten in Cartesia, and it's mine. I can have Council boys here with one word, and they'll take you out in chains. You could escape, I assume. You probably wouldn't end up in Malay, but they'd arrest you, beat the shit out of you, and all in front of Shal," she said. "Go ahead. Your corruption will be easier to sell."

His hands were boulders of trembling fury, his body so erect Shal thought her father might never bend again.

But he did. He was relaxed when he crouched in front of his daughter, his hands soft as petals against her cheeks. He held her, kissed her once upon the lips, and dropped his head with a sob.

Her mother stood behind him, arms crossed and body clenched onto the tension Marius released. She said, "Say goodbye, Shal," and the little girl lifted her father's face.

She kissed him back and said, "Goodbye, Daddy."

It was the only time Shal recalled seeing her father cry.

Time moved like a dream, with beautiful portals, cliffs, and avenues that went unquestioned as Shal sailed to the next forgotten memory. She stood in the hall of her mother's house, her mind whirring with the natural curiosity of youth and that of an amnesiac, waiting for this day to unfold.

She still sported the messy memory of her now dead father's fingers in her hair, though it was dulled by dirt and ragged strands. Her mother had tried to coax her to untangle it before today, but she'd refused. What was so important about today anyway?

A shadow stretched down the hallway, and Shal's eyes filled with tears. She knew what day this was now. It was the day she was brought to the new house in Ides, where she met Chancellor Doa. But more importantly, it was the day she met his daughter, Kati.

He stomped toward Shal, his face shrouded in gloom and finger pointed.

"You are going to stop bothering your mother and me," he said, his face a cold bulge of ferocity. "Repeat that."

Shal scrunched her nose and folded her arms over her chest. She thought it was answer enough, but when Chancellor Doa commanded her again, she curled her lip, stomped her foot, and said, "No."

He smiled. This man was used to hearing the word "no," but he obviously gave zero fucks.

He grabbed her by the chin, softly at first as if observing her potential as a good, sweet girl. Then his fingertips pressed into her jaw and he pulled her so close he wrenched a muscle in the back of her neck. She wailed when he tugged her. She decayed when he kissed her.

The kiss was hard and cold like a half-scaled fish pressed to her lips. *That* Shal remembered all her life. But as much hate as Doa seeded within her, there was a splendid speck of gratitude in knowing a decent man had kissed her once before.

"You're going to be a good girl, Shal," Chancellor Doa said. "Even if I have to do something bad to convince you."

His hand shot out like a secret knife that knotted and shredded Shal's messy braid, and she screamed as Rojer dragged her down the hall by her hair. He rounded the corner, flung open the closet door, and pushed her inside with his foot. With his fingers still clamped around the braid Shal's father had lovingly constructed a month prior, Doa slammed the closet door closed and flipped the lock.

Shal tried to pull her hair free, but it was hopelessly trapped, and so was she. The pull string for the overhead light was out of reach, so she felt around in the darkness for something that could aid her—a flashlight, matches, anything to shed some light on her dilemma. She felt the shelving beside her with cautious fingers, but blind caution stood no chance against whatever sliced open her thumb. She winced and sucked on her throbbing flesh as she patted the shelf, again discovering the offending pair of scissors. She gripped the handle and opened the blades as she guided the scissors to her wedged messy braid. With a squeak, she closed the blades, and sadness streamed through her veins.

It took several snips before the final, dry cut released her. She sprang to her feet and waved her hand overhead until she found the pull string. She tugged, and her eyes stung from the blast of light.

Shal pounded the closet door. She screamed for her mother. She promised she'd be good and quiet and never talk back to her stepfather again if someone would just let her out. But Shal convinced no one.

For hours, she sat on the floor, rocking and watching the walls inch ever nearer. They closed in on her in a way that thickened her breath and weakened her limbs. To distract herself from the shrinking prison, she continued snipping at her hair. One side, then the other, until she'd hacked away as much as she could. With nothing left to cut, she turned the scissors on the door.

After inflicting more than a dozen stab wounds, the doorknob jiggled, and Shal dropped the shears. She figured her mother would be her savior, that she'd throw open the door, enfold Shal in her arms, and beg her forgiveness for bringing such a mean man into their lives. But when the door opened, Shal instead looked up at the tan heart-shaped face of another little girl.

The girl's upper lip was curled in bewilderment, and she held the other end of Shal's braid in her hand. She passed it over, but it fell apart in Shal's fingers, joining the rest of the chopped locks on the closet floor.

"What're you doing in here?" the girl asked.

Shal shrugged. After so many hours of shedding tears and hair, she couldn't articulate the exact reason she'd been confined in the closet.

The girl stuck out her hand and helped Shal to her feet, her cheeks pink as the first strokes of sunset.

"I'm Kati," she said, giving Shal's hand a firm shake. "Are you Miss Luai's kid?"

She nodded. "My name's Shal."

A smile spread over Kati's face. "I knew that," she said. "Let me guess— Daddy locked you in there."

Shal tugged on her bottom lip, her face glazed with cold sweat. "I guess he did. I was bugging him and Mom."

"Something's always bugging him."

"Mom said they're getting married, so I figured I should get to know him. But maybe I know all I need to know," she said. "I'm sorry, but your dad is kind of—well—"

"An asshole?" Kati's eyebrows were raised, but her lips were pinched. They hadn't moved, but Shal had heard the girl loud and clear.

Kati blinked rapidly, and her mind spoke to Shal's. "Can you hear me?" she asked.

Shal furrowed her brow and thought, "Yes." She laughed out loud, and Kati hushed her.

"We should keep it to ourselves for now. Daddy wouldn't like it."

"Right. Because he's—" Shal closed her mouth and continued silently, "— an asshole."

Her new sister sighed. "Exactly. And you don't know the half of it yet."

"What do you mean?"

Kati Doa's lips pursed and she averted her eyes. "I don't think you understand what's going to happen now that you're his daughter. And I don't want to scare you." The girl sniffled and rubbed her nose, frowning. "Did you know I'm engaged?"

Shal squeaked. "To be married? How old are you?"

"Eight. But I've known about the marriage since I was seven."

"Who are you marrying?"

She shrugged. "I don't know yet. The bidding won't start until they're sure I'm fertile. Until I bleed." She gulped and balled her hands under her chin, which dimpled with a stifled lament. She breathed out slowly and steadied her trembling lips. "Let's talk about you instead. What happened to your father?"

"He left," Shal replied. "He left me with her—and with the chancellor—to be ignored, yelled at, torn down, torn up, and—" Shal tugged at her uneven spikes of hair, and her jaw quivered. "I don't think my daddy's coming back. My mom said he's probably dead."

Shal flinched when Kati draped her arm around her shoulder and pulled her into an unexpected hug. She wanted to pull away—her father was the only person who'd squeezed her like this. He was the only one who actually cared whether the gesture fixed her. But this girl cared, too. She felt it in the way Kati rubbed her back, how she hooked her chin to her stepsister's shoulder and sang softly a song about the Capesman.

*"From the herald's wearied eye
Breaks a new sunset and dawn.
The Capesman stands at the Crossroads
To carry us all ever on."*

Kati released her new sister and towed her down the hall. She was taller than Shal with more control over her body, but her gait revealed her tender age. Though she held her head high as she walked, her steps were short and timid, especially before turning corners. She threw multiple glances back at Shal as they walked, though, smiling as if to say, "It'll all be okay."

But Shal knew it wouldn't. She knew the future too well.

Reminiscence took flight, and Shal's knowledge accumulated. Even with her brain still hazy over the following three years, Shal was neutered into lucidity, forced to watch the young girls grow up suffering and crooked. There were many nights she would've been happy leaving in oblivion—evenings of rage and violence that ended with Shal and Kati scarred by the malicious Chancellor Doa—but with each vomitus memory, new objectives pooled in Shal's young mind: *Save your sister. Save yourself. If you have time, try to save your mother.*

The latter would eventually float off her to-do list. Luai discounted the pain her new husband inflicted upon the girls, distracted by baubles and decor and the promised majesty of life as the chancellor's wife. There were times when Shal caught eyes with her mother and thought she felt a stream of silent apologies, but neither silence nor remorse could save her. The young girls needed bellowing action.

Three months after moving to Ides, Shal confronted her mother and begged for help. Luai said she'd do what she could—which proved to be little when she moved out of the house days later and into Skylark Tower with her husband.

Two Council soldiers took her room in the house to ensure Kati and Shal remained safe, and surprisingly, the girls relished that time. Rojer spent much of the next few months in Skylark trying to impregnate his new wife and didn't visit the house often. Luai's fertility had been one of the major selling points, and when she didn't conceive immediately, the entirety of Cartesia felt the chancellor's frustration. Evictions became more frequent, more people lost their jobs to Council men, and the Capesman had a lot more work to do.

Luai's relationship with her daughter deteriorated to the occasional vitriolic visit. She threw many barbs Shal's way, ranging from her appearance—"Can't you even attempt to look like a girl?"— her mental capacity—"You're too stupid to know you sound insane"—and Shal's place in the spectrum of humanity—"You're defiant, mouthy, and infertile. You are obsolete."

Still, Shal believed her mother had simply been corrupted by the Council and begged her to leave the chancellor, to flee Ides entirely, so they could return to a normal life.

"We could be happy somewhere else, maybe even underground. We can take Kati and go today. The King will protect us."

"There is only one King, and he is my husband and Chancellor of Cartesia," Luai said, glancing back at the soldiers rifling through her former cabinets. "You two. You shouldn't be letting her get swept up in this King's Men nonsense."

"Our apologies, ma'am," said one of the soldiers, his eyes averted.

"Apologies won't stop it. She needs a good whack to teach her a lesson."

The soldier cleared his throat. "If you think that's necessary."

Luai marched to the Council boy, her eyes narrowed and lips tight. "Are you questioning the chancellor's wife?" She looked him up and down and inspected his cherubic bronze face. "You're young for a soldier, aren't you? Maybe you need some more time in the trench to harden up."

"I might only be sixteen, but I've proved myself repeatedly in the field, ma'am. My father was Council and his father before him."

She sneered like she might spit in his face. "What's your name, boy?"

"Mason, ma'am."

Luai grabbed Mason by his chin and hissed. "Shape up, or I will have my husband find a job better suited to your porridge spine. Cleaning the Pit in Malay, perhaps?"

"Yes, ma'am. I will do my duty, ma'am."

Mason grabbed Shal by the arm and whipped her against the wall.

She wilted to the floor, and Kati ran to her side. Both girls wept as Luai stomped out of their lives, leaving them alone with the ambitious Council boys.

Shal feared the soldiers in the house. Though the rash of beatings and violations occurred less frequently in the Ides Quadrant, she figured the chancellor wouldn't kick up a fuss if the soldiers made a move on her, but the boys kept their distance. Mason, especially, had been kind, even respectful, before Luai suggested he toughen up. Even after, the slam against the wall wasn't repeated, and he expressed his guilt over the incident in whispers that found Shal alone one night.

She sat on the porch, watching the plumes of Ides steel industry disappear into the stars, when Mason approached, timid and nearly inaudible.

"I'm sorry," he said.

Shal didn't turn her head to him. "I'm surprised Council boys even know that word. I figured they erased it from your vocabulary as toddlers. Especially a hereditary soldier like you." She expected the incensed man to leave her then, maybe throttle her on his way, but he exhaled a shocking truth instead.

"I hate them."

Shal finally gave Mason her gaze.

His eyes gleamed with regret, and his breath was deep and slow like he was holding back a career-ending sob. He licked his lips and directed his words at the ground.

"I hate Chancellor Doa," he said. "I hated Chancellor Bakkus before him. I hated my father and his father and all the way back to the first fucks who worshipped Chancellor Payne."

Shal's face crinkled. "You're trying to trap me. You heard me talking about the King's Men, and you're trying to get me to say something that'll get me arrested. I won't fall for it."

"If I wanted you arrested I wouldn't have to trap you. I could lie and say you attacked me. I doubt Doa would take much convincing to throw you in Malay."

"Then why—"

"Because I've heard stories about the underground, how bare it is, how hard, and I've still wept wishing I were there instead of Grace City." Mason lifted his gaze and stared deep into Shal's eyes. "I think you feel the same way."

She shook her head. "I don't want the underground. I want Cartesia. And I want the Council as dead as God."

Mason laid his hand atop Shal's, and she flinched. "Please don't be afraid of me."

She said, "I'm not," but her palms perspired with the lie. She was more scared of Mason than ever. If he was honest about his hatred of the Council, he was the first soldier of his kind.

But over the next several days, she learned Mason wasn't alone in his dream to leave the chancellor's employ. Dozens of heredity soldiers wanted out of the family business, along with their sisters, mothers, and whorehouse brothers. And Shal wanted to meet them all.

Within one month of secretly allying with Mason, Shal had built an army fifty strong and counting. The second soldier watching her and Kati had an "accident" on the basement stairs and was promptly replaced by a Council boy dedicated to Shal's cause.

As for what she would call her army, Shal turned to *The Complete Works of William Shakespeare*. It felt to her like the pages never cooled. Each sheet was a lively ghost of her father's memory, radiating love as she selected the perfect name for her hate.

Gathered in the basement of one of the chancellor's many homes, Shal stood before her diverse throng of allies, rift gold in hand, and proclaimed: "You're here because you want a better life—a world without the Council. But like me, you aren't willing to hide underground until things change. You want to exact change yourself, and you refuse to let any of those Skylark fucks stand in your way. You will not hear their weeping. You will not bend to their pleas or promises. You will spill their blood with joy. You are Tamora," Shal bellowed. "Queen of the Goths, and Shakespeare's most merciless cunt."

The Tamora cheered, and Shal kissed the soft leather cover of her rift gold. She thought of her father then, but her mother's face appeared in her mind when she said, "Now let's get out there and show those fuckers who's obsolete."

She was a thirteen-year-old woman commanding warriors thrice her age, but no one contested her authority. She demanded respect, and the army gave it willingly.

Mason also gave himself willingly. He offered her everything he had—his heart most of all, which Shal admitted she didn't know how to handle. She wasn't sure if she loved him, but she let him love her enough for both. They were inseparable in the early days of the Tamora, slaughtering what Council they could and returning home to convalesce in each other's arms. Shal relished every drop of Council blood she spilled in those days, and though she lost a significant amount herself, the trails of ink Mason tattooed over her veins, down her arms, up her throat, and across her heart, reminded her she always had more, pumping hot and hard, like a raging moat between Kati and Rojer Doa.

It wasn't long before the Council found them at home. At a moment's notice, Shal and Kati had to leave everything behind—the book of Shakespeare, included—to flee the chancellor's wrath. The girls and Mason led the Tamora from Ides for safety, to expand their numbers, and to protect Kati Doa from her suitors. When the girl bled, the bidding war kicked into overdrive, and Council boys ventured out like caustic fingers to comb the world for the chancellor's daughter. The Tamora were always on the move, and though they never joined the King's Men in battle, both armies understood that anyone under orders to deliver Kati Doa to the chancellor should be eliminated.

The search intensified when Senator Danzig won the honor to marry the illustrious Chancellor's daughter, but—as Shal frequently proclaimed—he'd have to find her first.

The dream machine roiled Shal through the next eight years. News reached Shal of Luai's confirmed infertility, and she returned to Ides for a last ditch attempt at saving her mother. It was not a day she wanted to revisit. When the memory unfolded, Shal shut her eyes to that day of begging and butchery. When it ended, she only had one eye to open.

Time sped as she readjusted to monocular vision. Once it slowed again and propelled the next memory into her senses, Shal found herself in Cessa County Park mere weeks before her incarceration, leaning against a rusted thresher.

Kati stood beside her, wringing blood out of a washcloth. As she cleaned and applied antiseptic to the wounds Doa's men had dealt her sister, Shal grunted and pulled away.

"Hold still," Kati said. "If you'd cleaned up after the fight like I told you, it wouldn't hurt so much."

"Addressing my army was more important."

"Especially with a bloody face, right? It makes you look tougher," Kati murmured.

Shal flipped up her eye patch. The fresh stab wound still oozed, and pain flickered through her face when she waggled her eyebrows. "What, you don't think I look tough right now?"

"This was never about what I think," Kati said. She dabbed antibiotic on her sister's wound, and Shal hissed.

She snapped her eye patch in place. Bolts of pain shot through her brain as she squinted at her sister. "You think justice isn't a good enough reason? Okay. Have at it, Kati. What do you think?"

Kati screwed the cap on the bottle of antiseptic and dropped it in her knapsack. "I think 'justice' is a funny word for 'bloodlust.'"

"You think that little of me?"

She shook her head. "I think that little of me. I'm the reason you started fighting. Whatever you are now, it's my fault."

"No, Kati. It all goes back to Doa. He hurt you. He hurt me, all of us. He started this."

Kati crouched as she buckled her knapsack, her voice a somber whisper. "But I can end it."

Captain Xula jogged to the pair, tying her long onyx braids into a tight ponytail. She was glazed with sweat and wiped it away with the back of her hand, thumbing the looping scar below her left eye. A soldier named Helena, just up from the underground and eager as hell to issue some familial revenge, tailed the Captain and joined her side with a timid salute.

"What do you have, Captain?"

"Good news for a change," Xula said. "It took almost a decade and a dozen peace offerings, but it finally worked." The Captain's face brightened in pride. "They're coming, General."

"Who's coming?" Kati asked.

Shal beamed at her sister, unpegged her sword from the dry Cessa County soil, and said, "I'm finally going to meet the King's Men."

The King's Men and Tamora's objectives were aligned, but they kept their business limited to specified quadrants so neither would complicate the other's machinations. Shal's soldiers were typically younger, more rambunctious, brothel escapees and underground rebels, so convincing them to check their egos in favor of the Council's systematic disablement took numerous negotiations and correspondence. In the end, it was decided best for all that the veteran King's Men keep watch over the most Council-laden quadrants, Cascade and Ides. The underground bases surrounding Skylark were the King's strongholds, and Shal was still too raw a leader to prove her worth to that exceptional man.

Until now. And she didn't want to blow it.

Shal beckoned Kati and Xula to follow as she marched through the park. "Xula, communicate our gratitude to the King and let him know we'll secure a safe place to meet. I'll send word—"

"You don't have time," Helena said.

Shal stopped and snapped at the new recruit. "Did you just you tell me, of all the things I've lost, I've also lost control over my life?"

"No, General."

"Then you're saying time doesn't favor me."

Xula stuck her head into the standoff. "She's saying the King's Men are already here, General."

Shal's back straightened, and she scanned the expanse of Cessa County Park. While some of her soldiers were leaned against playground equipment as they prepped their weapons, the brunt were gathered on the precipice of the crested park, sharpening, buffing, and stowing as many blades as they could carry. No sign of the King's Men yet.

"How close?" she asked Xula.

"Mason was scouting, found them half a league away."

"Why isn't he telling me this himself?"

Helena snorted. "It doesn't take a genius to figure that out, after the way you dropped him."

The girl wasn't wrong, but one twitchy glare from Shal sent her into an apologetic retreat.

"Excuse her, General. She can make a drunk bonecruncher look graceful sometimes, but she'll learn. I promise you that," she said. "Anyway, the visit's a good surprise for once, don't you think?"

Shal exhaled dryly. "Put the Tamora on alert, Captain. Make sure every soldier is armed."

"Why?"

"Because I don't trust good surprises, either," Shal said. "How many of our guns aren't for show?"

Xula lifted her chin. "Six with yours. Three pistols. Two blasters. We don't have the bullets to blast much, though. One line, maybe two. But—" Xula's brow furrowed, the looping scar pinched tight against her cheek. "You don't think the King's come to kill us, do you?"

Shal inched the handle of dagger out of her boot, making it easier to grab in a dash. "It's not the King I'm worried about."

She pointed her captain away, and the Tamora quickly broke into formation, freckling the pitted plains and corroded playground toys in Cessa County Park.

As Shal marched across the park to the rusted thresher, Kati pursued her closely.

"You went after him, didn't you?" Kati asked her. "After I begged you to leave it alone, you still went to that meeting."

Shal grunted. The "meeting" was supposed to be Kati's wedding to Senator Danzig—or a hasty honeymoon, more likely. Shal had promised her sister she wouldn't go, and she hadn't gone...into the hall. She'd merely discovered the Council boys sent to abduct Kati, asked them politely where the ceremony was being held, asked a little less politely when they didn't answer, and then followed their trails of blood when she allowed them to "escape."

Cartesia elite were gathered in the pop-up hall for Danzig's special day—many of them having attended his four previous special days. While they enjoyed the constant breeze from their fanners, Shal remained at the perimeter brush, observing. She'd read of weddings being things of pomp and fanfare in the old days, but from her vantage, the hall's gilded exterior appeared the fanciest part of the affair. The inside men conducted business and gazed around in impatience for the ceremony to commence and quickly conclude—until the boys Shal bloodied whirled into the hall, spewing apologies.

The Council erupted with questions and accusations, teeming and tugging at their failed agents, which Morchai used as his opportunity to enter the hall on Shal's behalf. Wearing a dapper disguise and carrying a case of explosives, Morchai snaked his way into the skirmish and dropped his baggage among the others.

It was just too bad the explosives had been duds and the bloody boys mentioned Shal. Once her name left their lips, Senator Danzig and his cohorts were on alert, their weapons withdrawn and soldiers cast outside to scour the surrounding brush.

As Shal explained the skirmish, Kati shook her head. As much as her sister's face scrunched or fists clenched in rage, she didn't raise her voice to Shal. She didn't snipe or hiss, not even in their typical sisterly brawling way. Instead, her shoulders drooped and she sighed.

"I can't do this anymore," Kati said.

Captain Xula called for Shal, but though she waved an acknowledgment, Shal's focus remained on her sister.

"We've talked about this. Fighting is harder than giving up, but it's worth it."

"Don't speak to me like I'm a child."

When she turned, Shal spotted the cuts on her sister's thigh. They were back. How long had they been back?

"Why don't you heal them?" Shal asked, pointing to the fresh gashes. "Why don't you try harder to hide them from me?"

Kati clenched her jaw as she glared at Shal. "I don't want to hide my pain. You should understand that better than anyone," she said. "It's not just mine, either. Every soldier I can't heal is another piece of my heart that rots away. I don't know how much I have left to give. I'm not happy, Shal. And thanks to me, neither are you."

Shal touched her sister's face and smiled. "I hold the world but as the world, Kati. A stage where every man must play a part, and mine is a sad one. I'd be a miserable cunt no matter what."

"You know what I mean."

"Yes, I do, and surrendering to Danzig wouldn't change a thing. Even if they had you, they'd pursue the Tamora for crimes against the quadrants. And if they didn't, *we* would pursue *them*. More people than you need protection." Shal gazed across the playground at the King's Men surmounting the hill. "But I have a bad feeling about this. I don't think we've seen the end of bloodshed today."

The army of seasoned fighters, two hundred strong, strode into the shafts of moonlight spearing Cessa County Park. The infamous King, a soldier for the poor who'd battle the Council in various capacities for over two decades, led the crew into the park, his bearded chin cocked high and knotted gray hair tied back in a bun. Scars old and new twisted through his face, and he wore a piece of crimson cloth around his forehead—to staunch a wound or to catch his sweat, Shal wasn't sure. And there, in his right hand, was his legendary sword, gleaming in its bloodlust.

She marched to meet her lifelong idol—not to congratulate him on the destruction of the Cascade Quadrant pier a decade prior, or for orchestrating the recent assassination of Secretary Blount, the scribe of the Captivity Act that banished all "non-patriots" underground. She had to warn him that she'd attacked the Council earlier that day, that she'd spilled blood and followed them, and it was possible they were watching her right now, waiting for her to slip up—say, to invite the Council's oldest enemies into her hideout.

She raised her hand and shouted, "Peace!" to the King. Then Shal drew her sword.

Those who hadn't promptly drawn in defense had their weapons out by the time the shadows encircling the park shifted into the cloaked bodies of Council dogs. The armies roared at each other. Shal dove into the Council's front line and chopped through four soldiers before they could reach the King's Men. It gave the King time to draw his army back with the Tamora, to blend and arm themselves in preparation for the soldiers streaming at them in mindless bloodlust.

Shal spun through the fray counting men and swords, guns and ammo pouches. She darted through the clashing hordes and out of the fray to the thresher. Kati had dug out enough earth to wriggle under the machine, her face and dagger hidden in the dirt.

"Stay here. Stay quiet," Shal whispered. "If anyone tries to pull you out, stab them in the throat. If that doesn't work..." She clamped her gun to her sister's palm and looked her in the eyes. "Aim to kill, shoot, and burrow deeper. There aren't enough bullets for mistakes."

Shal kissed her fingers and flicked Kati's cheek before scooting away from the thresher on her hands and knees. She drew her sword and wheeled around the park's seesaw in time to block a Council axe falling on a wounded Kingsman. She pushed the Council soldier back and kneed him in the stomach, giving her time to help her bleeding comrade to his feet. In that second of aid, a blade caught Shal's shoulder and spun her around with a shriek. She clashed against the Council boy's sword and pushed him so hard his blade dropped and chopped the meat from his chin. He squealed and stumbled backward, tripping over one of his dead friends.

A female Kingsman with black and red hair braided in a high knot dashed past and stabbed the gurgling soldier in the throat with a dagger before Shal could thrust. The soldier flicked off the blood, tilted the blade in salute to the Tamora leader, and stowed it in her belt. She choked up on her sword, and leapt away to drive the blade through a Council boy's belly. Dragging the sword horizontally, she rushed across the battlefield, spilling the boy's guts behind her. This Kingsman was beautiful in her brutality and one of the strongest warriors Shal had ever seen. But resilient as she was, she couldn't outrun a bullet. It nailed her in the back of the head, dropping her like a sack of wet laundry onto a pile of her warrior brethren.

Shal roared as she propelled her crouched body at the gun-wielding assassin. He fired once, too high, and Shal dove at his legs. She tackled him, took his gun, and before he could get out a full pleading sentence, her blade opened his throat. She remained crouched as she surveyed the human wreckage in Cessa County Park. Few were left standing, and the majority belonged to Chancellor Doa. But several from the Tamora and King's Men remained, including the King himself. He spun in place, his dual swords slicing air, flesh, and tossing soldiers aside like hapless trash. Two Council boys approached, still clad in their night cloaks and hoods obscuring their faces.

Shal thought wearing a shroud that could cover the eyes at an inconvenient time was a terrible military tactic, but since the Council didn't treat their soldiers as precious or valuable in most capacities, she supposed anonymity was better than skill. If one happened to survive hooded, it meant he could enter his enemies' company without detection later.

Captain Xula's voice rang out above the cacophony, screeching a warning at Shal, but it came too late. The bullet tore through Shal's calf, and she sank to the ground. The Council boy marched to Shal, his hood torn, nose pouring blood, and a crimson grin from ear to ear as he knelt beside her and pressed his gun to her head.

"Welly, welly, isn't this a treat?" he said, wheezing. "Doa's gonna promote me outta the trench for sure once I bring you home to Skylark."

Shal grunted and spat dirt from her mouth. "Then you better put that gun down before you accidentally blow the brains out of your bounty."

He snorted and lowered his weapon. It was time enough for Shal to nab the pilfered gun from her waistband, press it to the soldier's cheek, and pull the trigger. The last bullet in the chamber tore through his head, dropping him instantly to the ground, and Shal crushed the pulpy mess under her boot as she limped away.

The playground was bogged with blood, and the King stood in the middle of the mire, wobbling as two assassins advanced.

Between swinging blades as common as water in a storm, Shal raced to the King. Every step was a new battle and a new flush of pain, but she gritted her teeth, took torment as a reminder, and left the Council dogs puddled like rotten fruit across the park.

The King chopped into one of his assailant's necks, tossing him aside, where he stumbled and collapsed onto the top half of the new Tamora solider, Helena. Her bottom half was nowhere to be seen.

Shal grunted at the girl's slack face, hoping Xula wouldn't find her like this, and rushed past to aid the King.

But she was too late.

His eyelids drooped, he dropped his sword, and he stumbled from foot to foot. His shirt was soaked black with blood, and he spat scarlet as the Council boy plunged his sword into the King's belly.

The King howled, and his attacker tugged his weapon upward before ripping out the meaty blade with whooping triumph.

Shal cut off his celebration with a shocking slice to the back of his thighs. His legs buckled, and he collapsed face first to the ground. She advanced on him, her mind awhirl with fury and sword primed.

Then the King moaned Shal's name, and her heart jumped to her throat.

She halted the Council boy's escape with a swift kick to his skull and dashed away to shoulder the wilting King. She laid him on the earth and clasped her hands to the burbling wound in his stomach. She shouted for help, but the other survivors were busy tending others, and she couldn't call Kati out of hiding.

The King groaned, his teeth clenched as he kicked at the ground in fury.

"Don't move. You'll bleed out faster," Shal said, and the King chuckled dryly. "I know this part, kid."

"If you did, you wouldn't move," she said.

The King wheezed amusement, then sputtered up blood. Shal tried to wipe it from his face, but he turned his head away, his features crumpled in pain.

This underground hero whom she'd admired for over a decade was broken beneath her, a wispy breath from becoming rat food, and it was her fault.

How could she have allowed this moment to vanish into the recesses of her mind, to steal her rightful guilt over indirectly killing a great leader and warrior like the King?

The rest of the memory permeated Shal's brain like slivered glass. Trapped within her younger self, she pleaded for time to speed her along, to spare her the torment of the next revelation. But time was not merciful, and the King's hand was soon upon her face.

"I waited too long," he said. "I wanted to come soon, but I was afraid."

"You're the most fearsome soldier in the world, sir. The greatest ally of true Cartesians. What could possibly scare you?"

He hummed as he exhaled. The color had fled his face, and his scars and contusions were less pronounced in the waxy paleness.

"I've spent my whole life battling the Council in some capacity, to dethrone them and restore the sense and joy humans had before the rift and the Last War."

Shal shook her head sadly. "Even you can't unmake the evil they've done us," she said. "But we can raze Doa together and build a new regime on his comrades' bones."

"It's a nice dream," the King said. "One I shall not live to see come true."

"Not that with that attitude, sir. Negativity heals no wounds."

"Nor does false hope." The King's fingers fluttered against Shal's cheek. "Yet I could never shake it from my life, either. I couldn't shake a lot I should have. My fear of you, especially."

Shal gritted her teeth and swallowed hard. "And you were right to fear me. It's my fault you were attacked, my fault you're lying here now."

The King coughed deep and wet, then smiled. "No. I should have come sooner. I can never fix that." His voice hissed, but not viciously; more like cold air slipping through the crack in Shal's first cell at Malay. She used to sit beside that crack on her worst days, when she thought she'd never again breathe air that wasn't farted by prison masonry.

The King's voice comforted her likewise, though only the elder version of Shal knew why. When he touched her eye patch, she shuddered in her young skin and wept.

"I shouldn't have left you with her," he said. "I thought I'd ruined you, but you would've been better off with me. I can't fix that, either."

"Sir?"

"I should have taken you. Then I could have told you every day."

Shal gripped the King's hand to her heart. "Told me what?"

He exhaled heavily, clutched her fingers as tightly as possible, and whispered: "O beauty, till now I never knew thee."

Oxygen gelled in Shal's lungs and gummed up her throat. She dropped the King's hand and pounded her chest until air broke through viscous shock. With shaking hands, she wiped the remaining blood from his face and squinted. The scars had changed so much of his appearance that only squinting to blur her vision revealed the beauty both father and daughter had lost to cruel time.

Shal's lips trembled, and she whimpered. "Daddy?"

His answer was a smile. "I didn't want this life for you, but..." He touched her face again, his fingers now stunning cold. "I'm so proud of you, Shal."

His icy hand fell to his side, he blinked slowly, and his lips uncurled to a blank expression.

"Daddy?"

Silence. Stillness.

Shal collapsed forward and cloaked her dead father in anguish. She clutched and kissed his hands—the same hands that had turned the pages of *Twelfth Night* and clumsily braided one side of her hair every Friday night. How many men had those hands killed in the time since father and daughter parted?

Shal remained by his side, begging in the futile hope he would awaken. When he didn't obey her quiet pleas, she shook his slack body and screamed for him to come back, to get up, to stay with her and make up for lost time.

When she was quiet again, a small moan rose from the cloaked body on the ground beside her. The Council soldier twitched and grunted and shuddered as he stood, still drenched in the King's blood.

Shal grasped for her sword and leapt to her feet. While the assassin struggled to regain his senses, she slashed at him and sent him retreating on his heels. He tripped over a corpse and wailed as his hood fell back, and he crashed to the ground.

His bloody teeth were clenched at the fearsome warrior descending upon him, not a modicum of fear in his eyes, and though Shal had no external reaction to the boy's face, it was quite different inside her mind. Shal's father was not the only one she found and forgot that day, and as she raised her sword to terminate her father's killer, she screamed at knowing she failed.

The blade fell, but so did a sudden darkness. She couldn't see or move—a fact that froze her blood on its own—but she heard, quite clearly, a bonecruncher's roar, followed by the howls of death.

Chapter Nine

Shal's body jerked with nauseating spasms, and blood poured hot from her nostrils as she fell out of the Doc's wooden throne. As tremors jostled her again, she realized the room was shaking too. Chunks of steel and stone fell from the laboratory walls and beyond, echoed by panicked screams. Through the haze of destruction, a shadow darted across Shal's eye line.

"Doc!"

He stopped in his tracks and spun as if spring loaded.

Shal gripped the chair and pulled herself to her feet, her brain buzzing with stinging pain. "What the fuck is going on?" she demanded.

"Bonecrunchers," he said. "Four of 'em."

Shal's squeezed her eyes shut. *Not today*, she thought. *I can't do this today. Not now.*

When she opened her eyes again, the Doc and his lab were gone. She instead saw the bedroom she shared with her stepsister, Kati. And there in the dark, Rojer Doa stood grinning like a wild beast. Shal dove at the shadows and closed her grip on his throat, but his rictal face abruptly plumped into that of the Doc.

Pain careened molten through her mind, and she released the Doc as she staggered backward. "What just happened? I was back in my old bedroom, I saw him, and then—" She glared at the smirking Doc. "What did you do to me?"

"What you asked for," he said. "Your mind is completely open now. You're free to run rampant through your memories and they through you. And you didn't even get through half the process, so it'll just keep on going." The Doc bobbed his head smugly. "It's a fun trick, don't you think? Destructive, yes, but fun to watch—for me, at least."

Shal grasped his collar and yanked his body to hers. "How long does it last?"

The Doc smiled and tilted his head. "That depends. How long do you expect to live?"

Malay's foundation rocked violently, knocking Shal and the Doc to the floor. The ceiling whined, and they both looked up as the stone above them cracked. Shal scurried away, pressing her back flat against the wall, but the Doc's retreat was less successful. The massive slab broke free and landed on the man, crushing him from the waist down. His arms jerked upon impact, his eyeballs bulged in Shal's direction with an unnatural squeal, and he exhaled his last breath like choking on seaweed.

She gazed up through the hole, and the terrified faces of cons and guards gazed back. Behind them, like living prison bars, the immense fangs of the bonecruncher opened then slammed closed. The bonecruncher tore several faces away, and they disappeared into a gory void of mastication, as the monstrous worm slammed through Malay's foundations.

"Shal!" Morchai called her name from the entrance to Doc's office. "Thank the Capesman you're here. She's looking for you."

"And not alone, I see. The root—"

"First thing I did, General." Morchai handed over the small, chapped root, and Shal rubbed it on her skin. "We've lost a few, and I'm looking for more, but the majority of your people are marked. The bonecrunchers should avoid them now." He clamped his hand to her shoulder. "This is the beginning. You will lead us to a better world, Shal."

She smiled, but Morchai's face suddenly shifted into that of her father's assassin. The Council boy sneered, his bloody teeth bared, but Shal clawed the expression from his face. She grabbed a hunk of his hair and pushed him against a wall.

"Shal!"

Morchai stared at her, panting. His face was normal again, though more flushed than before.

Shal released and backed away. "I'm sorry, Morchai. I don't know what I'm doing. Some leader of the new world I'll be." She wiped a fresh trickle of blood from her top lip and turned to the Doc's cabinets.

Morchai tossed her a knapsack, and she filled it with whatever medicine and instruments she could. He filled up his own, cinched it onto his back, and handed Shal a steel shiv.

"Thank you. With all the chances we've been given to betray each other, you're a loyal soldier and friend, Morchai. You always have been."

A man cleared his throat from the doorway and said, "And he always will be."

The gunshot rang through the Doc's lab, and the bullet blasted Morchai's nose clean off his face, ripped off a panel of lip skin, and twisted his head backward as he fell.

Shal wailed at Warden Grejous, his pockmarked face blood-spattered and bruised but righteous as ever. He gripped his side as he limped into the lab, the gun shakily aimed at Shal.

"This is your doing, isn't it?"

She hid the shiv behind her back as she stood against the wall. "No, this is far better than what I planned," she said. "I thought there'd be one bonecruncher at most."

"You sick bitch." He kicked aside the Doc's arm and stood in the shaft of light shining from the hole in the ceiling. "I don't care if Doa wants you alive. I'll be a hero no matter what. I'll be the man who killed the Council's greatest enemy. Hell, even if the chancellor does punish me, he'll probably promote me after. Then I can get out of this pit and back to Skylark where I belong. They might even write songs about me. *Ode to Shal's Slaughter*. What do you think?"

She shrugged casually and gazed up to the ceiling. "I prefer *No One Grieves for Grejous*."

He snorted and stiffened his arm, his finger on the trigger. "Goodbye, Shal. You're the Capesman's problem now."

The shaft of light went dark, and the bonecruncher hovering over the hole in the ceiling dove through. The warden spun around to fire on the beast but didn't get a single shot off before the creature's jaws snapped closed on his torso. Its fangs stabbed through Ty Grejous's body and, when retracting its head, ripped his waist apart like warm bubblegum. His legs held the dead weight for a second before his knees bowed and his remnants collapsed forward.

The bonecruncher gobbled its snack and snaked through the ceiling again, tearing down more chunks of stone. Shal dove under a cabinet, and the bonecruncher followed. Its silver eyes flashed as it neared, but with its belly slithering across the floor, only its gargantuan fangs were visible from under the cabinet. She squeezed the root in her pocket, and the bonecruncher snorted through a pair of slits on either side of its face before retreating. It smashed and slithered through the opposing wall and into the corridor.

Shal ran to Morchai, but there was no reason to waste time on his corpse. She took his knapsack, belted his shiv, and dashed out the new tunnel the bonecruncher had busted through the blocks of Malay Prison. Guard Toye was howling on the bridge as a bonecruncher bisected him at the waist, the remains of Rashus still hanging out of the animal's mouth like a wilted stalk of broccoli stuck in its teeth.

Some cons screamed and fled and tucked themselves into balls, while others fell in line behind Shal. Her army of cons followed close, pausing intermittently to kick the deserving dead. She stopped herself to deliver Guard Camden a skull-rattling punch as he died on one of the slicer's arms, wielded by Myrrah. Shal's heart warmed, and she nodded to the healer. The bonecrunchers had started the affair, but the cons of Malay would be the ones to end it.

The world suddenly drained to white. Pain cracked through Shal's head, and her knees buckled. Her brain exploded with memory, and though she sensed someone grabbing onto her, lifting and enfolding her, she couldn't see his face.

With each blink, patches of contrast returned, but she couldn't make him out. She reached but couldn't feel him—only the cloth hiding the truth. She pushed and pulled at it and got lost in the hood. She screamed as she thrashed, unable to find her way out until he grasped her face with both hands. Once their eyes were locked together, the hood vanished, color and contrast returned in bold, and she looked upon the face of the King's murderer in the here and now.

Shal grasped Raoul's throat and squeezed with everything she had. Rage, hate, love, fear tightened every finger and crooked every tip into his collapsing windpipe. He wouldn't have been able to cry out even if he had a tongue. But his mental pleas rang out clear as a truth she now remembered.

"It was you, Raoul," Shal growled. "You killed my father."

His eyes widened, and his mind pleaded. "No, Shal, you don't understand."

She understood enough. Raoul was there that day in Cessa County Park. He'd been a Council assassin. He'd torn her father open and left him bleeding out on garbage soil a life his daughter had barely known.

She hadn't known Raoul either, it seemed. What other betrayals would the Doc's dream machine reveal? How many traitors stood beside her? How many cons in her crew had killed for Chancellor Doa?

She tightened her grip and snarled. She knew Raoul could read the murder in her mind and so stitched an imagined tapestry of bloody ways to end him. But she didn't get to enact any.

A bonecruncher smashed up through the corridor, sending the walkway tilting forward. Shal released Raoul and tumbled down the stone plank until she latched onto the railing. Raoul clutched it too, gasping for breath as he begged for Shal's trust.

The bonecruncher twisted its face to Shal's thrashing legs and snuffled violently. Hunger glinted in its golden eyes, and it slowly opened its mouth.

Shal exhaled. This was it. She wouldn't avenge the King today. She wouldn't witness every death of every person in Malay who deserved a torturous end. It was over. She had to let go.

She looked up at Raoul, who shook his head and pleaded madly for her to hang on, but she deliberately lifted her fingers one by one until only the middle digit remained. Glaring, she mouthed the word "murderer" and released the railing.

Raoul screamed in horror as Shal plummeted into the throat of the aurous-eyed bonecruncher. When the beast's jaws slammed closed, his mind spun with chaotic thoughts of fear and guilt.

Shal wasn't wrong about him. He deserved to die in all the ways she'd envisioned. She didn't know the whole truth, but it didn't matter now. She'd died hating him, knowing he'd killed her father.

It became difficult for Raoul to hold the railing. The bonecrunchers slithered past, their silver eyes flashing as they gnashed guards and stone with equal disregard.

Raoul stared at the bonecruncher below him again, and his lungs emptied. He'd gotten what he needed from the chancellor's con collection, but what good was the badge now? Now that Shal knew he'd killed her father, holding on to this piece of his own seemed pointless.

But he couldn't relinquish it to the bowels of Malay. He instead kissed the sheriff's shield, whispered, "I'm sorry" to the Crossroads, and slid it into his pocket.

Raoul's belly tensed, his fingers relaxed, and he let go too.

There was no pain in death—only darkness and the cool swish of Raoul's clothes against the bonecruncher's startling metallic throat.

Chapter Ten

Raoul had killed so many fathers. He'd had no choice in the matter, and none of their deaths had pleased him consciously, but he couldn't rationalize away his guilt. It burrowed to his marrow, leveed his veins, and cast nets of rot about his organs until his body felt as putrid as his soul.

If he still had one.

He didn't want to be this person—a murderer, a liar—so he hid his crimes as best he could with more lies. He was naïve to think he could hide them forever, but he'd survived this long and suffered this much. What the fuck worse could happen?

There was a time when he was good, when his crimes were age appropriate and quickly forgiven. His family lived frugally in the Cumulus Quadrant, but the love in Raoul's childhood home was anything but meager. There was warmth and song, and he sat for hours at his parents' feet, cradling his baby sister and listening to tales of God, of the Capesman, of the fairy stories he'd since lost to future sorrows. His parents rarely quarreled then, and his sister Maribel was so small and soft, like a warbling ball of cotton, he couldn't help loving her. Raoul's life, in all its joyful ease, was uncomplicated, even lackluster to outsiders.

Soon after Chancellor Doa assumed control of Cartesia, he visited every Sheriff's department in the quadrants. Raoul's father, Jakob, had run the largest department in Cumulus for over a decade, but neither seniority nor practical experience saved his job. More than a dozen officers were discharged from service and replaced with good old Council boys. Some of the original officers flipped and declared loyalty to Doa. Others battled their dismissal to death. Jakob accepted his release without argument, but he refused to return his badge.

"Isn't that stealing?" Raoul asked him.

Jakob's face relaxed like it did when he wanted to tell his son a secret. His mouth straightened, his eyelids drooped, and his voice wafted into Raoul's mind with cajoling warmth.

"I earned it, son. I put everything into getting it, all my heart and soul. I need it to keep going."

"But—"

Jakob pressed his finger to his lips and blinked.

Raoul tried again, this time silently. "Won't you get in trouble if you steal it?"

"Not if we leave the quadrant."

"Where will we go?"

His father sighed. "Where we can."

Within the week, Raoul's family moved from Cumulus to the low-rent town of Burberry in the Diem Quadrant. But with his father's non-patriotism on record, it proved difficult for Jakob to find work. He eventually found a job cleaning carcasses from city streets—"Rodents, mostly," he told his children. The explanation made Raoul wonder what kind of carcasses comprised the minority of his father's work.

Within a month of moving into the new house, Maribel's caught a cold she couldn't shake. After a week of sniffling and coughing, her fever spiked, and bouts of alternating tremors and unconsciousness besieged the eight-month-old girl. Raoul's parents rushed her to an urgent care center in Burberry, which unfortunately considered "cut-rate" a compliment. After several unsuccessful treatments, Maribel was transferred to Diem's only hospital. There, she was diagnosed with an aggressive kidney infection, and the bank accounts were drained to treat her. There were few noticeable improvements in her condition, however, and Raoul's family ascended new levels of anguish each day Maribel's heart lagged just a little more. The small girl was no longer cotton to Raoul. She was emaciated and hard, her body trapped in a clenched sort of existence. The family was further tortured when debt forced them to mortgage their Burberry hovel to buy Maribel's tiny coffin.

The fairy stories ended there. What tales Raoul caught through the wafer-thin walls had no happy endings—middles, either. There were only tales of harrowing regret recited over the lamenting music of liquor bottles. Few boxes had been unpacked or furniture replaced in the new house. No one saw any point in it. In Diem, suffering came fast, like a poisoned bullet to the knee.

Less than a year after the move to Burberry, Raoul lost his mother to suicide, and his father, mired in grief and rage, left his son alone to die.

Raoul didn't witness his father's departure. He pretended to be asleep on his makeshift mattress in the living room while the once great man gathered his belongings. Through the muttering, the weeping, and the last moments when Raoul realized his father no longer fought the decision, he squeezed his eyes shut and tried to freeze out the farewell.

But he couldn't. Raoul's eyelids were paper beneath his father's goodbye kiss, crumpling with the wetness of the man's liquor-sick lips, cold and abrupt as crib death. He wished his father had died of the same infection as his sister, or that he would've taken his own life. There was honor in that at least. Better to sacrifice one's life than continue on knowing he sold his son to death. In that action, his father erased any sweetness he'd shown his son, and for a fiery moment, Raoul envied his dead sister.

The front door squeaked, and daylight filled the rancid house. Raoul opened his eyes at last moment, but there was nothing left of his father except a shadowy hunched body, swallowing the light.

Rather than weeping for his fate, Raoul closed his eyes and imagined sleep again. It was better there—cleaner and more sensible, a guiling place where fake laughter was still medicinal.

The electricity was long defunct, but the house was colder and darker than ever when Raoul finally forced himself out of bed. The empty rooms were smaller somehow. He thought it would be the other way, that he'd feel like an ant in a colossal palace. But with nothing on the walls, no voices to fill the spaces, no clothes or toys haphazardly strewn around a room's perimeter, there was only the vising hollow. Raoul's echoing sobs tortured him so relentlessly he resorted to making as little noise as possible. Silence was the only peace in his control, and he reveled in it for nearly a month. Survival depended on quiet, on slipping in and out of bakeries and butcher shops and gathering roof rainwater in the night. He avoided all contact he could, with the rats breeding in the walls of the house as an occasional exception. He bounced his eyebrows at them and wiggled his ears. He shared crumbs of food with them when his stash was new. When he spoke to them, he felt heard, and heard them himself, squealing and snuffling in ratty vernacular. He was reminded of his father then, sharing silent secrets. Raoul thought they made a decent go at their quiet life and hoped they could all live that way forever.

Silence broke with the evening.

Raoul was nibbling from a stolen carton of rice when a gargantuan boot broke through the front door, and a man with barrel-chested girth stomped into the house. Ominous beads of red sweat jeweled his cheeks, and his fat, upturned nose made every grunt hoggish.

"Time to vacate, kid."

Raoul slept with kitchen utensils—butter knives, forks, whatever he could find to defend himself—but the man's rippling bulk, as well as the serrated dagger in his belt, made self-defense pointless.

"You hear what I said?"

Raoul's tongue was dry and dead in his mouth like a lump of clay on a sun-drenched beach. He waggled and curled it to form words, and his throat creaked and hissed before he replied. "This is my family's house."

"Not anymore," the man said. "Where is your family anyway? They gotta go, too."

Raoul lowered his eyes and tugged at his ratted shirt. "They already did."

The man snorted. "Fortunate for you. Less baggage." He grabbed Raoul's arm and pushed him to the door.

"Where am I supposed to go?" His voice wavered, and his eyes filled with hot tears. Everything he'd done to survive meant nothing. Even when he was hungry, he still had that house—a place to hide, and to reminisce. They didn't have many good memories there, but the imprint was undeniable, like a baby song with lyrics he never quite knew. He'd lost it for good now, along with the maturity he'd gained over his father's abandonment. He was just a kid again, and now he was homeless.

"You'll find a place. There are plenty of people itching to lodge a boy your age." He twitched his snout. "I could recommend a few places if you'd like. You don't mind kneeling for long periods of time, do ya?"

Raoul wrenched his arm free, and the man chortled like a drowning piglet. It echoed in the empty house, louder than the place had been in months. Scared as he was to leave, the noise drove him faster from the place, down the streets to the bakeries and butcher shops where he'd had the most luck finding food. But a lot had changed in the days since Raoul's last forage. The bakery's usual cinnamon steam was dead smoke now, so thick he could taste it, like the burnt crust he used to scrape into the trash when his dad made toast.

Raoul shook his head. He didn't want to think of his father or the nice baker, Mr. Tremaine now lying face up on a doorstep, eyes open and oblivious to the fire consuming his flesh as hungrily as his home. The burning houses and stores of alleged non-patriots spiked Raoul's will with lanterns of violence he carried like new friends along his path. This street had long nourished his aching belly, as well as the belief that he could survive this frightening world alone, but now the ache stung deeper and broader than hunger or loneliness.

Raoul traveled from the fires toward Mr. Cryster's butcher shop on the edge of Burberry, where the lights were low and danger swelled. He'd noticed the gaggle of shop hands during previous forages, but he hadn't realized the privilege they received in Cryster's employ. The shop hands, thirteen children learning and growing through testing and rotation, were given room and board in exchange for their services in the butcher shop. Even if Raoul didn't want to work as a butcher for the rest of his life, he was glad to swap a few months, maybe even a few years, for Cryster's scraps of security.

Smoke snaked from the corner of Calis and Arqam, but the butcher's smolder was a tic-tac-toe board compared to a rugby match, and he had no choice but to trust it. He stuck to the left side of every avenue, afraid of what lay to the right—a mere wobble might drop him right into Arqam Avenue, where the men called "the Rats" were significantly less pleasant than the rodents he'd befriended in the walls of his family's house.

Mr. Cryster looked bookish. He was a sweet-faced man with a dewy complexion, who said more than once he'd lop off his left leg for an hour alone with rift gold marked "Ernest Hemingway" or "Edith Wharton." He wore brown plastic glasses with square frames, and his arms waved like a conductor's when he directed the shop hands around the meat locker. His elbow-length rubber gloves and fat crimson freckles gilded his manner with the shades of violence befitting a Diem Quadrant butcher, however. Cryster's gray eyes glinted when he smiled, and he smiled most while lopping off a hunk of meat. The man pulled in fresh slaughter without resorting to baser sources, however, and business was consistently good.

Due to the steady stream of stock, Raoul assumed Cryster was a Council sympathizer, but the man flew no flag, wore no insignia, and though he was kindly and submissive to Council soldiers, he mocked them the moment they passed.

Five beds were open in the boarding house when Raoul entered asking for work. Cryster looked him over, pinched his biceps and calves, and smacked his back until Raoul straightened it, then flew back to his hock work. "You'll do," he said. "Your house is out back, through the freezer."

Raoul hadn't spoken for months, and the first time he tried, his voice had been a wet mewl, the sound of dreg a loving father could easily leave, but Cryster's acceptance validated him. Maybe getting banished from his house wasn't such a tragedy after all, and maybe it didn't say as much about him as a person as he'd feared. The other recruits were much like him—young, strong, without home or family, two without proper names until a week of socialization in the frosty meat locker earned them playful monikers.

Raoul named one of the new shop hands himself.

A teenage girl with long braids of thick, black hair and a slick scar like an infinity symbol under her left eye made her presence well known on her first day of apprenticeship. If Raoul lifted a fifty-pound cut over his head, the girl lifted fifty-five. If another boy impressed Cryster with a well-carved shank, the girl would carve a trickier section, thinner and with greater finesse. When Glau confronted with her blatant one-upmanship, the girl answered by smacking the ever-loving shit out of her accuser.

Raoul called the girl "Bruiser." He was afraid she'd be offended, but she chuckled at the nickname. Then she pinched a hunk of flesh on his bicep, twisted it with a ruthless finger snap, and dashed away. He cherished the resulting bruise. It seemed so long since anyone had touched him substantially enough to leave a mark. He pressed her signature in secret, trying to deepen and extend it, but the spot soon yellowed and vanished, and he brainstormed new ways to earn her shiners.

He teased her, competed against her, messed up her bunk in the boarding house, and all the while, he took stock of the contusions she gifted him. Each shape and size and various shade of blue had its particular place and lifecycle. Playful bruises bloomed on his biceps, dark and concentrated but brief, like the first. Outward mocking earned him a kick to the shin, as well as the occasional belly bruise—usually an undercut jab to the side that painted his abdomen in creeping cobalt venom.

Bruiser only twice struck Raoul in the face—the first time, open palmed, when he said she was good at butchery "*for a girl,*" and the second, close-fisted, the day she disappeared. She must have known how much Raoul valued her throttles, because the final bruise she gave him that morning lasted long after he'd forgotten her.

That morning, her skin was clammy on his wrist when she pulled him into the closet. He thought she was fed up with his flirting, that she might really hurt him this time, but he felt no pain then—just a hint of wetness when Bruiser pressed her lips to his.

Raoul smiled, his face redder than when Bruiser slapped him for tickling her.

"What was that for?" he asked.

She responded by slamming her fist against his jaw.

Pain jostled Raoul to the bone, and his eyes filled with hot tears. He wailed louder than he wanted Bruiser to hear, and grabbed his aching face like it might fall off.

The closet door squeaked and slammed, Raoul opened his eyes, and Bruiser was gone.

She'd given him the slip by the time he cleared his head enough to pursue her, but she wasn't anywhere in Cryster's shop or the boarding house. When he set to surveying his fellow shop hands, he discovered three others were missing, too: the stout, tattooed young man Glau, and a pair of twin girls who linked sausages with lightning speed.

"Where's Bruiser? Where are Glau, Bella, and Braxton?" Raoul demanded of his fellow shop hands.

Most kept their heads down. Only the oldest boy, Shiza, stood and gingerly touched Raoul's shoulder.

"Don't let it get you down. It happens."

"What happens?"

He shrugged. "The Council needs men, women, all ages, all kinds."

"For soldiers?"

The shop hands exchanged glances before Shiza replied. "And other things."

"Like what?"

Palo sighed and threw her hands in the air. "The kind of shit most people don't know they're doing until they've got a cock in the ass."

"Stop," Shiza snapped. "We shouldn't talk about that. We're not supposed to talk about that."

"The Council took her? And the others?" Raoul asked.

No one answered outright, but sad gazes from Shiza, Palo, and Yanui confirmed Raoul's fears.

He shook his head. "This is insane. We have to tell Cryster."

Danna swung his arms as he stood. "No point telling the man what he already knows." His body swayed like cobra's hood as he advanced on Raoul and said, "This ain't a really a butcher's, friendo. It's a meat market. The difference is we're still breathing when Cryster decides he's done with us. The best of the best are the biggest targets. The worst are next. It's better to be mediocre if you wanna survive long enough to reach the underground."

"How long has this been going on? What happens to them?" Raoul demanded.

Palo chewed the inside of her cheek. "Can't know for sure. Men can be soldiers in Skylark and guards elsewhere—at the prison, factories, and mines—or they can be whores. For women, the options are more limited. You breed or you don't, and you're fucked either way. I hear the Skylark brothels have a hell of a high turnover." Her hands were shaking, and she pinched alternating fingers, agitated as she spoke. "I've also heard the Council sends the most disappointing shop hands back to Cryster—minus the breath and ready to butcher."

"No." Raoul's bruised jaw throbbed with an ache that branched down in his whirling stomach. He leaned against the wall, his breath like threads of flame. "No, Bruiser wouldn't let them take her. She's too strong. She'd fight."

Shiza stood next to Raoul, his back against the wall and head cocked to meet his gaze. "She might get away. People have escaped Council abduction before. Even joined the King's Men."

"Have you ever seen someone who got out?" Raoul asked.

The older shop hands looked to each other, silent.

It was all Raoul needed. He stood tall, his chest puffed, and hands clenched. "I won't let them hurt her," he said and strode to the door.

Palo stopped him halfway out, her eyes glimmering with sympathy. "It's too late, Raoul. If Bruiser's as tough as we all think she is, she'll get through this. She doesn't need you risking your life for her. You're safer here."

"For how long? When will Cryster decide I've gotten too good, and it's time to swap me to the army for a pork loin?" he replied.

"The army, if you're lucky," Yanui said. "Breeding isn't Doa's only concern, you know. That man has a large appetite, and I'm not talking pig's feet." He tossed a gnawed pig hoof into the bin. "And I hear he's not picky when it comes to his whores."

"But getting tossed in a brothel would probably put you closer to Bruiser," Danna added.

"Still a stupid idea, if you ask me. Why fight for a complete stranger?" Palo asked.

"Everyone's a stranger now. I don't know anyone like I knew my parents or Maribel or—" Grief stabbed Raoul's throat as he gazed out upon the teary vastness of the Burberry night.

The boarding house buzzed with whispers but fell silent when he looked over his shoulder.

"Maybe it is stupid to fight for someone I don't know. Or maybe it's the only chance I have left to know someone. Or for me to be known."

Shiza heaved a nostril-flaring sigh. "It's your funeral."

"More like 'it's your rat-eaten corpse in a ditch,'" Danna added.

Palo grunted. "A Rat like Akron."

"I meant rodents, but I wouldn't put it past Akron, either," Danna replied. "He has disgusting appetites, too."

"Who?" Raoul asked.

"Akron is the leader the Arqam Rats. They're the Council's biggest Diem recruiters."

Raoul bit his lip and peered out to the dim street. "So if I want to find Bruiser, I ask for Akron."

The kids chuckled. "Walk Arqam long enough, and the rats'll find you," Palo said.

Shiza slapped a hand to Raoul's shoulder and said, "I think it's noble what you're doing, kid. You're braver than me, that's for sure. I hope your bravery doesn't get you killed."

Raoul shook the boy's hand, said, "I'll see you underground," and walked out the door.

Raoul's heart was a drummer telling the idyllic story of Boy becoming Man. Surviving alone in Diem was nothing. Working for Cryster was nothing. But saving a would-be friend from worse than death would be a victory that sent childish ways into retreat and carried Raoul to the precipice of a new world. There, he would imbibe and even instruct the springtime of his life.

The task illuminated him with courage, but—and he would not know it for years—the decision to pursue Bruiser led Raoul into a darkness that would unhinge him over the few decades.

Eyes peered from secret war rooms behind moldering walls, and whispers stripped Raoul to chapped bone. He wore Arqam like a clammy gray coat burdening each subsequent step. The looming street spires were mountains he couldn't cross, the holes in the asphalt were gaping charcoal chasms. But there were greater obstacles in his way than the boulevard's broken down buildings.

Shiza was right about Arqam's Rats. They were upon him before he could conjure an opener that didn't make him sound like a baby. But he did, with a shuddering squeal that incited cackles from the trio.

Akron was the husky, ruddy-skinned spearhead of Arqam's Rats. He had a convivial crudeness stirred to the surface by the wild gestures he made with thick, callused hands. Bry was quietest of the three, but his eyes were chatty emerald orbs, twinkling with secret psychoses while the others conversed. Twiller was a slip of a man clad in a gray suit disproportionate to Burberry's dubious pretense. But while he appeared the most gentlemanly of the troika, his attitude was most lurid, and his grin like a greasy smear prickled Raoul's skin.

The men sidled up to him like lava bubbling over a blade of grass, and Raoul cleared his throat.

"Good evening, sirs."

Akron chuckled and elbowed Bry. "The young pup finally barks."

"Just as long as he doesn't bite," Bry said.

Twiller winked and crinkled his nose. "I might not mind." He danced his fingers over Raoul's shoulder, and the boy violently shrugged him away.

"I'm not here for that," he said.

"But you want something from us," Akron said. "You must, otherwise you wouldnta walked up here like you own the world." He peered at Raoul, his shadow cloaking the boy as he snarled. "You don't own it, you know. *We do*."

"And Chancellor Doa owns you," Raoul said.

"True," Twiller said, and he tickled Raoul's chin. "But there are many worlds within one, and Burberry's where you be, my boy."

When Raoul pushed him away, Akron jumped forward and put a knife to Raoul's throat. Bry and Twiller curled around Akron's shoulders as he hissed through a yellow grin.

"The pup thinks he can get something for nothing. Pups are stupid like that, yipping and scrapping and forgetting—" The blade drew blood, and Akron licked his lips. "A pup's just meat. A pup can't hunt, can't pull weight. A pup ain't shit but frolic and food to us, boy."

Raoul stared straight ahead, deep into the man's pale eyes, unwavering.

Akron snorted. "You think living out here made you hard? You're softer than you was at your mama's titty. Cuz you got no one now. I bet Mama woulda torn the Capesman a new asshole if he'd come for you."

"But Mama's not here," Bry said.

Twiller hissed a giggle. "And if the Capesman's coming for you, puppy baby, you best believe I'm coming first."

Raoul grunted his name through gnashed teeth, and Twiller fluttered his eyelashes.

"Pardon?" the slight man asked.

Raoul flared his nostrils, tightened his belly, and said, "My name isn't 'pup' or 'puppy baby' or 'boy.' It's Raoul. And I have some demands."

Akron bobbed his head and lowered his knife as he and the Rats backed off. "Let's have it then. I could use a good laugh."

Raoul considered telling them the truth. Maybe they'd be more receptive to honesty. Or they might laugh in his face, figure him a weakling for chasing someone who was no less dog meat than he, maybe even kick the shit out of him.

"I need food," he said instead. "Water, shelter—"

Akron waved his meaty hand. "Let me stop you right there, pup. Your needs don't mean shit without fulfilling a few of ours."

"What do you want?"

"What does anyone want? Allegiance. Devotion."

"Fine. Consider me devoted," Raoul said. "Now about the food—"

"Not good enough," Twiller said. "True devotion requires action."

"What sort of action?"

"It's not us you gotta convince," Bry said. "Allying with us requires allegiance to the Council as well. You want food? They're the ones to ask."

When Akron wrapped his arm around the boy, Raoul's stomach constricted with an acidic clench. The man's teeth were sparse and rotten and his stench none too appealing. But, unlike Raoul, he was clearly well fed.

"We aren't that different, kid. I used to have a family too—a wife, a daughter, even a prissy cat my wife used to tote around to competitions. But the Council took all of that away, and bless 'em for it. I was trapped in that life, a prisoner of mediocrity. I was a nobody, and now I'm a king. People know me. People fear me," he said, puffing his chest. "It was evolution, Raoul. The strongest survived, just as you survived what obliterated your family. You might think of yourself as a lone wolf, but I'm here to tell ya a wolf needs a pack. True strength lies in numbers, and in who you know."

"And you know the Council," Raoul said.

"Indeed. They can give you everything you need, want, or—hell—what you hate, too. Besides, what do you really have to lose?"

Raoul opened his mouth, but no sound came. He lowered his eyes, head shaking.

"You think they're evil?" Twiller asked. "You think they don't care about anyone but themselves? You're right. They don't. But we're part of the 'they,' pup. You could be, too."

It nauseated Raoul to think of allying himself with the Council, but if he could survive, if he could find Bruiser, how could he possibly refuse? Akron was a filthy man, but he sure as hell didn't spend his nights face down in the gutter. Disgusted as he was, Raoul couldn't deny the lure of betterment, of evolution. Plus, these men had taken Bruiser. They had to know where she was now, or at least what she'd been drafted for. If he could find that out, maybe he could escape before he had to prove his allegiance.

"You're right," Raoul . "If my father had gone along with the Council's changes, we never would've had to leave Cumulus. Maribel might've never gotten so sick, and even if she had, it wouldn't have broken us like it did. Mom wouldn't have—"

The lie stuck in Raoul's throat, bitter as truth. He didn't want to believe what he told the Rats of Arqam, but he couldn't deny his future had hinged on a choice his father made without consulting the rest of the family. At the time, Raoul had thought it a noble decision and morally sound—even with his choice to steal his badge—but how moral was it to shove your loved ones into damnation and then run away when life became the Capesman's dank waiting room.

Akon wrapped a beefy arm around Raoul. "You won't have to worry about that anymore. Anything, really. The Council takes care of its devotees. After all, you're the future, Raoul. The better fed and better educated you are, the grander this world will be."

Raoul couldn't trust Akron or his cohorts, but he allowed them to lead him down Arqam Avenue anyway, toward darker and more rotted dilapidations.

Chapter Eleven

The Rats led Raoul to a crooked shithole with boarded windows at the end of the street. The door hung a half-inch off its hinges, so the series of six rusted padlocks seemed like overkill. Twiller, Bry, and Akron had two keys each and unlocked the door, then stood back with eager grins as Raoul reached for the knob.

His palm perspired against it, and pink flecks of rust stuck to his skin when he twisted and pushed into the crumbling brick high rise.

A soft but awing glow greeted Raoul as he entered, cast by overhead chandeliers and stylized candle sconces upon the scarlet walls. Drawing closer to the walls, he found them speckled in gold flakes so sculptural he wondered if they were real gold. When so many people were starving throughout Cartesia and the underground, why had someone tossed a fortune in gold shavings at an insignificant red wall? He ran his hand over the décor, and his fingers came back dusted in gold, a stark contrast to the rust on his palm. His gaze rolled over marbled floors and vaulted ceilings, the latter decorated with mirror panels reflecting his amazement.

"What is this place?"

Twiller whispered, "Home," and draped his arm around the boy.

Raoul shook away the slimy man and gravitated to Akron for protection. It surprised and amused the rat, who cackled and pointed Raoul up the gilded staircase spiraling to the building's apex.

Fueled by wonder, Raoul bounded up the stairs, flight after flight, enthralled by the décor and glittering trimmings. On the fifteenth floor, he stopped to catch his breath. His lungs burned, and his tongue stuck to the roof of his mouth. He tried to wet his lips, but they gummed with his dry saliva and made him thirstier.

"Care for a nip?"

The silver flask a dapper man shook in Raoul's face was embossed with a frilly "D." Raoul grabbed for the flask and pressed the cool metal to his lips. As he tilted it, his gaze climbed the stranger—from his freshly buffed wingtips to his exquisite suit, perfectly hugging his substantial belly, and up to his solicitous smile. The fluid hit Raoul's tongue with a surprising sting, and the intense aroma filled his eyes with tears. He'd never tasted it before, but he recognized that smell from the fog that so often surrounded his father after Maribel's death.

Raoul spat out the whiskey filth, as well as the new saliva he desperately wanted to swallow. Then he froze. His spittle shone on the strange man's shoes and the plush carpeting on the fifteenth floor.

The dapper man's head resembled a boiled red cabbage, and his eye were daggers aimed at the three panting men ascending the stairs to join him and Raoul. He snatched back his flask and grunted.

"If this is a new recruit, he's going to need some serious tutelage in manners," he said.

"He's a scrapper for sure, sir," Akron said. "But I've no doubt you can make good use of him."

"Doing what exactly?" Raoul asked.

The moment he finished speaking, Bry smacked Raoul in the face and barked. "Have some respect for the Senator, pup."

The dapper man's face cooled from scarlet to pink. "That's all right. It's natural to be concerned about your future, especially after spending significant time in the company of these scoundrels."

The rats snickered, honored by the compliment.

The gentleman bent to Raoul. "Do you know who I am?"

"A senator," he replied matter-of-factly.

"You only know that because I said it," Bry muttered.

"That's not important," the senator said. He pinched Raoul's chin and pulled him closer with an awkward tug. "But let me assure you, *I am*."

He led Raoul up one more flight of stairs, into a room cloaked in darkness. The Arqam Rats ignited the wall sconces, and light trickled through the room. The color scheme continued from the first level, but where there'd been golden flecks were now dramatic shimmering ribbons of paint and ostentatious accents. Even the boarded cathedral windows were high-class with diaphanous scarlet draperies.

While the rats sloppily hunkered down on the regal furniture, the dapper man sat gently, with intent, and folded his hands on his lap.

The senator cocked his head, blinked slowly, and smiled. "What is your name, son?"

"Raoul."

His head righted. "Hello, Raoul. I am Senator Danzig, a member in high standing of our illustrious Cartesian Council, and a close friend of Chancellor

Doa. If I wished it, I could put in a good word for you with the chancellor. Or..." He clicked his teeth. "...I could not."

"Suppose I don't want your recommendation," Raoul said.

Senator Danzig's brow creased with confusion, and he glanced at Akron.

The man shrugged at Danzig with a dismissive grunt. "One of those," he said. "Hand to the Capesman, I thought about sending him back to the butcher in paper sacks."

Raoul gulped hard. "Is that what you did to the kids you took? You killed them? Cut them up?"

Bry tongued his teeth. "Not all of 'em."

The Senator cocked an eyebrow and leaned across the marble coffee table. "Why are you so interested, Raoul my boy?"

"How can I be sure you'll make good on your promise if I don't know what happened to anyone else? For all I know, I could be signing up for certain death."

Danzig expelled a throaty laugh and pulled a pale blue handkerchief from his breast pocket. As he dabbed his spit-speckled lips, he nodded at Akron, who leapt to his feet and clobbered Raoul's left cheek with a downward jab that slammed Raoul's face against the plush chair's wooden skeleton and bounced him, limp, to the floor.

Senator Danzig stood and crossed to the boy sputtering on the blood pouring from his nose. Pressure squeezed both sides of skull, and for several minutes he feared it was his brain leaking down his face.

The rats lifted him up and dropped him back in the chair. Danzig dabbed his lips once more, then tossed the handkerchief at Raoul's purpling face.

"First off," the Senator started silkily, "I didn't, nor do I aim to, promise you anything. Is that clear?"

Raoul clamped the cloth to his nose and stretched his aching jaw. "Yes, sir."

"Good." He nodded to Bry and Twiller, who scampered out of the room while Akron cracked his knuckles. "Second, I suppose I can't blame you for being curious. A modicum of curiosity is healthy, even inspiring," he said with a whimsical lilt. "Under the right circumstances of course. But you, my friend, have given healthy a miss and gone straight to being a cat on its ninth life."

The door swung open, and Twiller and Bry entered, each carrying a large silver tray with a great dome for lids. They set the trays on the table, but only Twiller lifted the lid with the gusto befitting the roast chicken, braised beets and potatoes, and jug of fresh sparkling water with iced condensation streaked on its glass skin.

Raoul's jaw dropped with the handkerchief, and his tongue pooled with metallic saliva. His belly growled furiously and he lunged forward, but Akron grabbed him by the hair and forced him back in the chair.

"There he goes again, wanting something for nothing," Bry said.

The Senator poured himself a glass of water like a diamond waterfall of God's legendary grace.

"That will change in time," Danzig said and enjoyed a long sip of water as he stared at Raoul. "I bet even someone as stubborn as you can admit you don't know what life'll be like a month from now, a year from now. You don't know where or who you'll be. One day you're—" Danzig fired a finger-gun at Raoul. "—Where are you originally from, friend?"

Raoul dammed a fresh trickle of blood with his forefinger to his nostril as he said, "Cumulus."

"My, my, what a fall." Danzig shook his head with his bottom lip protruding. "What caused a good Cumulus kid, of proper age and a valuable asset to our continued existence, to wind up penniless in the Burberry pits?"

"My father lost his job at the sheriff's department."

"I see."

"Thanks to the Council."

The senator sneered and glinted a few ivory teeth. "He wasn't offered a job in the new regime?"

"Yes, but—"

"He turned it down because of his dusty old principles, thereby sentencing you to death." He raised an eyebrow. "And your mother?"

Raoul lowered his gaze to his bloodstained hands. "My sister went first," he whispered. "She wasn't even a year old."

Danzig filled a glass with water and pushed it to Raoul.

He grasped the cup with both hands and slammed it to his mouth so desperately his skull vibrated with pain. After the first gulp it occurred to him the water might be drugged or a diversionary tactic, but it was cold and wet and Raoul couldn't be bothered with the deadly little details while he guzzled for dear life.

Not one drop of water clung to the glass's slippery cliffs by the time he returned the cup to the table. He reached next for the platter of chicken, but Senator Danzig clucked a chiding song.

"Not yet, my dear boy," he said. "First, answer me this: when your father lost his job, when he refused a new one, when he uprooted your family and handed them over to a garbage quadrant run by vagrants and rats, you must've been awfully angry with the Council. The Chancellor especially."

"I suppose," he said, his mouth filling with saliva.

"I wouldn't be surprised if you're still angry. I know I would be," he said. "My entire family dead and gone... Anyone would be angry."

Raoul pressed his body to the chair back, his feet tucked up and head lowered as if hiding when he said, "They didn't all die."

The Senator batted his eyelashes and clapped his hand to his chest in shock. "What do you mean?"

Raoul exhaled a shuddering breath. "My sister and mother died. My father left."

"Left? A teenage boy, sick at the death of his mother and baby sister, and he left you alone in Burberry? Why?"

Raoul shrugged and sucked on his bottom lip.

"No reason?" Danzig shook his head then smacked the arm of his chair with a grunt. "That is unacceptable. I'm sorry, Raoul, but I can't fathom it. Your mother and sister die, and your father—the rock, the savior—runs off without a word? I've seen many shades of cruelty, even perpetrated a few myself, but I would never run out on someone I love. It's shameful, just shameful." Danzig pushed the chicken platter closer to Raoul and wiggled an eyebrow. "Don't you think?"

Raoul nodded and said, "Yes, sir, very shameful," then ripped a glistening drumstick from the bird and shoved it in his mouth.

The meat tasted of fire and fat and dripped hot juice down his chin. His face still ached from Akron's blow, but the meat and honeyed skin proved an effective distraction. It dulled his pain as he chewed and mulled over his past and, more importantly, his future. It was a future Raoul's father had pretended for years he wanted to see—to nurture his son's growth, to share in working days and storybook nights as they had when Raoul was young. But Jakob would have no part in it now, except as Raoul's inspiration to be a better man than his father.

Senator Danzig smiled, his lips nearly as greasy as the stripped bone Raoul sat on the platter.

"The Council works tirelessly to rid the quadrants of such shameful people, son. People who drag society down and stand in the way of our survival. Say, like abandoning a precious child without cause. We don't want to hurt the innocent—far from it. Our objective is salvation and restoration. But a person's true colors shine brightest under stress. Your father's obviously did," he said, cheeks pink with sympathy. "That's what we do. We stress the limits. We test the foundations. Some people are built stronger than others, but we don't tolerate those who are strong solely because they feed on the weak. One must be noble to possess real strength. People like you, Raoul."

Raoul didn't want the man's flattery, especially because—deep down— he *did* want it. He wanted kind words and a warm hand patting his back like his mother did when he was ill. He wanted Maribel's soft coos again and his father's fairy stories. He wanted a family. He wanted the kind of love that stayed.

He didn't thank Danzig for the compliment, but his chest swelled and he found his knees locking, pointing forward, the thought of leaving the company of these Council men no longer sailed his thoughts.

"You're special," he continued. "Anyone can see that."

"Except Daddy Dog," Twiller remarked, picking chicken from his teeth.

"His loss," the senator said. "The ex-sheriff clearly had no vision."

"And you do?" Raoul said.

The Senator's eyes crinkled, and his lips spread to boast his tight rows of uniform teeth. He opened his arms and laughed. "I'm the King of Vision."

"And you use that to steal kids from their beds and place them...where?"

"Back to the butcher," Bry said, groaning. "That's a hard-on talkin' for sure. No one cares that much about his fellow man unless he's hoping for a poke."

The senator pushed the platter closer to Raoul, but he waved it away. After months of scant meals, one drumstick stretched the limits of his stomach.

"What *are* you hungry for, son? What is it you really want to know?"

Pussyfooting wasn't working. Deception wasn't working. These men liked him, respected him, and he figured he'd show them the same courtesy by being honest.

He pushed the tray of food to the Senator's side of the table, leaned forward, elbows on knees, and stared into Danzig's eyes with a razor focus he'd given no other man.

"A woman was taken from the butcher's," he said. "She was young but tough. Nameless but unforgettable. Senator Danzig, I need to know what happened to her."

The man nodded, tented his hands at his lips, and hummed. "I suppose she's in Ides. Grace City, most likely," he said. "Which would prove quite a coincidence since I'm hoping you'll head to the same place."

"Grace City? To do what?"

"There's a training program at Skylark I think you'd be perfect for. After the training is complete, you'll be able to do and have whatever you desire. This nameless woman included."

The Council represented everything Raoul's parents taught him to hate, but he didn't want to gamble as his father had. He didn't want to embrace pride over sense or abandon his only chance to save the girl who'd pummeled a living Heaven into his heart. Besides, who was he to listen to his parents now? They were cowards, selfish in their respective exits, and while he doubted Senator Danzig would become a hero to him, at least he'd given Raoul a viable future.

Chapter Twelve

It would be his first time in Ides. As a child in Northern Cumulus, Raoul used to boast that he'd been to the ritziest quadrant dozens of times, as he and his father frequently played along the border. Those were some of his happiest memories and he accessed them often after his family's relocation to Diem, but reminiscence brought contempt and shame now. It was as if that love was merely for show. He would have to redefine love, and Grace City seemed as good a place as any to begin.

Accompanied by Senator Danzig, Raoul ascended the staircase to the roof where a helicopter sat humming, almost eager to whisk the lowly orphan boy to Council grandeur. The pilot represented that thought perfectly in his Diem scruff and grime and pressed jumpsuit completed with sparkling medals. They could've been fabricated for all Raoul knew, but they dazzled him nonetheless. With the alien swell of flight swirling and tossing him to and fro, he could focus on nothing but the wonder of his new life.

From hundreds of miles above the earth, Ides bragged its opulence. Its largest metropolis, Grace City, was a hotbed of classy corruption and the heart of the Council's main operations. While many of the councilmen spent their evenings relaxing in the northern shore of neighboring Cascade, they were back at work by morning, weaving salvation and restoration in Skylark Tower. Unlike Northern Cascade, Grace City satisfied business in triplicate as Council men lived, worked, and played in Skylark Tower. Chancellor Doa included. He, like many of his cohorts, had multiple quarters in Ides and across the quadrants.

As their transport neared the Skylark helipad, Raoul gazed down upon the rows of varicolored antlike people filing obediently into little boxes. Some of the boxes were residences, but if they belonged to simple citizens they were a different breed than those in the other quadrants—and an entirely different species than the Diem dregs. Those people were needed to power Ides, the north of Cascade, and various spots across Cartesia. They were needed to chauffer the Council-owned vehicles, to build the electronics and communication devices they, as dregs, were forbidden from using otherwise. They were servants of the rich, and sadly, many felt grateful for the task.

Raoul's stomach lurched with pity and vertigo as the helicopter landed on the illuminated pad atop the tower. The ground felt like whirling sand underfoot when he stepped out, slowly adjusting to gravity, as men in gray jumpsuits approached. They had bludgeons at their hips, and their collapsible batons sustained a steady rhythm against their oily palms as they strode to greet Senator Danzig.

"He in?" Danzig asked them over the roar of propellers.

One guard nodded while the other rushed to open a door and lead the visitors down a hall. He turned a key in a metal wall plate and opened the elevator doors. The men sneered at Raoul like he'd emitted a foul odor, and one tripped him as he followed Danzig into the elevator. He skidded on his toes and bashed into the Senator's side before smashing against the glass wall. Pushing away from the wall, he caught a dizzying eyeful of Skylark's interior below.

The largely translucent elevator sailed through mirrored levels and rooms fogged with the steam of leisure and industry, and Raoul's skin glazed with a sweaty fear that made his hands squeak as he clung to the slick walls.

Danzig laughed and handed Raoul a handkerchief. "Does it live up to the rumors?"

Raoul dabbed his forehead, his eyes aimed at the opaque ceiling. "My parents avoided talking about Grace City whenever possible. They didn't want us to know."

"But you did, didn't you?" Senator Danzig squeezed the boy's arm. "Don't be ashamed. Your parents couldn't possibly keep such entertaining yarns a secret. Which have you heard?"

"I heard a rhyme about Chancellor Payne and his seven wives. He hired the staff and cut the ribbon on the first brothel in Skylark Tower." Raoul cleared his throat and recited.

"Chancellor Payne,
A braggart, a brain,
Gave Skylark a new piece of Heaven.
He said, 'When it comes to sex,
It's best with an ex,'
So Payne gave his friends One through Seven."

Danzig cackled. "Haven't heard that one in ages," he said. "It's not true, though. The honorable Chancellor Gose Payne did have seven wives, but only six worked in the brothel. The seventh was fertile and too precious for such work."

"Didn't she also kill him in his sleep?" Raoul asked.

The Senator nodded. "But he sired more than most before she slit his throat. My great grandfather, to name one." He grinned. "A dear, brave woman Great Great Granny was."

The elevator vibrated as it slowed, and with a lilting hum, the Senator pressed a blue button.

"He'll be expecting you," Danzig said to Raoul. "I'd get more of that sweat off your lip if I were you."

Raoul frantically wiped the moisture from his face. "What's he like? The Chancellor?" he asked.

Danzig grinned and said, "He's a teddy bear."

"Really."

"I learned early on never to speak ill of bosses, friends, or future father-in-laws."

The elevator stopped and the doors opened to a corridor lined with bustling glass rooms. Raoul glanced at Danzig, and the Senator snorted as he shoved him out. A combat class executed precise kicks and jabs to his left, and to his right, a similar cluster of young men meditated peacefully.

"What is this?" Raoul asked.

"The heart of our military training program," Danzig said as he led Raoul down the corridor, pointing out the varied activities in which Council boys were immersed: a literature class comprised of young boys reciting from rift gold, a ferocious round of calisthenics, even a gaggle of hooded soldiers roaring with joy as they guzzled ale. Raoul stopped and stared in at them. They clinked mugs, high-fived, and were in all ways brothers. They didn't see him, but he saw his old life in each stranger, for they smiled in a way he hadn't seen in years.

"A good soldier needs more than battle skills. While you strengthen you body, you will also strengthen your mind, and your bonds to those who truly value you. Our men are well-rounded and respected members of society, Raoul."

"And dispensable?" he asked. "Otherwise you wouldn't need so many."

Danzig eased him from the tavern with a sigh. "Regrettably, our enemies are numerous and many of them skilled in warfare. We do what we must."

A bronze door with ornate scrollwork stood at the end of the corridor, leading to the only room not comprised of glass.

"This is where I leave you." Senator Danzig clamped a hand to Raoul's shoulder and said, "It's been a delight knowing you, son. I have no doubt I'll see big things from you."

"You're not coming with me?"

"I have business on another floor, I'm afraid."

"Not Payne's House, I assume."

The Senator twiddled his fingers. "I'm practically betrothed. Those dark days are behind me. Like yours."

He pinched Raoul's chin and smiled. He spun and sped to the elevator, eyes forward, chin high.

The sleek leader of Cartesia wore a gunmetal suit with a rose-pierced lapel, further shaming the plainest room in Ides. Dry iron walls enclosed him, and dim skeletal bulbs hanging overhead granted his black hair a radiant glaze. He stood, hands folded at his waist, and blinked slowly like a cat with a belly full of fish.

"Raoul, is it? Come in, come in," he said in amicable falsetto. "Once you've made it this far, there's nothing left to fear."

Raoul closed the door behind him and strode to Chancellor Doa. "I'm not afraid, sir."

"I'm so pleased. I am also Rojer Doa, Chancellor of the Four Quadrants of Cartesia and Curator of rift gold."

"I didn't realize that was a job. How much rift gold is there, sir?" Raoul swallowed hard. "If you don't mind me asking."

"Of course not. And there's more than you'd think."

Doa smiled and gestured to the modest table and chair set beside the drab room's cathedral window. The ostentatious tea set looked foreign on the rickety wooden slab, especially with fresh plumes of steam leaking from the spout. He hadn't seen a reasonable place to steep, let alone boil water, but the chancellor wore such an accommodating expression, and he gestured to Raoul's seat as if the boy were of equal stature. As much as he hated to admit it, Doa was right—he'd come too far to allow fear an equal say in this choice.

The Chancellor pressed his clean, tapered fingers to the teakettle's lid and poured the tea like an amber waterfall into a white stone cup with pale green trim. The liquid issued a cloudy breath and deposited droplets on Raoul's face when he leaned over the yawning cup. But it wasn't sweat, or the steam's fragrant dew. The mug was surprisingly cool to the touch, and the liquid rolled cold down his gullet with a refreshing minty sting.

He sighed as the cool tea permeated every pore and sense with a grateful lull he hadn't felt since Cumulus. It was a fairy story comfort, a wave of tranquility that came in the middle of those tales, when the bad people still had the upper hand but you knew the hero would break free or find what he wanted—who he wanted, even—and live happily ever after. He gazed about the room as if the flourishing feeling would recolor the drab walls.

"Every room's a boast but this one. There's nothing in it," Raoul said.

Chancellor Doa chuckled as he refilled Raoul's tea. "Ah, but *I* am in it."

"But you're not boasting, either. You're not trying to sell me on the Council or flatter me. Why bring out the biggest of all big guns if you're not going to shoot?"

"Who's to say you're not already riddled with bullets, Raoul, son of Jakob."

"How—" Raoul's tongue was dry and sticky. He downed his tea and cleared his throat. "How do you know my father's name?"

Doa grinned. "I knew him, of course. Issued the order that put him out of work myself."

"You knew—" Raoul's mouth went dry again.

"Yes. Senator Danzig, too. Your father's well known around here, my boy. He's been a thorn in our side for months, ever since we picked him up for burgling a bank," Doa replied.

Raoul's head drooped, and his spine suddenly weighed too much to stay erect. He moaned as he tried to fill his lungs with air, but they felt like dry, stained paper, thick and stiff in his chest.

The Chancellor slithered to Raoul and pinched his chin to lift his lazy gaze. "He was a fighter like you. He begged us to let him go. He said he had to get back to his son, a boy he'd left all alone in Diem."

Raoul smacked Doa's hand away and spat at the floor. "He's here? My father is a soldier?"

Doa snickered and shook his head. "You're both fighters, but I'd never let a dreg like that in my army. You're a better man than him, Raoul. A strong man, a smart man. You could even be *my* man."

He pinched the boy's chin again. This time Raoul didn't have the strength to slap him. All he could do was obey the fatigue in his limbs and slide from his chair to the floor.

The Chancellor of Cartesia stood over him, and his words radiated at Raoul in viscous Council waves as he said, "You're one of us now. Forever."

"What did you do to me?" Raoul asked, aching for breath.

"Drugged you," he replied in a nonchalant chirp.

"But I was going. I was willing."

Doa pulled Raoul up from the floor. His hands were soft and sweaty, and his crow's feet streaked his face with glistening color when he grinned at the woozy boy.

Raoul's ankles bent, and his feet flopped as Doa towed him out of the room, into the glass-enclosed corridor. The studying soldiers had set aside their books and the men in combat training stopped mid-kick and marched to the wall, fingers splayed over the glass. Every eye fixed on Raoul, following him to the floor when Doa released Raoul to gravity.

The glass gleamed as Raoul swept his gaze about the corridor, but the Council boys on the other side were brighter, washed out and flickering.

Raoul felt like his cheeks were dripping off the bone when he said, "What's happening?"

"The truth," Rojer Doa replied.

The flickering soldiers, gifted with both education and leisure, vanished before Raoul's eyes. The rooms were empty; not even the beer and rift gold remained.

"You said you were willing," Doa started, crouching beside Raoul, "but I wonder how far that willingness would take you once you got what you really came here for."

"I didn't—"

Doa pressed a solitary finger to Raoul's lips and hushed him. "I've seen thousands of you in my life. I can spot your kind from miles away, and I've taught my men to be just as keen. You act tough as nails, but right now, your conviction is aspic. When you're boiled down, you're nothing but the resin of your forefathers' false courage." He petted Raoul's damp hair and said, "It's not your fault, though. God's death, the rift, the tectonic shift—they pulped mankind, reduced us to sentimental twats. Well, a goodly portion of us. There were, of course, a select few who rose above the tears and regret to create a new world." He smiled and waggled a finger at the boy. "You were raised by the wrong people, kid—by the kind who value honor over longevity and order. We were all the latter kind long ago, Raoul, and we've returned to reclaim the world.

We have scraped ourselves from the ashes and built our smolder to a blaze that's reignited the glory of men. It's because of people like me, like my father and his forebears, that all this is possible. I see that same spark in you, son."

Raoul's face wrinkled with disgust. "We're nothing alike."

"But we will be, and you'll be grateful for it."

"Never. I came here out of honor, to save her."

Mirth illuminated Doa's expression. "Who?"

"No one," Raoul said, shaking his head. "I won't tell you. I won't let you punish her because of me."

The elevator slowed at the end of the corridor, and the doors opened with a slick swish. As a masked man in a black jumpsuit approached holding a silver suitcase, Chancellor Rojer Doa laughed.

"It doesn't matter. In a minute you won't remember her name, your mission, or how much you hate me."

The masked man set the suitcase beside Raoul's rolling eyes. He popped the latches and opened the case, which contained four primed hypodermic needles.

"What is that?"

Doa plucked a needle from its foam cradle, flicked the syringe, and crinkled his nose as he cleared the bubbles. He fixed one eye on Raoul and pursed his lips.

"You'll believe it to be a great many things," he said. "A vaccine against every known disease, steroids to increase your strength, drugs to boost your intellect. But none of that's true. The truth is this serum will keep you obedient. It'll keep you loyal to the Council, even to your death."

Raoul growled. "I would never die for the Council."

"You'll die for me if I command it." Doa's voice was cloying velvet in Raoul's ear. "When I'm done with you, you'll kill yourself if you think it'll make me smile. You'll do whatever I tell you the Council needs, and I'll reward you every year with another dose of liquid devotion. You'll ache for it, because you know it pleases me."

Raoul tried to stand, shuddering, pouring sweat, and his hands slipped across the glass floor. His arms felt stuffed with soft cheese, and his breath clotted until the masked man flipped him onto his back.

Doa placed one hand on Raoul's chest, the man held Raoul's head steady, and the needle punctured Raoul's neck with a flush of vibration. The Chancellor pushed the plunger, and the serum exploded like fireworks throughout Raoul's body. His gaze rolled to Rojer Doa, whose sinister grin and wrinkles softened to angelic clarity.

Doa pushed the rest of the serum inside, and the firework embers radiated to the tips of Raoul's extremities. Warmth filled every pore and coated his body in a cool, sticky glaze.

Raoul was effortlessly happy. But there was still a piece of him hidden behind the smile, trembling, alone in the dark. He couldn't let that piece disappear. He had to hold onto who he was. There was still time to fix everything. He could live up to the good life his father had wanted for him. And he could save her. He could remember her, find her, and save her.

"Bruiser..."

Doa withdrew the needle and placed two fingers over the throbbing puncture wound. His touch was a goodnight kiss, and his voice curled around Raoul's name like a blessing.

"Who?" Doa whispered.

Tears drained from Raoul's eyes, and with a stinging blink, his brain cleared of its pesky past debris.

"Who's Bruiser?" Doa asked again.

Raoul shook his head. "I don't know, sir, but I can find out."

The Chancellor cradled his new soldier's face, stamped his forehead with a wet kiss, and said, "Thank you. You've pleased me greatly."

Raoul could've sworn he'd known happiness before this but couldn't conjure the will to ponder it. Happiness had a new definition in the sacred saliva drying on his brow.

Chapter Thirteen

Life was best with a goal that couldn't die. The Council needed tasks completed, people silenced, and desires fulfilled at a gloriously incessant pace. There was always someone new to please, some lower man to outshine. Raoul became a ladder builder of sorts, using whatever backs and bones he could to climb higher in Chancellor Doa's esteem. He was, for the first time in his entire life, serving his beloved government. He was a happy man. His sister never died—was never born, either. His mother hadn't committed suicide, nor had his father run off. Raoul had always been a boy of the Council; he'd just never been recognized for his ambition and talent before. That, he declared to his fellow trench mates, would soon change.

As promised, the Council provided the soldiers with education and entertainment, though not as well rounded as advertised. A normal day consisted of martial arts classes and strength and agility training. There was leisure time, but it paled in comparison to lessons in weaponry, combat, and field training with real dregs. Despite the occasional blackout from ostensive exhaustion, Raoul loved every minute.

For the first few months, Raoul remained in the background observing seasoned soldiers, learning from their loyal brutality. In his first year of service, he was inducted into a battalion specializing in eviction. His team trouped through the quadrants, forcing families from their lifelong homes, delighting in how easily they could squeeze tears from otherwise strong men and women. He wished he could collect them, become curator of sorrows with a collection as grand as Chancellor Doa's legendary hoard in Malay Prison.

A few weeks after passing into Cumulus, the veteran squad leader, Kala, celebrated a recent eviction with every ounce of alcohol and medication he could find in the house. After a long night of helping themselves to whatever the ex-residents couldn't carry out, the eviction squad rose to hit their next assignment—all but one. Kala was bloated blue when they found him curled up in the bathroom, a creamy foam dripping from his gaping mouth. It was unclear whether Kala's death was accidental or intentional, but no one wasted more than a minute debating the issue. Picking a new leader was more important, and Raoul knew it. He nominated himself for the position and strongly encouraged his fellow evictors to second the motion. When Hisani, a scraggly man missing his nose contested Raoul's claim to the position, he was quickly persuaded to change his mind. He valued his remaining facial features too much to continue the argument.

Raoul held the position for two years, the boyish face behind banishment in Cartesia. It earned him more respect, extra food during meal distribution, and the biggest perk of all—private time with Chancellor Doa. It was a rare privilege he fought to keep. He evicted faster, was less forgiving, and shed unnecessary blood in the name of the Council. No one was surprised when Raoul was promoted in his third year of service. Though the Western Ides Battalion was small, winning the position of Captain was certainly not, and neither were the power and prestige that followed his elevation.

The battalions teemed with envy and one-upmanship, and while most soldiers were friendly to one another, reveling in their duties and amicable competitions, Raoul considered no man his friend. He exulted in disconnection from everything but his true objective. For eight years serving the Council, advancement through bloody repetition was his greatest comfort.

Every night, Raoul would look out upon the world, over its squalor and suffering, and be thankful he was no longer a part of it. He belonged to a better world now, and he served an integral purpose. He grew from boy to man, from mercenary to Captain, and hoped to give Chancellor Doa all the blood he desired. Raoul had delivered his idol plenty of King's Men over the years, plus some of the new dregs comprising the Tamora, but their leaders would bring the fattest rewards. As much as Raoul loved the spirit of violence and its artistic barbarism, he ached for a promotion out of military service. To be out of the trench full-time, to orchestrate and dictate with the men he so admired, to finally gain the Council's permission to bed a woman. While he'd had opportunities and the torturous urge, he also knew Chancellor Doa's opinion on militia taking too many liberties with the Council's generosity.

"You certainly could," Doa said as Raoul filled the chancellor's glass with burgundy wine. "A desperate widow, a desperate widow's daughter? I'm sure some of your men have done just that."

"I discourage it, sir," Raoul said.

Doa sipped his wine. "Of course you do." He gestured for Raoul to sit, to fill his own glass and drink in the heady intoxication of fidelity. "The soldiers who disobey aren't just lesser man, they are thieves as well, claiming precious wombs needed for elevated stock. Perhaps yours. You're special, son. You understand such privileges must be earned."

"I understand whatever you tell me understand, sir."

Doa clinked his glass against Raoul's and laughed. "Good man. Of every dreg to slither into my presence, you most deserve the frills of Council life. You should lead armies, not that thickheaded brute the insects call 'King.'" He gulped his wine and danced his fingers against the lip of the glass. "Perhaps his followers would follow you, given the right motivation."

"If you wish it, Chancellor."

Raoul still hadn't touched his glass of wine. Rojer nudged it to his hand and bounced his eyebrows as he said, "Make it *your* wish, Raoul. Kill the King for yourself."

The soldier lifted and tilted the glass against his lips, swallowing the wine with a hard swig. He'd already resolved to deliver the heads of every enemy to please Rojer Doa, but as he envisioned disposing the King and stealing his devotees, pleasure swelled in his own chest.

"Yes," Raoul said. "I will kill the King."

"*King*! Ha!" Josha, Captain of the Southern Ides Battalion, scoffed as he grinded his blade on the whetstone. "Who's that man to call himself 'King'? We're more royal than that rabble of underground trash."

Raoul chuckled as he slicked his hair into a tight bun. All around him, soldiers prepared for the night's battles. The trench was a factory for death and debauchery that stunk of blood and sweat, but Raoul loved its aroma, even mused about bottling the sweet scent of brutality and selling it to dregs as a cure-all.

"As long as they're deluded enough to think they're the superior species, they're more dangerous than a drunk bonecruncher."

"Bullshit," Josha said. "I've lost count of how many SI has silenced under my command. How about WI? How about you, single-handed?"

"Rebels are like roaches," Raoul said as he chapped his bludgeon for more abrasive blows. "Even if we eliminate the King's Men, more vigilantes will rise. That Shal bitch finds more followers every day."

"Not for long. My team's going after her stepsister tonight, and you know Shal never leaves her stepsister alone." He grinned and blew steel dust from his sword. "We'll get Kati first, then we'll take out Shal."

Raoul sneered. "WI is tailing the King's Men to their hideout, and then..." The homicidal reverie flushed his cheeks. "It's going to be beautiful, Josha, and the chancellor will be so grateful. I can taste the champagne and snatch now."

"As if you've had either," Josha said with a snort. "Hey, let's meet for a drink after assignments, toast our victories?"

"Can't. I've got my yearly tonight," Raoul said. "We can celebrate tomorrow if you're still in the mood."

"I'll be in the mood." Josha grabbed his groin and grunted as he humped his palm. "A good battle gives me a week-long hard-on."

Raoul snickered. "Oh, I know. The entire trench knows when you've had a good kill. Fuck, we all know when you prick your finger, Captain. You've got a hell of a blood boner."

"Death lifts me up in more ways than one, bud," he said with a smirk. "You're no different, you know."

"I don't pretend to be," Raoul replied. "Just thinking of the King's head on a spike, me the one to put it there, gets me harder than any of your haggard whores."

"Hey, they do fine work. Better than nothing anyway. And better than paying Skylark prices."

"They're dregs, Josha. They should be dead."

"With the shit they've got in their veins, they probably will be soon."

"You know that, and you still screw them?" Raoul said, shaking his head.

Josha clamped his hand to Raoul's shoulder. "I got my yearly last week. I'm immune to rotten snatch. If I could get Skylark snatch for free—and without the big boys knowing—I would. Wouldn't you?"

"I'd rather channel everything into ensuring the King writhes beneath my blade in a pool of his own blood. Then I wouldn't have to pay for women."

"What about writhing with one of Skylark's whores in a pool of the King's blood?" Josha nudged Raoul's chest and bounced his eyebrows.

"Even better."

An emissary approached the men and saluted. "Captain Raoul, you have an urgent call from the chancellor on the second deck."

"Second deck? Must be important," Josha said.

"I hope the King's Men didn't hear of our attack and commit mass suicide," Raoul said sarcastically.

"What a shame that would be," Josha said. They clamped arms in camaraderie, and he wished him luck.

"May the Capesman have a busy night," Raoul said.

"For you, too, Captain."

The second deck consisted of broadcasting stations from every Council post in Cartesia—and several private rooms in Skylark. Guards stood outside of every room on the Second Deck, which stood on the last floor of the trench and three floors below the cheapest Skylark brothel. It made the Second Deck the most revered place in a Council soldiers work world. More than a few boys who'd been called to the Second had taken the opportunity to slip upstairs for a quick and dirty splurge. But Raoul was honored just to get a call from Chancellor Doa, and ignored the guards' suggestions he would "sneak three more."

The guard wiggled his brow, scanned Raoul, and allowed him into the Skylark screen room. Doa was triple Raoul's size on the screen as he sipped scotch and tapped the arm of his chair.

Raoul stood at attention, hands behind his back. "You look well, Chancellor," Raoul said.

"I'd look better if you hadn't made me wait so long. It is a big day for me, Captain. For my daughter, too...once they find her."

"Apologies, sir. I was discussing tonight's plans with Captain Josha."

"Yes, about that," Doa began, his lips shiny with liquor. "My rats tell me the King's on the move—toward the Tamora."

"They've never collaborated before. Why now?"

"I suspect the King knows how close we are, and how doomed he is. He's a tired, desperate man, Raoul, with nothing but his hate." Doa sipped and licked and drummed his glass with his middle finger. "Like us all, he wants an heir, and Shal is a reasonable one. She's strong, courageous, a right cunt when she needs to be."

"Isn't that always, sir?" Raoul asked.

Doa grinned and tilted his glass to the screen. "Indeed, son. A fine point."

"Thank you, sir. There's no need to worry. I can handle the King's Men, even if they do reach the Tamora."

The Chancellor's mouth straightened to a dry rope, and he lowered his glass so fluidly the ice didn't clink the sides. "You do not appreciate how dire this is, Captain Raoul, so I will forgive that nonchalance...once."

"Yes, sir. Apologies, sir."

"If the King and Shal are permitted to reunite, our regime will face its most precarious time since our installation after the Last War."

"What do you mean 'reunite?'"

"Shut up and listen, dreg."

Raoul's organs shriveled in his gooseflesh body, and his gaze plummeted to the floor. He apologized but Doa didn't speak until Raoul met his gaze again.

"This is important, Captain."

"Yes, sir."

"This day of all days."

"Yes, sir."

"I don't want the King captured. I don't want him maimed. I want his body strung up at my daughter's wedding—hell, at her *bedding*, if it keeps that long." The Chancellor wheezed a laugh into his glass, a glorious devilry glinting one eye, but the smiling beauty fell to sorrow, and he drew a longer sample of his liquor. "Of course, I need my daughter first."

"Captain Josha will not fail you," Raoul said. "And if he cannot rescue dear Kati from her captors, I promise I will."

"I trust you, Raoul. More than many others," Doa said.

"Thank you, sir. I will not fail you. I swear the King's Men will be dead by dawn."

"I only care about the King."

"Then the others will be a lovely bonus." Raoul grinned. "I will kill them for you, Chancellor. I will bring even more glory to this day."

"I would expect no less from you, son. You are truly a man after my own heart," he said. "Do you understand how much I treasure you?"

Doa's voice sent symphonies of devotion through the soldier's flesh, and he found himself suddenly woozy from the chancellor's affection.

"Come to me after your yearly," he said, and Raoul bowed.

"If it pleases you, sir."

"Yes," Doa said. "You will."

Chapter Fourteen

The Western Ides battalion found the King's Men on the southern edge of the forest outside Cessa County Park, but they wouldn't be stopped for long. Raoul ducked behind the brush and pulled up his hood, watching the King with ravenous curiosity. He'd seen the man up close a dozen times, even clashed swords with him once or twice, and thought the same thing he thought now as he sized up the venerable warrior: "He doesn't look so tough."

The King had an inch on Raoul, and his biceps were slightly larger, but he didn't have Raoul's speed or agility, and he sure as fuck didn't have his stamina. Even now, while the King rested beside the stream, the sallow weight of exhaustion dragged his weathered skin from the bone. This was a man at the end of his rope. It was looped round his neck, and his toes inched off the wobbly block keeping him alive. He was just waiting for someone to kick that block out in cold mercy.

Raoul glared at the man and whispered, "Wait no more, old man."

The King's Men resumed their march through the woods, and Raoul's men hung back.

"They'll follow the stream," he said. "And the King's too careful not to notice a tail."

"Captain Raoul." A masked soldier saluted. "Our spies have spotted the Southern Ides battalion approaching."

As much as Raoul wanted to take out the King alone, he had to surrender to the truth that he stood no chance against the unified vigilante armies. He pulled his soldiers back to meet Captain Josha in the woods outside Cessa County Park. Blood striped the Captain's face, and his left eye was swollen shut.

"What the hell happened?"

"Shal got the drop on us," he grunted. "The Senator's wedding is ruined."

"Then we're going to need a hell of a lot of corpses make up for it." Raoul called both battalions' attention. "You hear that, boys? Kill them all! For every

Tamora and Kingsman left standing, I will kill a Council boy myself. Survive this battle, and you might yet die. Is that understood?"

"Yes, sir!" they barked.

"What about the King?" Josha asked.

Raoul grinned, his teeth bared and fingers itchy. "Leave him to me. Leave no others but Kati Doa. If you need to hurt her, so be it, but use force sparingly. Senator Danzig doesn't want to marry a bruised peach."

"Speaking of which..." Josha pointed to a rusted thresher where the leader of the Tamora was crouched.

Shal's lips moved swiftly as if coaching the thresher on how to keep being a corroded piece of shit. Once she dashed away to meet the approaching King's Men, Josha signaled for his men.

"Key, Bracken—follow me." He fired a look at Raoul, and they both knew: at least one of these boys would die tonight.

Key had been shit since he arrived in the trench the previous month, and his only mastery was in complaining. Bracken was quieter for a new kid, better at sharpshooting, but Council had little use for a green sharpshooter when they needed hand-to-hand cruelty.

Bracken went first, with deliberate gesticulations like he had time to pinpoint exactly where Kati Doa was secreted under soil and steel. Her dagger was too fast to catch the light, but the curtain of blood from Bracken's throat was bright enough, as was Key's in the prolonged spurts before Josha subdued Kati and dragged her out from under the farm equipment. As half of the WI and SI clambered at the dregs in Cessa County Park, Raoul led in the other half from behind, closing in with furious howls.

Bodies fell against playground equipment, sliding down colored plastic with wet squeals. Raoul chortled as dregs from both enemy armies rushed at him, and he took them down with barely a sweat broken. He spotted Shal across the park and felt an ache to pursue her, but a bullet tore past and bit her leg, sending her wailing to the ground. As a Council boy approached her with a readied pistol, Raoul shrugged and turned his attention to the King. The panting man looked like he might collapse, but when the WI warrior faltered his strike, the King swung his massive blade and decapitated the boy with one ferocious chop. His gaze followed the dead soldier to the ground, and when he lifted his chin again, Raoul stood opposite, a grin slicing his face.

"You look familiar," the King said.

"We've fought before," Raoul replied.

The King spat blood at the ground and tongued his swollen lip. "Then we've both failed in our tasks to this point."

"Not for long. Besides, I never wanted to kill you so much as today. Today is special. Today is beautiful."

"Today," the King said, "your beloved Chancellor gave you some particularly heartfelt words that made you want to please him even more. And what would please him more than my demise? He's got you trained proper."

"I enjoy serving the chancellor."

"And I'm sure he enjoys your service. In the field, face to face, on your knees—"

Raoul growled and lunged at the King. His sword chopped the shell from the King's ear, sending him back a few stunned paces. Raoul rushed and knuckled an uppercut beneath the King's jaw, followed by a flatfooted kick to the stomach. The King fell to the ground, moaning, and Raoul circled him, disguising his gasps as amusement.

"Who's on his knees now, old man?" Raoul wheezed. "I gotta say, I'm disappointed. I thought you'd give me a better fight than this. I've heard so many grand tales of your prowess, of your eternal strength in battle. But you and I had better scraps than this in my first year. I guess it makes sense. I'm in my prime, and you're—" He chuckled. "Well, you're a sack of scars and hope burning low, you crusty old dreg."

The King stood slowly, without threat, his muscles relaxed and eyes focused on a world past Raoul's blood-speckled face.

"Don't you have anything to say, King?"

He stared past Raoul, his eyes like fogged glass, and shook his head.

Raoul advanced with his sword readied but first whispered in the King's ear. "Say hello to the Capesman for me."

He plunged his sword into the King's stomach and ripped the blade upward, slashing and spilling flesh and innards before tearing it free. The man wavered, his jaw slack, as Raoul hooted and danced in victory.

Stripes of pain suddenly flamed in Raoul's thighs, and he collapsed. He twisted to inspect his slashed legs but instead saw the blood-drenched leader of Tamora, her muscles knotted to steel and face like a madhouse ablaze. She keened as she raised her sword, but the King's dying moan seized her attention. Raoul crawled away, clawing dirt and pleading for mercy, but he didn't gain two feet before Shal was upon him. Her boot cracked the back of his head, his face collided with a rock, and darkness swallowed the world.

Raoul awoke tasting copper and salt. After Shal's blow, the enduring battle had squeezed and shoved his limp body down the hill, into a corpse-strewn ditch beside a storm drain. He'd drifted in and out of consciousness for four days but remembered nothing. The passersby must've thought him the lowest of dregs, trembling in a urine and blood-encrusted fever sleep.

The experience varied greatly in Raoul's mind. In his dreams, he was home in Skylark, and the greatest of spoils were his. Victory was the closest and brightest star, casting a golden glow about his body, and it was greatly admired by the free, breeding women of Grace City. By the person he most admired, too.

Chancellor Doa cradled Raoul's face and kissed his cheek—soft, like an angel's lips—but when he disconnected and saw the man unpuckered, there were only the cold black guts of a devil. His desiccated fingers scraped Raoul's cheeks, and every congratulatory word reeked of sulfurous bile, of death, of a nasty, diseased morning in Diem Hospital.

Diem Hospital...

What was in Diem Hospital? Why would Raoul be there? And whose baby was that, bloated and vomit-drenched on the bed?

The Chancellor was beautiful again, and so was the needle in his milky claw. Raoul tilted his neck to the syringe, the blissful anticipation of his yearly inoculation flooding through him in the aching, itchy prick of pre-orgasm, but the release never came. It shed its assumptions of pleasure and virility and warped Raoul's belly with strange new rage.

No, not new.

Raoul cleared the gunk from his eyes and peeled them open to a world overrun by sewage with fishy crimson skin. Cool wind prickled his soggy body and stiffened the pearls of pus on his wounds. His legs ached horribly, stiff as his shivering propelled agony from head to toe. He yowled as he pushed himself from the cadaver-choked ditch, pebbles, grass, and dead insects glued to his face. Wiping it away smeared his face with more street shit, but it was better than the strings of rotted hair from the scalps of his lifeless allies in the ditch.

He flicked the hair from his fingers and juddered at the word "allies." They wore Council insignias, Council cloaks, and with Council expendability. Raoul's legs throbbed with infection as he stood and beheld the hazy playground at the apex of the hill. Confusion swarmed his mind like a fever. It beaded his brain with hot droplets of half-thoughts that he was both at home and in prison, that he'd been left behind and just where he needed to be. He was both lost and found, both hurt and validated by his pain, and as his mind cleared, he felt like a twelve-year-old boy again. Alone.

He couldn't deduce why he was in Cessa County Park—or Ides, for that matter. He surmounted the hill where the death-rot was strongest, and his gaze sailed over the corpses. One in particular inspired powerful stirrings in Raoul's gut. He knew of him, admired him. So why did he have the sinking suspicion he'd had a hand in this heroic man's demise?

Gripping his belly, Raoul swung his gaze from the lifeless King and the littered dead. Disoriented and mind combatting itself, he stumbled out of the park with two maps stamped on his brain. It was as if he'd forgotten something, missed something, or was extremely late for an appointment, but he couldn't recall what.

Deep down, from a mental lockbox that now popped open with a rusty judder, those memories escaped. Two lives stretched out before him, one consuming the other and regurgitating blood in steaming splashes through Raoul's mind. The sickening crack he'd dealt disobedient dregs, the screams and pleading for mercy, the malice thick and hot as porridge in his veins, and all the while, such heart-fluttering mirth expanded in his soul.

It seemed to Raoul a violent story of some other wretch's life, that he'd been imprisoned in a robotic shell of himself that craved only murder and the chancellor's approval.

He gripped his head. Could the chancellor hear him now? Could he help him remember his lost life? Did he even want the man's help if...if...

Raoul gritted his teeth. Could Doa have done this to him?

Yes, of course he could. He was a vicious, self-serving man, a demon who cared nothing for people like Raoul or his father.

His father. Where in the world was Raoul's father?

Faces of allies and enemies flashed through his mind, people he'd hated and vice versa, and though he couldn't differentiate between them, he tasted blood and vomit and the sweaty viscosity of the inoculation, protecting and intoxicating his every inch.

"The yearly," Raoul whispered. "I missed my yearly."

With that realization came countless others. The Rats of Arqam, the helicopter ride to Ides, zooming through Skylark Tower with Danzig. Truth was a palpable sludge dripping from his brain, filling his sinuses, and glutting down his gullet in acidic tears wept by men, women, and children he'd put out of house and existence. Those dregs were his people, and he'd slaughtered them with a Council man's mirth. He still felt twinges of it now, peeking out between massifs of disgust.

It seemed so long ago that he was the young boy who woke up alone, innocent and afraid. How many boys just like him had he sent to early graves? How many families had he forced onto the street, how many had he forced into criminal survival, how many children orphaned and parents made childless?

If truth was a sludge, guilt was the epoxy solidifying it to jagged planks that stabbed his guts. Doa had done this to him, reprogrammed his true nature with the yearly serum, but Raoul had allowed it to be done. He'd sought out the Rats of Arqam and welcomed whatever danger followed. He'd given himself over as readily as a brothel boy, like his mind, body, and the last six years of his life meant nothing.

Perhaps it was now true. Murder had corrupted what good there had been in his youth, and now that he was wide awake, again able to execute free will, he saw little point in it. Nothing he did would change the horrors he'd inflicted upon the people of Cartesia. Though the Council would no longer use him for their murderous agenda, he couldn't forget what they'd taught him. He was forever a killer. When he killed someone now, it would be of his own volition.

That notion inspired a surprising smile as Raoul imagined his sword gouging a hole in the chancellor's heart.

Chapter Fifteen

Skylark Tower had been so immaculate before, awing Raoul to his core, but it now appeared an ideal glass coffin for the Council's golden gods. He marched to the entrance, focus fixed, but a guard leapt into his path.

"Captain Raoul? Is that you?"

He blinked, his face blank. "Open the door, Gus."

"We thought you were dead. Everyone did. The Chancellor made an announcement."

"I'm sure it was very touching. Open the door."

"Yes, sir. Of course. I just need your destination code."

"Wherever the fuck Chancellor Doa is right now."

Gus chuckled. "It's Sunday, Raoul. The Chancellor is at church services. They all are."

Raoul grabbed the man by his collar and pushed him against the door. "We all know church services are no more than extended brothel visits. He's deeper in pussy than rift scripture right now—and when it comes to the business he and I have, neither the Capesman nor pussy are more important."

Gus's face creased in disbelief. "Captain, I don't understand."

Raoul sighed, reeled around, and punched the man square in the jaw. His head cracked on the door, and he slumped to the ground. Raoul quickly gathered Gus's weapons, two pistols—one empty—one machete and a bludgeon. He'd have to move faster now, and with a dozen places Doa could be in divine worship, he'd have to guess right. He dashed for the stairwell and burst through the door just as a captain was exiting.

"Raoul, is it really you?" Josha's sight zigzagged over Raoul's face, and he smiled. "Holy shit. You magnificent bastard. I thought you were worm food by now, maybe even captured by that one-eyed cunt. Please tell me you found her and fucked out the other eye."

Raoul's body churned with nausea. "Stop it," he hissed.

Josha chuckled. "What?"

116

He shook off the sickness and forced a smile. "Sorry, I'm a bit out of sorts."

Josha squinted, and his hand moved to his bludgeon. "Does the chancellor know you're back?"

"I was on my way up to forty-two to join him for worship," he said. "A welcome home treat."

"Then you won't mind if I claim whatever masseuses he's got waiting on seventy-three."

Raoul pulled a hard smirk. "Shit, that's a hell of a present. I'm glad I didn't go to forty-two. Thanks for that."

"You're not going to walk, are you? You'll tire yourself out."

Josha pushed open the stairwell door and followed Raoul out into the hall, toward the elevator. He looked down through the glassy floor. The alarm was not yet raised. Now if he could just ditch Josha…

"I think I can take it from here, Captain," Raoul said as the elevator doors opened.

"Unless you need someone to hold your girl down for you. The unsuspecting ones can get a bit feisty."

Josha winked, and Raoul's stomach burbled again. He couldn't remember everything from his years of living as a Council puppet, but he knew he would've laughed at such base jokes a few days before. He forced a smile, and Josha patted his back as he accompanied him to the elevator.

Raoul pressed the button for the seventy-third floor brothel. It had the highest turnover of them all, as first-time employees thought they were hired to work in a legitimate massage parlor rather than a brothel. His heart broke for those women and men. It broke for the King and his soldiers, for Shal and her followers, for Bruiser—who he'd long forgotten—and lastly for the life he'd thrown away so carelessly years ago.

The button Senator Danzig had pressed to activate the false training sessions had a fresh, greasy thumbprint. Some poor bastard was about to lose everything.

"Hey, are you listening to me?" Josha asked. "You're acting like returning Kati Doa to her father isn't a big deal. Now Senator Danzig can finally have his young bride."

Raoul's heart broke for the chancellor's daughter, and he replied stiffly. "Of course it's a big deal. Congratulations."

"I couldn't have done it without you. Or the hundreds of good boys who shed blood in Cessa County Park."

"Their sacrifice was worth it in the long run," Raoul said. "For the greater good of the Council."

Josha's face flicked with amusement. "I don't believe you."

Raoul's throat tightened. His fingers twitched, and his inner killer howled. "Bash his face in," it cried. "He's not your friend—never was—and he'll slaughter you with less thought than you're giving him."

He considered appealing to Josha—or to the part of him unmolested by the Council's mind control—even trying to convince him he wasn't operating on his own impulses, but deep down he knew it wouldn't work. He instead puckered his lips and glowered at the SI Captain.

"I don't care what you believe, only what the chancellor believes," Raoul said. "And he holds me in higher regard than he'll ever hold you."

"Until I delivered him his daughter. Now I'll get the good whores, maybe even a few wives," Josha said. "You're a failure, Captain, and what's more, I can read the treachery in your eyes. You have some foulsome deeds in mind, boy, and I refuse to let you carry them out."

Raoul snickered. "Let me? Oh, Josha, you senseless pawn. I didn't wait around for your permission while I was drugged, and I sure as shit am not starting now."

Captain Josha ripped the bludgeon from his belt and swung it at Raoul's head. Raoul ducked, and the baton bounced off the glass behind him, sending painful vibrations up Josha's arm. He swung again, but Raoul was ready for him, catching the baton with his left hand and pressing the pistol to Josha's eye with his right. He smashed the Captain's face against the elevator wall as his finger teased the trigger.

"Real or fake?" Josha asked, his breath fogging the glass.

"You'll know in a second, won't you?" he said, grinning. "If you can know anything after I've painted the walls with your brain."

"Why are you doing this? I looked up to you, Raoul. Your strength, your cruelty."

"All false. All forced into my soul by the Council."

"Was it?" Josha asked. "Or did they just open something the outside world forced you to keep locked away?"

"Cruelty isn't natural."

"It is to the King's Men and Tamora. It is to anyone who kills to survive," he said.

"We don't kill to survive, Josha. We kill for the control to choose who survives."

"But you'll do it now, won't you? If you don't kill me, I guarantee you won't survive. I will empty every last vein, laughing, singing. I will surpass cruelty when I end you."

Raoul couldn't deny the twitchy feeling in his gut urging him to follow through on his threat—to watch in boyish glee as Josha's brain dripped in lovely pink chunks down the glass elevator, for all of Skylark to see. He drew back the pistol, covered Josha's eyes, and said, "Goodbye."

The empty pistol clocked Josha's skull with enough brute force to knock him out cold. His face smacked the glass and he slid to the floor in a slack lump as the elevator slowed at floor seventy-three.

Six guards of varied stature stood along the corridor leading to the Doa's Sunday service. The men held their batons waist high, but they appeared more annoyed than threatening when the elevator doors swished open. Raoul holstered the empty gun and removed the bludgeon, but kept it hidden behind his back. If he could get through this without killing anyone—

"What the fuck is that?" The lead guard barked and pointed his baton at Josha's crumpled body on the elevator floor.

Raoul hissed, "Shit," and whirled out his bludgeon as he dove from the elevator.

He suspected at least two of the guards' guns were fully loaded—likely the pair closest to the brothel—but were under strict orders not to discharge unless absolutely necessary. That meant the first line was likely skilled at hand-to-hand combat, thereby preventing the release of precious bullets. Six years in the Council's militia had taught Raoul many things, including the staff hierarchy. It wasn't known to many but had been confessed to Raoul during his hazy days alone with Doa that Skylark was the only place where the man felt truly safe. While he traveled the building with a convoy of guards, he was confident the King's Men or Tamora wouldn't have the balls to strike on Council turf. It was why the trench, a musty hole fit for a lower quadrant, remained in the heart of Grace City. But even the filthiest of trench boys were valued higher than Skylark guards. These men were least trained and least educated, and though many were naturally proficient in combat, they had nothing on a man who'd served as Captain of the Southern Ideas battalion.

The first pair of guards lunged at Raoul. He dodged and ran between them down the corridor as fast as possible to the wide-eyed men aiming guns, their fingers still hanging off the triggers. He smacked the gun from the leftmost guard's hand before whipping it upward and cracking the man under his chin. He collapsed, moaning, which Raoul stopped with a swift boot to the face. He yanked the man's gun from the floor and spun just as the other guard closed one eye to aim. Raoul pulled the trigger, but the pistol dry-fired. The moment the hammer dropped on the empty chamber, he dropped to the floor—a millisecond before the other gun discharged.

The bullet cracked the glass behind Raoul and sprayed his back with shards. He removed his machete just as the first two guards tackled him—bad luck for the man who dove onto the waiting blade. As Raoul fought to pull the machete free of the dead guard's chest, the second man repeatedly slammed his baton against Raoul's right shoulder. He grunted and released the machete, scrambling backward on his hands over slivers of glass. He retrieved his bludgeon from the floor and swung it at the guard's head, sending him howling onto his side.

Pain rollercoastered up and down Raoul's right arm. He could barely lift it, certainly not enough to use a weapon. He kicked the wailing guard's baton out of reach and delivered him a brain-swelling blow with his boot heel.

There was only one guard left, his eyes filled with tears, his jumpsuit flowering urine down his left thigh. Raoul realized then that this man had the only loaded gun because he was the least proficient warrior, maybe even a brand new recruit. Now that he inspected him, he recognized how skinny the man was, how pale with terror. He wasn't a man at all. He was just a boy. Yesterday, he might've been a butcher's apprentice.

"Go ahead. Kill him."

The silky voice stroked a lovely secret place in Raoul, and he found himself striding, entranced, to the trembling boy who couldn't level his weapon. He ripped it from the young guard's hand, flipped it around, and gave the little pup a taste of the oily gunmetal. He fingered the trigger and glanced over at Chancellor Doa, shirtless and damp on the other side of the brothel's glass door.

The Chancellor's amusement was sensual, a hot vibration of chuckles that tickled the executioner within Raoul's throbbing soul.

"Kill him for me," Doa said, and the executioner nodded.

He stepped back a pace to aim, and the boy sobbed a prayer. Not to the Capesman. To God.

"Let me be as dead as God," he said. "Let me be snuffed out like God and Heaven so I will never meet my loved ones at the Crossroads, and they may never see what became of me."

Raoul sneered. As he pivoted his body, he pushed the boy to the floor, and fired two shots at the brothel door. The bullets cracked the glass but didn't penetrate it.

Chancellor Doa's grin was splintered as he laughed at Raoul. He spoke into his two-way radio, and a screeching alarm resounded through Skylark Tower. He turned his back on Raoul and walked away.

The door was locked. The elevator was moving, and trained soldiers were on their way. He didn't have time to waste. He beat the weakened glass with his bludgeon until a he spotted the scantily dressed brothel employees on the other side, creeping closer. He paused, and a mahogany woman dashed forward to let him inside.

"Thank you," he said, cradling his tender arm.

"Wait, sir, please." The woman grasped him by the forearm and shoulder and, with a grunt, forced his dislocated bone back into the socket.

Raoul's knees buckled, and he gasped for air like the stabbing pain might drown him. Several young women and men steadied and lifted him to his feet.

"We can help you," one of the boys said, but Raoul shook his head.

"You don't have the weapons, and the soldiers will be here soon," he said. "There's no reason for you to get killed over this."

"There's every reason," said a girl with a bloody nose.

Raoul wiped sweat from his brow and beheld the group of weepy employees. "Not like this. Run if you can. Go underground. Train and arm yourselves. Even if I kill Doa today, another man will take his spot, and you will be needed to fight."

The pleasing music from the speakers ceased, replaced by Rojer Doa's boisterous cackle.

"Stop putting impossible ideas into their heads and come to me, Raoul," the chancellor said sweetly. "I've been eager to see you since I learned you were alive. My beautiful, lucky pup."

Raoul's teeth were clenched as he spun around, his gun and bludgeon readied, and marched down the corridor of glass cages. The massage rooms were empty except for one. There, Doa sat upon a kingly bed with two shotguns trained on the open entrance.

Raoul smirked as he entered. With one weapon aimed at the chancellor, he closed and locked the door.

"I'll admit you look intimidating, Rojer. If I thought you'd actually shoot me, I'd be a little scared."

"You think I won't?"

"Have you ever done your own dirty work?"

The Chancellor pouted, but the frown quickly swirled into a smile. "It depends what you mean by dirty," he said. "But I know you won't kill me, either, Raoul. I'm your friend, your mentor. I've been more father to you than the man who left you to die in Diem."

Jakob's face bled into Raoul's mind, and sour guilt coated his tongue. He swallowed hard as he advanced on the bed.

"Did you know who I was when I was evicted from that house? Did the man who kicked me out know I was the Cumulus Sheriff's son?"

"We knew it was possible." Chancellor Doa rose to his knees on the mattress as he replied, his guns following Raoul's movements. "But we couldn't be sure, so he followed you all the way to the butcher, all the way to *Bruiser*."

Raoul cocked his head. "What?"

Doa's face twisted in sick pleasure. "You know she's probably dead because of you, right?"

"That's not true."

"You were correct in following her here—she was in Skylark when you arrived," he said. "But unlike you, she was smart. She escaped. She went underground and joined the Tamora."

"I didn't kill her."

"Probably not, but you sure as shit gave the order that night in Cessa County Park, and very few survived."

"*You* gave the order!" Raoul bellowed.

"I wanted the King. I believe I said I didn't care about the rest."

Raoul lowered the gun. Doa was right. It was Raoul who'd told those boys to slaughter everyone. He'd threatened their lives so they wouldn't leave a single Council foe standing.

Doa's face softened. "I'm sorry you have to go through this, Raoul."

"Don't you dare feign sympathy for me."

"Oh, it's not for you. It's for me," Doa said. "I had high hopes for you. I had so many plans."

"Plans to use a drugged-up version of me to collect every vigilante standing in your way of complete domination?"

"I won't deny that I made something great of you," he said, his face flushed with vanity. "You were well on your way to becoming one of the most powerful men in the world, my son. And you liked it, didn't you? You *wanted* to be more, to be elevated."

"I was under your control."

"But you don't have to be anymore." The Chancellor walked forward on his knees, his lips shiny with a fresh coat of saliva. "Admit you liked it, Raoul. Admit you were happier serving me."

The door wobbled violently in its frame, and the horde of soldiers with madhouse eyes glared at Raoul from the other side of the wall.

"I'll forgive you if you admit it. We can go back to the way things were—better, even. No serum, no trench, no more fighting. I'll do as I promised. I'll give you a title, a home in Grace City, and a fertile woman to love."

Raoul clenched his jaw, and the Council boys pummeled the walls with their batons.

"It's what you always dreamt of," Doa whispered.

It was the dream of an inoculated man, but now that Raoul was free it tempted him still. To be a real Council man was to live in peace disproportionate to the rest of Cartesia. That life could bring him happiness, but it could never be real. It would be the first symptom of a communicable disease, infecting any future joys.

"No," Raoul said resolutely. "I'll never be the man I used to be or the man you want me to be."

Chancellor Doa smirked as he aimed his gun. "Then you will be a dead man."

The shot rang out, vibrating the massage parlor's glass walls, and stabbing Raoul's ears with its echo. Smoke snaked from the barrel of Raoul's pistol, which he lowered as he stood beside the bed and looked down on Chancellor Doa. The man lay reclined on the bed, nostrils flaring and his chest awash with crimson from the gurgling bullet wound in his shoulder.

Doa grunted. "You filthy cockworm dreg. That was a stupid move."

"Missing your heart? Tell me about it," Raoul said and pressed the pistol to Doa's chest.

But he couldn't pull the trigger. His skin buzzed to numbness, and the weapon fell from his petrified hand. He tried to speak, but his jaw moved like rusted metal, and his tongue was no more productive than lint. His legs buckled, and he folded to the floor, groaning as the trench soldiers stormed into the room with masks clamped to their faces.

Raoul cursed, but it came out as "Fhmmf."

Captain Josha removed his mask and knelt in front of Raoul, his temple marbled cobalt and face stamped with dried blood. "You really should have killed me, pup."

"You should've stayed dead, son."

Pain wracked every suture in Raoul's skull. His tongue was as dry as sand, and his jaw felt overextended, just shy of its sockets. Raoul snaked his arid tongue around his mouth and felt steel rods propping open his jaws, crusted with blood. Black cloth covered his eyes, but the room smelled distinctly of the trench, with wafting hints of chemical char.

Someone ripped the cloth from his face, and Raoul's gummy eyes cleared as he gazed about the dim, slate room. Chancellor Doa stood before him, his suit of similar hue though possessing a luxurious sheen that made him appear glazed in stardust. He was still so beautiful to Raoul sometimes, so kind to those willing to prove their loyalty.

A masked man in the corner snickered as he advanced on Raoul, snapping a pair of metallic tongs.

"What is it?" Doa asked the man.

"He's considering begging for mercy, sir."

Raoul grunted and gurgled in dispute, but the man hooted.

"No arguing. I heard it all," he said, tapping his temple with the tongs. "Yeah, yeah, it's the serum. That's what they all say, boy."

"I would never beg for that monster's mercy," Raoul's mind hissed. "I'd rather be dead. So go ahead and kill me, because I'll never stop fighting the Council. I will never stop speaking out against the Chancellor's crimes against the good people of Cartesia."

The masked man relayed Raoul's words to Doa, who laughed as he took up the tongs.

He pinched Raoul's tongue and stretched it as far as the ligaments allowed.

"Fight? Maybe," Doa said. "Speak? Never again." The Chancellor's face neared Raoul's, his voice breathy and lilting with secret glee. "It's a shame. I liked your tongue, son. All those times we were alone—me sipping tea, you sipping me."

Raoul's eyes teared, and he struggled to break free, but the leather straps burned his wrist, and his jawbone thundered with pain.

"As much as I'd like to stay and say goodbye to that talented tongue properly, I'm afraid I must rest. You did quite a number on me, my boy." Doa eased his suit jacket aside and revealed the thick cast of gauze under his chrome-colored dress shirt. A pinpoint of blood appeared at the center of the cushion, and Doa groaned. "Shit."

He passed the tongs back to the masked man and winced as he readjusted his jacket.

"It's probably for the best I leave anyway," he said. "I wouldn't want to break my streak of having other people do my dirty work."

The Chancellor leaned in again and planted a cool kiss on Raoul's sweat-dappled brow.

"Tell Jakob 'hi' for me."

Raoul keened and thrashed as the chancellor turned on his heel, and the masked man filled Raoul's sight with his massive body.

He pinched Raoul's tongue, stretched it out again, and with a silver eyedropper dangling above the meat, he said, "Stop moving. You don't want this stuff dripping down your throat."

Raoul clenched every muscle, but the fibrous tissue tremored on, squeezing horrified belches from his tightened belly. He watched with peeled eyes as the dropper loosed a bead of pearlescent liquid that fell like the devil's own tear upon Raoul's tongue.

The drop struck the muscle with shocking cold. After ten seconds, the fire began, like molten pinpricks burning wider and deeper to allow intruding shafts of air. The holes in Raoul's tongue eventually merged, becoming an ambitious ravine longing to free him from the burden of speech.

The last threads snapped, the tongs released, and his skull hit the headrest with circles of red and black spiraling all around him. For a moment, though, before he blacked out, Raoul could've sworn he saw something small and pink tumble to the floor.

Chapter Sixteen

He awoke moaning but didn't recognize his own voice. The guttural grumbles sounded more like a wounded animal. Onyx bruises stained significant portions of his body, and his jaw felt like it hung loose of the right socket. He leaned his face against the cool window and blinked his vision sharp.

Malay Prison appeared behind the fog like a herald of despair. From the helicopter, the massive gray structure with spiny turrets proclaimed desolation and reminded Raoul of his first flight. How hopeful he'd been with Skylark's glistening glass in his future and his mission to rescue Bruiser still intact.

His throat seared as he whimpered for his many failures.

His lips were chapped and scabbed, but when he attempted moistening them he was woefully incapable. He'd prayed for his time in the mythical Muting Machine to be a nightmare, but here he was, a dead stump of flesh clotting his throat and the rest of his life in Malay's claws.

Then he remembered Doa's last words to him. "Tell Jakob 'hi' for me."

Could Raoul's father still be alive in Malay Prison?

He sat up straight and swallowed his pain. If he were to meet his father again, he would do it with what scraps of pride he had left.

The Malay guards didn't make it easy, though. As they dragged him from the helipad down into the scabrous fortress, they spat at him and bashed him into walls. They tripped him and then beat him for falling behind. The trek down winding stairs and musty corridors seemed to last forever, as if he were being towed through levels of a hellish fungal gorge where Warden Grejous waited to welcome the devil's latest spore.

The bottom half of Raoul's face was swollen from surgery. The top half had new thumping bulges, courtesy of the guards, including a contusion that had bloated his left eye shut by the time the men pushed him to the floor. There, shivering in pain and certain the rest of his life would be as cold, wet, and gray as the rest of Malay, Raoul spotted a gleam. A pair of shiny black wingtips winked at him, and he followed the cleanness up the stranger's perfectly creased pants to the crisp charcoal jacket, and then to the pockmarked face of Warden Grejous.

"Hello, Raoul," he said in a dry scrape of a voice. "Do you know who I am?"

Raoul blinked "yes," and Grejous smirked.

"Good. Then you should know I hold your fate in my hands. However," he said, followed by a dejected exhalation, "yours is a special case. The Honorable Chancellor Rojer Doa requested you be kept alive and captive for as long as humanly possible, which means I can't kill you if you annoy me."

Raoul's head wilted with the weight of pain, and he spat out a lumpy dart of blood.

The Warden cleared his throat, and two guards grasped Raoul by the arms. They pulled him to his weak, rolling feet, and forced him to look at Ty Grejous.

"That doesn't mean you should annoy me. There are things worse than death, my boy." He tapped his scummy tongue to his top teeth and dragged, cutting tracks in the thick, yellow film. "But you know all about that, don't you?"

Raoul wanted to spit in Grejous's face, but he didn't have the saliva. The reason why, he then noticed, sat in a small jar on the Warden's desk.

The Warden pressed a sausage finger to the lid and rolled it onto the edge of its circular base. As he rotated the jar, the severed tongue flopped against the glass, but Raoul could swear he felt it tingling in the basin of his mouth. Grejous rolled the jar to the precipice of his desk and yipped when he pretended to let it drop. He caught it before it hit the floor and guffawed as he padded to the glossy oak cabinet behind his desk.

He opened the doors to expose a trove of peculiar sundries, from pieces of clothing and weaponry to a plaited lock of blood-spattered blond hair. He sat Raoul's tongue on a shelf beside a pair of false teeth and what appeared to be a sheriff's badge.

Raoul squinted at the golden shield, and Grejous laughed.

"Caught that, did you?" He plucked the badge from the shelf and held it to Raoul's face.

The words "Cumulus Quadrant Sheriff's Department" shone as brilliantly as they had the first time Jakob let his son handle the precious symbol of his life's work.

Raoul reached out with a child's inquisitiveness and was promptly reprimanded with a bludgeon blow to the spine. He crumpled in agony, but the guards caught and held him up to face the warden.

"I take you recognize this piece of tin?" Grejous asked.

Raoul grunted.

The warden cupped his ear mockingly as he said, "Pardon?"

His wet growls came again, screaming: *Where he is? Where the fuck is my father?* But Grejous just chuckled and shook his head.

"Oh my dear boy, you really must try to enunciate." He placed the badge back on the shelf and closed the cabinet with a whiff of stale air. "It is too bad Jakob isn't here to greet you. Been a long time since you saw your father, hasn't it?"

Raoul gritted his teeth, and fresh torture racked his bones as he nodded.

"I thought so," he said, drumming his chin. "Six years or more, right? Yes, the chancellor mentioned that before we tossed Jakob into the pit."

Raoul's eyes widened and glazed with hot tears.

"Oh..." Grejous's face stretched to a rotten grinning grave. "You didn't think he was alive, did you?"

Rage and sorrow careened the boy's veins, and he thrashed against the chortling guards as Grejous slithered closer.

"He was yesterday, though," the man said in a gravely belch. "The Chancellor didn't like the idea of you two living in such close quarters, and since you're the one he wanted to keep alive, the old man had to go. But don't worry," the warden said, bopping Raoul on the nose. "We made sure to let him know you were on your way here. We told him all about you, Raoul, about how you helped the Council kill his allies, especially about how you killed the King." The warden whistled out a rotten breath. "I was impressed by that, I gotta say. The King was no spring chicken, but he wasn't a slouch, either. That took a lot of balls, kid."

"A lot of serum, most likely," one of the guards grunted.

"True, but we didn't tell your father about that part," he said to Raoul. "Just that you killed the King, and that you're the reason we had to put him down. He was disappointed to say the least. Another year, and he might've gotten released to the underground."

Raoul's fury was a tempest whipping his muscles into superhuman action. He ripped and shoved and knocked both guards from his body so he stood unrestrained before Warden Grejous.

It was the first time during their meeting that legitimate fear crossed the man's cratered face. The warden ran for the pistol in his desk, but he plucked it from the drawer too late. Raoul tackled the man's legs before he could get a shot off and punched him so hard his skull bounced off the floor like a hapless pebble. He ripped the pistol from Grejous' hand and cracked the man's cheekbone with the butt of the gun, safeguarding his unconsciousness.

When the guards shook off their dazes and stormed at Raoul, the killer assumed control. The first guard flew fast at Raoul, grabbing him from behind, but before the man could realize what was happening, Raoul reversed the hold, twisted the guard's arm back, pressed the barrel against his belly, and fired. The man fell backward in shock, clutching his stomach and Raoul, knowing the sound of the gunshot would draw more guards, locked the warden's door.

The second guard didn't attack. He panted, alternating focus between Raoul and his comrade burbling blackish blood down his face.

Raoul pointed the pistol and sneered at the guard trembling in terror. But terror drained from the man and sunk into Raoul when the door jolted with the impact of a Malay horde come to subdue him.

The second guard's scowl lifted, and fluttered his eyes.

"Give up, kid," he said. "You got enough bullets for me and maybe two more, and I guarantee there's more boys than that out there."

Raoul kept an eye on him as he checked the chamber. Two bullets, and the magazine was empty. The fucker was right.

The guard's face flushed a smug scarlet. "I know cuz that's the pistol we used on your daddy. Took only one shot, of course. The rest were for fun."

Raoul squeezed the trigger and shot the red-faced guard in the gullet. He stumbled backward a pace and collapsed dead against the door. The pounding paused then intensified, and not five seconds after the guard fell to the floor, the warden's door busted in.

Raoul stood, his eyes aimed at the dead guards at his feet. Though he'd only wanted Doa's death on his sober soul, he'd killed these men of his own volition, just like the boys defending floor seventy-three in Skylark.

He dropped the gun, and the gang of Malay men pinned him to the floor. He wouldn't fight them, but he didn't want to be beaten, either, so when one of the guards clobbered Raoul's nose and forced a gag into his mouth, he clamped his teeth onto the man's fingers.

Both fingers split at the joints, rocking and ripping free in Raoul's mouth as the man bellowed and bashed his face. Raoul unlocked his teeth, the last sinew snapped, and the man fell backward, spraying warm blood across Raoul's new contusions.

Raoul spit out the top halves of two brown fingers into a bubbly pool of red slobber. He grinned, even hummed a bit in the back of his throat when he beheld the man's blanching face. It was the last thing he saw before his brain sustained a blow rivaling the one Shal delivered in Cessa County Park.

As Raoul sunk into a cold stupor, he wondered if his father saw him suffering from the Crossroads. He wondered if he was glad.

Raoul languished in unconsciousness for three days, slept on and off for four more, and woke anything but refreshed on the eighth day in a six by nine cell in the segregation ward with the worst of Malay's crazies. He couldn't ask the guards bringing him food and water how long he would be there, and no one volunteered the information. He eventually stopped counting time and resigned himself to a cold truth: *This is it. This box is my life now. And I deserve it.*

Speaking to no one but the rats in the walls, their language returning to his disintegrating mind, Raoul began to believe he'd never left Diem. He was still in that house, still quiet and alone. Perhaps he'd even died there, and Malay was all in his mind—a gruesome metaphor for a soul in anguish.

But one day, which started like the innumerable others, ended with Raoul's liberation from the segregation cell. His throat seared with thirst, and the first sunlight pierced his eyes with blades of agony, blinding him as faceless guards corralled him and other solitary cons into the community blocks. The others bumped him, and he thought he heard one whisper, "You're a dead man," into his ear, but his lengthy conversations with the rodents in Malay taught him not to trust anything he saw or heard in the prison.

Raoul survived under that tenet for the next several months. News about his assault on the warden and the guards spread like wildfire, but he ignored every attempt to engage him in discourse. He wasn't interested in one-sided conversations, and with few incarcerated telepaths to interpret, that's exactly what Raoul would've gotten.

He became a deaf mute. As long as his past as a Council stooge didn't leak, he could accept being a topic of discussion. However, his refusal to offer any form of response earned him quite a few black eyes and bloody noses for being a haughty prick. He fought back occasionally, and other times took his lumps without a sound or punch thrown.

Suffering guilt in silence transformed Raoul into a collapsed husk of a man. He shuffled through the prison without thought or expression. He did his work, obeyed all orders, and even allowed himself to be used and abused by the guards. He didn't care, and he was resigned to his apathy for the rest of his days at Malay.

Before Raoul's first year of incarceration ended, however, fate revealed a spark of hope, building slowly as he watched Shal strut into Malay with gruesome purpose. He wanted to share that purpose, but he'd have to make amends first. He expected her to lash out at him, even try to kill him, but upon their first meeting, Shal looked at him as a stranger, and Raoul's heart soared at realizing he had a second chance.

But while Raoul watched Shal, another con watched Raoul.

He was observing her one morning when a woman sidled up on him in the mess hall and slapped the cup of murky, warm water from his hand.

She had a don't-fuck-with-me scowl and rippling iron arms freckled with sunburn. With scarred flesh and cropped hair, she resembled many of the soldiers Raoul had fought over the years, but this woman had one noteworthy difference. The scar like a capsized number eight had deepened with age, her homicidal squint further splintering the weathered flesh beneath her left eye.

"I know who you are, you tongueless freak," she said. "You worked for the Council. You were a fuckin' trench dog—an evictor, an orphaner, a murderer."

Raoul would've answered, "Yes, but..." to each one, but he could only nod and fully accept the blame. He didn't expect sympathy or forgiveness following the admission, but he didn't expect the woman to punch him in the mouth, either—except to cement the proof that she was, in fact, a girl he'd known long ago.

Blood poured from Raoul's split lip, but he didn't dam it. He allowed it to flow freely, then he wet his fingertip with the biological ink. He painted each letter stiffly on the wall, his wrist locked so it wouldn't shake, until his blood spelled out her former name: Bruiser.

The woman's eyes widened. "My name is Xula. I'm a Captain of the Tamora." Her jaw was clenched, but the slight tilt of her head betrayed her conviction. "No one's called me 'Bruiser' in years. Not since—"

Raoul tapped his chest. *Not since me.*

"I guess that answers the question of what became of you. You sold your soul to Chancellor Doa."

Raoul shook his head.

"No? Were you tricked?"

He nodded.

"Then you're too stupid for my sympathy, and I don't like the way an unsympathetic fuck like you is looking at General Shal." She clicked her teeth together, and her next words frothed out between. "So what's the plan, boy? Convince her you're a good guy now, then shiv her in the shower?"

He protested with wild gesticulations that Xula refused.

"You're a murderer. You killed people who only wanted to be happy, who *woulda* been happy if you hadn't been such a stupid, spineless boy." Xula's face crinkled as if knowing this intimately. She released him, and Raoul gasped for breath as he massaged his tender throat.

"How many?" she hissed. "Do you know, or did counting corpses become too troublesome after you and your friends killed the woman I loved?"

Raoul blinked wet and slow and tried to envision which of a thousand corpses had been precious to Xula. It hurt to sift through those faces, for the women blended into one another in recollection—a host of strong expressions going soft, and the light disappearing from their eyes in a more obvious way than it did with men. There was a misplaced sorrow then, when Raoul discovered his fantasies of Xula as Bruiser, which had populated his sober mind since the day he met the Rats of Arqam, inspired the poorest decisions of his life. His was the first happiness he derailed, for no reason at all.

He mouthed, "Who was she?" and Xula bristled. It was as if Raoul's lips inquiring her dead lover's name equaled defiling the woman's body after interment.

"No one you'd consider noteworthy," she said. "She wasn't a captain. Barely a soldier. But she wanted so badly to join me in battle. 'Just once,' she said. 'Just once, I want to see you save the world.'" Xula's face drained to a sick butter-beige, and she gulped repeatedly as she backed away. "Just once it was," she strained to say, eyes averted.

Raoul mouthed, "I'm sorry," and Xula sneered at him like this was her favorite part.

She slammed her forearm to Raoul's windpipe and pinned him to the wall. "Let's get something straight: you could never do or say anything to me that an apology could fix. You couldn't offend me, boy. You couldn't hurt me. I'm the lightning storm to your shrub. Or—" Xula snorted and flicked his chin, "—your stump."

He wanted to tell her she was the reason he'd gone to Grace City in the first place, but it wouldn't have changed her opinion of him for the better. This woman hated him, and with good reason. Nothing he could say, write, or act out with tears and remorseful gestures, would get the girl he'd known as Bruiser back on his side. And if she couldn't trust him, how could Shal?

"I want to hate you, and I will. You can hate me, too. I don't give a fuck. To me, you'll always be a murderous piece of Council trash. I don't care what penance you've done. A week of sport for you boys is enough to ruin your souls for eternity."

Her gaze crossed the mess hall, where Shal sat with Morchai, then swung back to Raoul.

"She's going to get us out of here. She's going to save us all. I know it," Xula said. "But she's going to need as much help as she can get. The Tamora and King's Men will rise again, but Shal needs to survive to lead them."

Raoul shook his head fervently. *Yes! I want that too, Bruiser! Please tell her I've changed, that I'll do whatever it takes to convince her I'm on her side!*

"But Shal's suffering has taken its toll. On her memory, specifically," Xula continued. "She doesn't remember the night the King died. She might not remember you. But if she does, if she hates you as much as I do and wants you dead, you're dead, boy. She just lost her sister, and I won't allow your shitty existence to upset her."

Raoul crinkled his face and tapped his ring finger as he mouthed the word, "Lost?"

Xula's face relaxed. "Oh shit. You are out of the loop, aren't you?" She scratched her face, nail against scar, and sniffled. "Kati Doa's dead. Killed by the good Senator before Shal could save her, and if you think that's not doing something to the bitch, you're crazier than everyone assumes you are."

He blinked and tried to propel his thoughts into Xula's brain. *I don't want to hurt Shal or anyone else! I want to atone for my sins. I can't be silent anymore. She makes me want to scream. I need to scream, or I'm going to die!*

Xula couldn't hear those thoughts, but someone could—fragments and fuzzy uses of her name that beckoned her from across the block.

Raoul felt it. He felt her head lift, her mind echo his voice, and her soft, unsure reply: *Who just said my name?*

Chapter Seventeen

He didn't expect such a laborious day. He'd hoped to laze around the pier, popping off for the occasional overdose and victorious infection—nothing like the abounding carnage at Malay Prison. He wasn't inclined to smile as he traversed such vast, unfolded cemeteries, but there, in his greatest enemy's lockbox, hints of the Capesman's humanity shone. It allowed the deaths of his former oppressors to curl his lips and fill his pores with a memory belonging only to him.

The smile fell fast, and the Capesman went numb again. Death had all but driven empathy from his heart. He could not feel for the deceased as deeply as he wished, but he remembered each one, every collected soul, even those taken by his predecessors. From his direct forebear to the first—the one, the original, the great god-killer—the heralds' lives and memories populated consciousness. Grave contemplation momentarily defined the familiar faces from his past, but they drifted off like aimless children, lost with ease in the web of conjoint retention. He held onto them as long as he could, sitting on the edge of the world with life on one side and the Crossroads on the other, but when he felt the wrench of fresh death, new ghostly faces bloomed in his mind, establishing duty's reign over his existence.

He knelt beside the corpses in Malay Prison and touched their cold skin. It took less than a moment for the wet electricity of the afterlife to spring from the carcasses and queue dutifully behind him, but it still caught him off guard. The transference had a smell he couldn't get used to, like charred flowers or grease-fire taffy, and the noise could be shockingly rude, sometimes sounding of bubbly trumpets or squelchy hisses. None of the afterlife conversions were identical enough for the Capesman's acclimation, but no corpse was unique, either. Death had razed every accomplishment in life to the final one: sloughing off the filthy chains of Cartesia. It was the truest equality. There were no quadrants in death, no classes, no wealth—just a lengthy line and the strangely beautiful herald at the lead.

Some of the deceased knew the Capesman immediately. Some needed convincing. But even those who didn't accept death followed him entranced, content, trusting as ducklings. He glided through the shambles of Malay with his line of souls, and though the few survivors paid him no mind, some appeared to detect his presence. Chins lifted, eyes shone with acknowledging tears, and stunted hairs stood endwise, but ultimately, they knew nothing of him except their gratitude in being left behind.

The train of dead stretched around the cellblock bend and down the stairwell—already too long, and the Capesman had more to collect. He commanded all eyes to him. The line turned in unison, and with a collective blink, the Capesman felt his feet upon the pier. In that same moment came the part he loathed the most—the instant when the corralled dead gazed upon the door to the Crossroads. Histrionics unfolded on him like a fiery blast—sorrow and fear and excitement bundled and blazing from every fiber.

He opened the crimson door and the cool breath of eternity curtained his face. The souls shuffled obediently through, the worry evident in their eyes when the previous person evaporated in the pier's misty terminus.

A terrified man with pockmarked skin approached, hands clamped under his trembling chin. The Capesman knew him all too well but refused to acknowledge the grievances screeched by the many voices in his mind.

"Where am I going?" Ty Grejous asked.

"I don't know," the Capesman said flatly and pointed him to the door.

He didn't know the ultimate destination. Skepticism and anger creased many faces when he admitted this, but it was true. His bargaining skills had years ago prevented him from taking that plunge, so he couldn't know what happened when someone stepped off the pier.

There was, however, one scrap of knowledge possessed by the Capesman alone: the memory of a land called Heaven and a being the world knew as "God." Though he was the last descendent of the original, it was as if his own lips had formed the words that negated God's omnipotence, blinking out Heaven and every soul within. He tried not to think about it, but as he sat on the edge of the world, waiting for the death call, the weight of his decisions crushed every mind within his own. Not only had he caused an entire world of souls to disappear, he'd simultaneously annihilated the cornerstone of faith for billions of people. Some Cartesians believed God endured in some way, that he dwelt within the Capesman and could be worshipped through the herald, but as far as the Capesman knew, they were dead wrong.

He couldn't blame them for wishing they'd known God and His Kingdom. The one Capesman who'd achieved that dream remembered the splendors of the afterlife, and every Capesman since reveled in his memories of the magical place, but then came the overwhelming sorrow of what he'd done, possessing those who'd come after. The first herald took comfort where he could, watching his growing children sweetly tended by the woman he loved. He wished he could touch them, let them know he loved them still, but shame prohibited such happiness. He could not sully their beautiful lives with the stain of his genocidal greed.

He did touch them again, though, years after his first Capesman breath. When his wife and children fell asleep with no hope of waking, he held their hands, and one by one escorted them to the Crossroads. He regretted challenging God's design for many reasons, but witnessing his wife and children walk through the amaranthine door, into the mists beyond the pier, where he could not follow, was the worst torture of all. It was also the last time the Capesman felt anything.

The current Capesman felt nothing now as the last in line passed through the door and into the mist, except the persistent tug from those still left at the prison. He wished he could leave them. Neglected souls without the Capesman or his horn as guide could eventually find the pier and the Crossroads, but it might take centuries—long, maddening years of invisibility and solitude. Some of the cons probably deserved to spend ages as phantoms searching for the elusive pier, but the Capesman would spare them the torment. Even to the dogs of Malay, he couldn't bring himself to be so cruel.

He returned to the prison, where the remaining dead had shrugged off their flesh without him and now meandered the carnage in confusion. Sounding his horn lifted the spirits' heads and drew them to him like moths to light. They followed, like the countless others, to the Crossroads and the mysterious land beyond.

When the dead were again quiet, and he was alone, the Capesman settled on the pier to conjure the dreams of the forgotten. He thought of those he'd heralded onward and those he'd yet to lead. When he thought of the past, he saw many faces scattered in the dark—strangers, friends, family—but there one face outshone all others. Sometimes he forgot her name or their personal connection, like he forgot them now, but a singular phrase clung to the edges of his mind. He didn't know what it meant to him, but it filled his heart with light to speak the words:

"Beauty, til now I never knew thee."

Chapter Eighteen

The autumn air smelled like snow. It was one of his favorite scents, and he looked forward to its first presence ribboning the air. But this time, the crisp promise of winter brought with it stormy colors that painted the sky and left bad omens on his doorstep. His marriage had been in jeopardy for a few years prior, but ever since Rojer Doa started polling the electorate, Marius's bed was in perpetual winter.

There was warmth elsewhere, though. He found it on the lawn, rolling in fallen red and gold, and in the kitchen, beating spoons against the floor to bless his aimless whistling with rhythm. He found it in the dark, where her innocence was like a beacon of light, and between the pages of Shakespeare, cuddled up and crying out for poetry. In the deepest winters of night, he found warmth wherever she was. Wherever Shal was.

He thought he'd achieved true happiness with Luai, but when their daughter was born, the concept elevated to a more vibrant, life-changing definition. One look from Shal was enough to quiet the most tumultuous storm within Marius, and when this new love enfolded and deepened prior his joy, he imagined it would last forever. Perhaps that's why he didn't notice Luai slipping away. By the time he realized how deeply she'd planted herself in the tangled garden of Cartesian politics, it was too late. The roots of power and cachet had already coiled around her as tightly as she used to hold Marius. That was over now. She made it clear that his love, this family, no longer influenced her heart, but Marius refused give up on her. She begged him to cast off his foolish dreams of winning her heart again, but he just smiled, drew her close, and promised he could become whatever man she wished him to be.

Marius never learned how Luai and Rojer met or when they joined together in more than opportunistic deviances, and it didn't matter. Marius knew how *he'd* met and fallen for her, and he couldn't fathom how a love that created something as beautiful as Shal could be dashed forever. Their old happiness lived in their child's smile. Surely they could learn how to extract and embrace that happiness once more. He recognized his thinking as delusionary, an admission that frequently made a midnight battlefield of his mind, but he'd rather be happy than right, and he'd rather try to rescue their love from oblivion than watch it burn to ash at the foot of a more prestigious man's bed.

Shal didn't care about her father's lack of prestige, nor could she understand *how* it was lacking. His peers respected him as a professor of Payne University, the only higher education school left in the Cumulus Quadrant, and the reverence lingered following his departure from teaching, when he opted to pursue politics. His wages were scant as an educator, and the accounts dipped into critical condition soon after, but if anyone asked Shal, she would gleefully declare her father the richest man in Cartesia. Her world didn't turn on finances or titles. For Shal, his talent in reading from *The Complete Works of William Shakespeare* made him a king amongst men. Marius was her cipher, translating the complexities of all men into one unwavering unity that stemmed from her father's examples of goodness, civility, honor, and diligence. And most important of all, his example decoded the importance of having a sense of self assigned from the inside, not from a gang of men who valued obedience over free thought.

Marius knew his banishment had a hand in dashing the world she'd built, but shaking those fatherly foundations was the least of offenders. Even if he hadn't challenged Rojer Doa following the death of the venerable Chancellor Pleskin, if he hadn't publicized his favoritism of democracy over oligarchy, Luai would've chosen Rojer over him just the same. Without a binding marriage agreement, she was free to do so, and Marius wagered she could've finagled her way out even if they'd been married. His regret never lessened, though, thanks to one small fear that if he'd just given up on her instead of challenging her lover, he might've been allowed to stay close by, to watch and guide Shal's life.

But that's not how it went. At least, not as prettily. After banishment, the idyllic man known as "the King" provided guidance to Shal through stories of valor and peril while her father, Marius, played dead.

That was after he'd been embittered by failure. When he first launched his campaign for Chancellor, Marius had all the hope in the world. More, actually. After the Last War, after God's death and the opening of the rift, the panicked world *needed* someone to step up. Someone had to prioritize Cartesia's needs and restore order. Someone had to collect and catalog what rift gold hadn't been stolen, as well as how many healthy citizens remained following the tectonic shift. Cartesia needed the Council's aid then. But deep into the second century of its dictatorship, Marius believed Cartesia needed something new.

He had no chance. An intellectual, an optimist, a follower of literary men like Earth's transcendentalists—how could the world accept a man like him when the majority thought life was excellent as is, and the rest were either underground or too fearful of being driven underground to announce their support? Nevertheless, he had to try. For a better world. For a happier daughter.

It was difficult summoning followers, especially from the ritzier quadrants. Legions of Cartesians were just trying to survive, glad to be miners and steelworkers, farmers and seamstresses, to be good and worship right. The Council instructed them exactly how to do this, of course, especially when it came to worship. God was dead, that much was true, but He could never really be dead if they kept Him in their hearts, as the Council kept Him in theirs. Then, with enough faith, God could return one day, and all of Cartesia would be saved.

While the Council didn't approve of Capesman-worship, they had a nebulous stance on whether they believed he or she or it was an angel, a devil, God's own kin, or something worse that slipped through the rift from even God couldn't know where.

It wasn't surprising that people secretly regarded the Capesman as the "new God," but neither God nor the Capesman were half as divine as the Council. They dictated who lived and died, who prospered and failed. They condemned and absolved, and then often condemned again. They lorded Cartesia in ways many of their followers outright refused to confront, while others shrugged and said, "What can you do?"

The words churned in Marius, day after day, year after year.

What can you do?

He tried explaining it to Shal when she was too young to understand. He just needed to say it, to tell someone who couldn't judge him that he was terrified. He didn't know how much longer he could "be good and worship right," and he dreaded the day he'd rebel and spill his truth.

Shal giggled and kissed his cheek and made his tears into a game, wet gems of costume jewelry she tossed aside in favor of squishing his face into the smile she loved so much. It assured her that peril could never touch them, not as long as Daddy and Shal were together.

His arms enfolded her, and he swallowed the urge to unfetter that darker chamber of his heart. It was silent for a while, reappearing in pale, sweaty dawns when vigilante communiqués listed the noble dead, or when Luai debuted an outfit she couldn't afford.

The terror wasn't so easy to shake. It stuck with Marius for his remaining time above ground, but it was worth watching his daughter grow a few years more.

The day of the election results arrived like a dark and whipping winter encroaching on October skies. As Marius stood beside Senator Rojer Doa, gazing out at the roaring crowd gathered for the polling and inauguration ceremony, he realized that the past year of speeches and promises had all been meaningless. Marius could shout his throat bloody, but he'd never be louder than Doa's title, and every heart-clenching distinction of every soulless politician on the inaugural podium screamed, "Obey, or be cast underground!"

Leaving the life he'd built with Luai festered cold in Marius's belly. Demented as it was, he still saw her at times as the girl down the road, the one with the mile-high legs and a devil's knack with a fiddle. She used to play it at night, in the red-veiled lamplight of her bedroom, and he'd been one of many boys and girls entranced by her.

Marius couldn't remember what became of the fiddle. Or of the girl.

She'd been replaced seven years ago, he supposed. It wasn't deliberate, but Marius had fallen so utterly in love with Shal that Luai's little affection got tumbled up and lost among her more frequent scowls and insults. He wasn't sure when her expressions became inconsequential as the wallpaper, because he'd cherished both and couldn't recognize that both badly needed renovation. It was no wonder she told Shal her father was dead.

He was, in a way. Marius, a man who had for years believed love, free thought, and value could return to Cartesia, was vanquished by the very hope that spurred him. He still believed the world could be liberated from the Council's tyranny, but he would not be a part of it.

Chapter Nineteen

Underground, he had no name. But he did answer to various monikers. "You" was fairly common, as was "the Quiet One." He worked his way through the underground which, much to his surprise, the people had excavated and colonized into a community more than half as large as Cartesia. He worked odd jobs in mining, engineering, and the pipeworks, as well as a few months as a hydroponic farmhand for a subterranean lake.

He spent a year working for and patronizing the warrens of underground life, all the while dreaming of the life he'd left behind—minus a few players. When sorrow became a noxious smoke, strangling his vision and making him feel he'd made a horrible mistake, he would center himself by visiting reader's row. The network of home-based libraries snaked along the stone bank of a serpentine river known as Bone Gulch, and thrived among the most bustling sections of the underground community. Depending on his mood, he could usually be found in the mystery house or the historical house, though he frequently searched the various houses for new poetry, which didn't yet have its own abode. The mythology and religion houses were the most popular, as was the rift gold house, curated and personally guarded by a man named Loche. All homeowners interacted with rift gold, however, as the librarians doubled as scribes: studying, duplicating, and binding copies of the precious pieces from other worlds.

It was there, at Loche's rift gold house, that a new underground citizen and fan of William Shakespeare's work learned more about who Shakespeare was.

"He was an actor," Loche explained as he flipped the yellowed pages of a William Shakespeare biography. The paper was in good condition, all things considered, but certain paragraphs and sentences were lined in orange; sometimes deliberately like a stab of color, and sometimes scribbled into confusing boldness.

"He was in a group that performed for a queen, even before his plays and poems were out in the world. Even more after, though. It says here the group was called the 'Chamberlain's Men.'"

Silly as the nameless man thought it was, he bristled at how the title "Chamberlain's Men" reminded him of the chancellor and his boys.

The gooseflesh softened when Loche stuck a thin, wrinkled finger in the air.

"Ah ha, the name changed!" he exclaimed. "It says here the group name changed to the 'King's Men' when the queen passed away." He blinked wildly and flipped several pages. "That's strange. Did the queen consider herself a Chamberlain? I don't think that's in here. I wonder if this William Shakespeare occasionally fancied himself the king of players. He doesn't seem the humble sort." Loche shrugged, smiling. "I think I prefer 'the King's Men,' anyway."

The nameless man turned the biography in his hands and said, "I agree, sir. Thank you for sharing this with me. I had a piece of his rift gold once—*The Complete Works of William Shakespeare*—and this reminds me of home."

Loche's eyes widened. "How many works?"

"Thirty-seven plays. One hundred and fifty-four sonnets."

The man staggered and fanned himself as he laughed. "Holy Crossroads. I haven't read half of that. Do you not have it anymore?"

"I left it behind."

Loche clapped his hands to his cheeks and howled. "Left it? Why?"

The nameless man passed the book back to Loche. "Someone needed it more than me."

Loche sneered, but it quickly morphed into a smile. "How kind of you. How kingly."

In addition to being a literary man and connoisseur of Cartesian lore, Loche had served as a heredity soldier in the Council's militia when he was young. He was skilled in various areas of combat, especially with a sword, and shared many lessons over the next several years with the man he dubbed "King." As his new protégé grew in strength and knowledge, the underground citizens were drawn to their labors. While men, women, and children had been training underground for years, no one was willing to assume the militia's helm until the King volunteered.

He promised them revenge, he promised them progress, and within a year of taking command, the King's Men had acquired numbers to rival the Council battalions occupying the lesser quadrants. It was then they deemed themselves ready to venture out of the hidden world to eliminate every Council soldier they could.

Tales of the King's triumph over Council boys in Diem and Cumulus reached Chancellor Doa, who disseminated squads to discover whether the

King and his men were more than myth. His soldiers stalked the army's rumored hideouts above ground but gravely underestimated their stealth. The Council and the King Men's would not meet face to face until the King wished it.

As he strode into the abandoned Chartreuse Distillery in southern Cumulus, the King knew what awaited him. He dropped his weapons, opened his arms wide, and welcomed the soldiers that streamed at him from behind rusted tanks and worm-eaten barrels. They towed him into the boiler room where tension and rage gelled with the shadows so horrifically the chamber appeared cobwebbed with threats. Chancellor Doa emerged from the dark, his head tilted and laughter dancing from his throat.

"What are you doing here?" he asked musically. "I was expecting a so-called king."

"Then your expectations have been met." The man lifted his chin with a smirk. "I am the King, Rojer. A rank higher than Chancellor and more beloved by far. I suggest you kneel to your superior."

Doa giggled, then widened his jaws to propel his amusement into wall-rattling mockery. He snapped his head to men with a wheeze. "Leave me with the dreg," he said, and the soldiers disappeared into the secret valleys and nests within the heart of Chartreuse.

Alone with the King, Doa shook his head, his face lined with morbid pity. "I don't believe it. All this time, and you're still trying to win Luai."

"This isn't about her. It's about you."

"Because I came out on top, I know." He chuckled as he fanned a fresh patch of sweat on his cheeks. "You must learn to let these things go, Marius. It's pathetic."

"If I were the only member of the King's Men, perhaps you'd be right, but I have a legion of followers, Rojer, and each one has a dozen reasons for wanting you dead."

"What a coincidence," he said, whimsically inflected. "I have just as many reasons for wanting them dead."

"And who do you mean to rule when your people are dead?"

"Those are not my people. They're dregs, and you're welcome to them, Ki—" Rojer bent at the waist with a soprano wheeze. When he lifted, he continued laughing but waved the tears from his eyes. "Oh, I'm sorry. It's just so funny thinking I should call you 'King' when you're such a worthless shit."

"And you're a monster," the King spat.

"I'm a politician," he corrected. "I'm not surprised you don't understand the difference. You've never had the stomach to do what this world really needs to be done."

"And what's that?"

In the low boiler room light, Rojer Doa's fingers were amber stems crooking to talons.

"A deluge," he said with a hawkish hiss. "To start from scratch."

The King's face scrunched. "You want to destroy Cartesia?"

The Chancellor couldn't have been more diplomatic in his swishing finger and pursed expression. "No, no, no. Destroy means..." He shrugged. "Well, it means *destroy*, and that's not we want at all. We want to *refresh* Cartesia. That's been our plan all along, ages before I took the reins."

"And the underground..."

Doa laughed and waved his hand as if smacking away a gnat. "We'll deal with them in time. And those who survive...well...the bonecrunchers will get hungry."

"You can't do that."

"It's practically done. A few more years, perhaps, and this world will be cleansed. We will start anew and prove to God that we are ready for His divine presence again. We will show Him we're worthy...once heathens like you are out of the way," he said. "In fact, it's probably best if my boys take care of you today. Then the dregs *like* you will quickly peter off to nothing."

The King cocked his head and spoke with a silvery lilt. "How do you expect your boys to kill me when they're already dead?"

The smirk dropped from Rojer Doa's face. "What?"

"You didn't really think I'd come without backup, did you?" The King tsked and shook his head. "Are you sure your type is the best to bait God into existence? I have a feeling He wouldn't be fond of your leadership tactics. Or lack thereof."

Color drained from the chancellor's skin. He backed himself against the wall but tensed his muscles to maintain his regal poise. "Call them in then," he said. "Let your army tear me apart if that's what you want."

"Oh no, Rojer," the King said as he advanced slowly. "I don't want them to tear you apart. I can do that just myself." He grabbed Doa by the neck and whispered in his ear. "And it'll be a lot more fun that way."

The King tightened his grip, and the chancellor wheezed, his skin gray and clammy as a dead fish.

"Have it your way," he squeaked. "But before you kill me, rest assured your daughter's corpse will make its way back to you. I've already made arrangements for you to receive it following my funeral. I know it seems like a long time to wait, but it's protocol in this sort of situation. I regret her body will be likely a bit rancid by then, and I can't speak for how...incomplete...it might be, but I promise you will receive the bulk, even if it takes several shipments."

The King relaxed his fingers and hardened his scowl. "You're bluffing."

"Am I? I'm her stepfather, Marius. Do you really think I don't know where my dear little girl is right now?"

"She left Ides," the King said as he stepped back. "She's in hiding."

"But she isn't hiding underground, which means she's on my turf," he said. "I see every move she makes."

"If that were true, you would've killed her already."

"Now that I know her connection to the King, I definitely want to keep her around, if only to torture you." Doa drummed his chin. "You know, I'd consider telling her the King's true identity, but she seemed so happy that you were dead. She never warmed to me, but Luai and I figure it's because you did such a number on her, leaving like that."

"It's because of you!"

"No, Marius. You brought this on yourself. You campaigned for her hatred." Doa licked his lips into a grin. "If you choose to kill me today, I promise she will know the truth before she dies. She will know the King is her father, living happily divided from the child he pretended to love."

The King's chin trembled, and he grunted as he turned his back on Rojer Doa.

"That's right. Run away," the chancellor said. "Hide underground, dismantle your army, and live out your days for as long as I allow."

"You don't control me," the King grunted over his shoulder, and the chancellor snickered.

"I just did."

The thick, coppery stench of blood flooded the boiler room when the King opened the door. His soldiers stood at attention, their weapons streaked crimson from the Council boys limp at their feet. As he walked away, Rojer called after him with a caustic address.

"Your Majesty!" Pausing to cackle, he continued. "You should know that while I acknowledge Shal's value, I won't protect her. If she and her middling little army attack my property, Council boys included, I will be forced to discipline her."

The King's Men exchanged puzzling glances, and Doa sneered.

"Oh dear, you didn't know she ran her own crew, did you? I suppose I'm not shocked, you being an absentee father and all. In that case, I won't elaborate. It's probably best you remain a ghost."

The King led his soldiers of the corpse-strewn distillery, but the chancellor's laugh chased him. It was a ghost too, haunting the King and his comrades— except for those he commissioned to scour Cartesia for information about a new renegade army built by a girl named Shal.

His soldiers returned underground with stories of narrow escapes and sneak attacks. He heard of her strength in battle, how she grew more menacing by the year and massacred Council boys who outnumbered her army five to one. Most inspiring were the stories of how she protected Kati Doa. Even when the fight seemed futile, Shal stood between death and the chancellor's daughter, immovable.

Marius didn't want that kind of life for his daughter, but each time he heard of her victories against the Council, his heart swelled with pride.

Chapter Twenty

He'd died nearly a decade ago, but acrid blood still flooded his tongue when he thought of that day in Cessa County Park.

"Killed by a Council boy," he spat. "It's shameful, Marius."

He didn't want to recall that moment when his body became useless meat, but sometimes when the mists of the Crossroads were so high they billowed over the amaranthine door, he found himself enveloped by death. In that fog, his mind swam with visions of every Capesman's death, including his own.

The death itself didn't pain him. It was the last face he'd seen before his demise that whipped his heart into a sickening agony. Though many faces appeared to him as the Capesman, Shal's blazed singularly in Marius's mind after expiration. It weakened him, like a blade of glass diving in and out of his heart as he stood in line on the pier. His knees trembled, then buckled. Sandwiched between a Tamora soldier and a weeping Council boy, Marius collapsed like a ragdoll.

The line kept moving, and despite all efforts to stop, turn around, or reverse, Marius moved with it. He wasn't the only one who crawled to the edge of the pier, but he was the only one who recognized the Capesman was wilting, too.

Five souls ahead of Marius, the trim Capesman with dewy amber skin grunted and directed the dead to the Crossroads with lackluster waves and head bobs.

The closer Marius got to the herald, the more he panicked. He'd done everything wrong. On the pier, with his soul at its most honest, he knew he wasn't 'the King' he'd pretended to be. Not at the core. Marius's truest self began and ended with his child. All those years when they were apart, he'd been incomplete.

He realized it now as he approached the Capesman. He hadn't been happy a single day without his daughter. "It was for the best. For her protection," whispered the memory of every underground morning. "Don't go to her. You'll get her arrested. You'll get her killed. You'll ruin her life."

But what life was there to ruin? While separated, they hoed the same rows, cultivated the same sins, and hated the same men. Shal's life was as ruinous as her father's before her. Living apart had done nothing but plant more seeds of sorrow to flower in full before the Crossroads, plaguing Marius in cold, petaling regret.

With his head bowed, the Capesman pointed at the swirling mist beyond the red door, but Marius didn't move. "Go on," he said, eyes still directed downward.

Marius stood up and shivered out one word: "No."

The Capesman's eyes lifted. He hunched his back and huffed loudly. "I don't have time for this."

"How long have you been the Capesman?" Marius asked quickly.

"I don't know."

"You look tired."

The Capesman's chest rose and deflated with a puff of air. "Yes. I'm tired of people trying to talk their way into a job they don't understand."

"If it's so horrible, why did you talk yourself into it?"

"Because I was a fool."

"So am I. What better replacement than a likeminded man?"

The Capesman shook his head. "You don't know what you're asking for, friend."

Though sorrow weakened his muscles, Marius straightened his spine and stared into the Capesman's rich chocolate eyes. "I'm asking for the chance to see my daughter again."

"You won't know her as you do now. Your priorities will shift, and her face will dissolve into the billions of others populating your mind. I can't remember what my family looked like, let alone if they ever loved me. A human loses everything in becoming Capesman."

"For you, maybe, but my daughter is everything to me, and she's in danger. I can't leave while I can still help her. Please. Now that I'm dead, I realize I have something to live for."

"Just like everybody else," the Capesman replied blankly.

"Maybe, but *she's* not like everybody else. She's unforgettable."

A pitying smile bloomed on the Capesman's pale pink lips. "You really are a fool, and you will realize all too soon how dangerous that is."

Marius's throat went dry. "Are you saying you'll do it? You'll make me the Capesman?"

He nodded, eyes closed. "I've held out as long as I can, but it's time for me to walk on, to finally see what lies on the other side of the mists." His smile abandoned all notes of sadness then, and when he opened his eyes they glistened with tears. "I hope when I'm there, I am me again. Only me."

"What do you mean?" Marius asked.

"You'll see."

The Capesman grasped the former King's hand, and heat charged through him like a thorny fever that punched holes in the very fabric of his being. Each new pit filled with eons of knowledge until the man known as Marius shrank and thinned until he existed only in the spaces between the holes, flimsy as used thread.

He knew he was important. Powerful, too. The Capesman had a strange feeling like his power was needed elsewhere, something about a girl and an army far from the pier, but he shrugged it away. Nothing was more important than heralding the dead.

When the former Capesman let go, the man heaved a sigh that brought a truer smile than any that had graced his face since bargaining his way out of death. He hooted and embraced the new Capesman, and the souls still in line glowed rosy in shared jubilance. As the man who'd been herald disappeared into the mist, the dead knew they were headed for a better home than they'd ever had in life. Those who'd been scared of the Crossroads now jittered in eager anticipation, and no one sought to barter their way home.

The new Capesman felt the same truth glow in him, but there was no jubilance. When the souls were gone and the door closed, he retreated into his collective memory. He swam through tumultuous fathoms of faces and places, and though there was familiarity in many of the images, he found himself incapable of distinguishing his contributions from the pool.

He swam those busy waters following his recent heralding at Malay Prison. The souls had left something at the pier—a scent, or an aura—that troubled his oceanic mind and summoned from the depths an unforgettable face he'd long forgotten.

Whatever madness had transpired at Malay Prison, his daughter had been there, and she'd survived.

Chapter Twenty-One

Raoul opened his eyes to a gun barrel. Beyond it, fingering the trigger, Shal stood with vengeance gleaming in her good eye. He raised his hands in surrender. He wanted to explain his part in her father's death, but he knew she didn't want to hear it. He was terrified, pouring sweat, and every organ like a raisin of its former self as his eyes wandered from the pistol to his bizarre surroundings.

Shal quickly curtailed that curiosity by slamming the gun against his head, and he crumpled to the rubber floor, his mind pleading. "Shal, I beg your mercy."

"Tempt not too much the hatred of my spirit for I am sick when I do look on thee," she growled. Her finger curled around the trigger and she held out her hand to block the brain-spray.

Slender fingers fell upon Shal's pistol and forced it down, sparing Raoul's life for a few seconds. As Shal turned to quietly bicker with a young woman who crinkled her heart-shaped face, Raoul watched in wonder.

"I thought you wanted him here," the girl said. "You said he was your friend."

"I was wrong," Shal replied. "He's a liar. He killed my father."

"How? When?"

"That night in Cessa County Park, the night the Council abducted you."

The auburn-haired girl peered around Shal at Raoul. When their eyes met, they shared a gasp. Raoul hadn't met the girl, but he'd seen her enough—especially in the chancellor's familiar face.

"Kati Doa," his mind whispered.

She squinted at him. "I don't know you. If you know me, it means you've watched me, and if you've watched me, it means someone told you to."

Raoul nodded sadly, and Kati sighed.

"That's a shame." She beckoned to three large men in dingy jumpsuits. "Throw this traitor into the dirt."

The men tromped to Raoul, grasped his arms and legs, and hauled him toward a large circular door.

"Shal, I never wanted to hurt your father!" his mind screamed. "I never wanted to hurt anyone! I admired the King. I admired you for as long as I could before—" He swallowed hard. "I was drugged. Doa, all those Council bastards—they had control over my mind."

Shal signaled for the men to halt. They set Raoul down, but one man kept a large boot on his back, pinning him to the floor. Shal crouched beside him and said, "Explain yourself. Quickly."

"The Council made me a murderer. For years, I slaughtered innocent people believing it was right, that it was what I wanted. That day in Cascade when you left me for dead, you saved my life, Shal. I missed the yearly inoculation that kept me subservient to the Council. I sobered up, became myself again, and realized the truth. I tried to get my revenge—I tried to kill Doa, but I failed. That's when he took my tongue."

"Why didn't you tell me any of this before?" Shal asked.

Raoul looked to Kati Doa. "Why did you tell me your sister was dead when she wasn't?"

"To keep her safe. I didn't know who I could trust, and obviously, I was right to be cynical."

He nodded. "I'm sorry, Shal. I was ashamed. My past is a graveyard I've tilled and filled with carcasses I once called free will and honor. I've hated good men and women, some my own blood, but nothing compares to how much I hate myself."

"What's he saying?" asked the man with the boot on Raoul's back.

A smile bloomed on Kati's lips, and her talent with telepathy permeated Raoul's mind in silky, feminine tones. "He says he hates himself."

Shal narrowed her eyes at the former Council Captain. "I know how he feels. I hate him, too."

Kati waved at the man with the boot on Raoul's back, and he stepped away.

Shal squealed, "What are you doing? He admitted to killing the King—my father." Her voice dipped into a soundless ravine mossed with sorrow, and Kati patted her back.

Raoul reached out, but she refused his sympathy. "I haven't been under Council's control for almost a decade." With hands clasped and pleading, he appealed to her. "I promise you I'm the same man I was in Malay, the man who loved and supported you for years. You trusted me yesterday, with so many intimacies of your life."

Kati's eyebrows lifted, and Shal grunted as she turned away, planting her forehead on the slick wall.

Raoul stood, aching from head to toe. While Kati leaned against the wall beside her sister, the three men in jumpsuits grunted as they extended their hands to Raoul in hesitant camaraderie. Fleck, Greyer, and Ilana introduced themselves individually, but their identical mannerisms betrayed their shared genetics.

"Triplets?" Raoul asked Kati.

She nodded. "They were the first multiples in almost a century."

"How is that possible?"

Kati's lips were pinched as she spoke to Raoul's mind with a smirking lilt. "How is telepathy possible?" She spoke aloud again. "We lost so much after the Last War. Even what we gained from the rift hasn't helped the common people much, but we've been learning underground. We've been dissecting and building and isolating the rift gold among us. We've found God in our blood again."

"The underground is fertile?"

The triplets smiled together, and Ilana said, "More than you'd think. It's funny how escaping constant trauma allows the human body to heal."

"And the mind to bloom," Fleck said to Raoul's mind.

Raoul stared at him. "You're telepaths too?"

"Only Fleck," Kati replied, and Raoul's brow crinkled. "Odd, I know. We've come a long way, but we haven't figured everything out yet. And maybe we're not supposed to. Many of the doctors believe telepathy is an innate talent like singing. One can be taught to carry a tune if he or she really concentrates, but it's never natural or quite as beautiful as a natural born telepath."

Raoul's cheeks filled with air, and he exhaled. "There's so much I have to learn. And now that you're not going to kill me—"

Shal glared at him, her face knotted as a devil's backbone. "Don't be so sure of that."

"Fair enough," he said, hands up in surrender. "But may I ask a question?"

She looked over her shoulder and said, "You may."

"Where are we?"

"You dove down a bonecruncher's throat," she said. "Where do you think you are?"

"Citizens of the underground built this replica over the past few years," Kati said. "We call it the Tempest. It's our primary mode of travel these days and, surprisingly enough, well-liked by authentic bonecrunchers."

"Sometimes a little too well liked," Greyer said. "We've had more than a few try to fuck us in transit. Nearly killed the lot of us."

Raoul squinted at Kati. "Aren' t you already supposed to be dead, Miss Doa?"

She smiled and embraced her sister. "We're all supposed to be dead now."

"I don't understand. I thought your beef with the Council was about avenging your stepsister's death, Shal."

The Tamora leader pushed off of the wall and stomped to Raoul, her face tight as a coiled snake. "Do you only want the Council destroyed because they took your tongue?"

"I see your point," he started, "but then why lie to your allies in Malay? Why say she's with the Capesman and fake the grief?"

"Because death was the only way we could think of to free her," Shal said, brushing hair back from her sister's face. "And it was never fake. Kati was alive, but I still couldn't be near her. I couldn't live with the comforts of her kindness and logic. Mourning her was easier than missing her."

The girls crisscrossed arms around each other's waist, and Shal leaned her head on her sister's shoulder.

It was the only time Raoul had seen Shal adopt a softer air than those around her.

"Besides, real trust can't thrive in captivity," Shal continued. "As much as I trusted you and Morchai and Xula—" Her sight fell to the floor at the mentioning the dead—"I couldn't let any of you in on the plan when I didn't know if Kati could carry it out. I couldn't risk that one of you would betray me for something as trivial as an undosed meal."

"And it's a good thing she lied," Kati said. "Otherwise you'd still be stuck in Malay."

Shal smirked with pride. "How goes the rest of the rescue, by the way?"

"Underway. The Snug is on the job."

Shal cocked her head. "Snug?"

"The Tempest isn't our only transport. It is the best, however. The Snug will need a bunch of repairs after this is said and done, but it's one of the many things I'm eager to show you, sister." Kati squinted one eye as she pointed at Raoul. "Have you ever been underground?"

"Never," he said. "And I can't believe I have to go now with all these sins on my soul. I should've gone with the other shop hands. I should've saved my muscle and money to leave Diem for that life."

"Were you one of Cryster's shop hands?" Fleck asked.

"Briefly."

"Some of our best soldiers are Cryster stock, especially those who escaped the trade," he said.

"Like Bruiser," Raoul whispered.

"Who?"

He raked his top lip with his bottom teeth and clenched his jaw. "Xula."

Fleck nodded. "Yes, like Xula."

Ilana grunted. "Could you guys clue in the linguistic, tongued freaks over here?" he asked.

"He knew Xula," Fleck said.

Greyer nodded sadly. "I can't help but notice she's not here. Was it the bonecrunchers? Was it our fault?"

"No, it was mine," Raoul said, head bowed. "Indirectly at the very least."

Shal's focus shifted, and with surprising sympathy, she touched his shoulder. "A lot of people could take credit for that. Myself included." She wiped budding sweat from her upper lip and unclenched her jaw. "I can't pretend I'm not angry you lied, Raoul, and I haven't forgiven your grievous crimes against Cartesia, but if what you say is true, if you were drugged and coerced to kill, you can't take the blame for everyone's deaths. Not even the King. It wasn't you who killed him. It was a Council puppet, and that flunky dog is long dead." She squinted at him. "Right?"

He nodded emphatically, his mind ballooning with gratitude.

"Then let's just rejoice that the asshole's gone and move on. You've done enough penance for your sins. We all have. Now's the time to focus on making Rojer Doa pay for his."

Her face was relaxed, even glowing with sympathy, but her eyes shut abruptly. She slumped onto a rubber bench and massaged her temples with a moan..

Kati crouched beside her, a hand on her knee. "Are you all right?"

"My head's been pounding like mad since the Doc." She folded her body over her thighs and dropped her head between her knees. Exhaling through pursed lips, she wiped rivers of perspiration from her forehead.

When pain released her, she lifted her head with a trembling half-smile. She stood again, but acute agony returned with a sudden wallop that knocked her to the floor. She gripped her face and wailed, jerking uncontrollably.

Kati screamed her sister's name as Fleck brought Kati her medical kit.

"What's happening to her?" she asked.

"I knew this would happen. It's that crackpot's damn machine," Raoul said.

"What machine?"

"Some cons develop amnesia from the trauma in and out of Malay, but Shal's got it worse than anyone I've ever seen," Raoul said. "She couldn't remember huge chunks of her life. She can now, obviously, since she finally recognized me as the King's murderer after all these years."

"So all of her memories are coming back in force?"

"I'm not sure. Most people come out of the dream machine mad or brain dead."

Blood trickled from Shal's nostrils and her body convulsed. Kati and Raoul held onto her as she writhed, mumbling to herself strange words Raoul couldn't understand.

"What's she saying?" he asked.

Kati leaned closer to her sister's whispering breaths, closed her eyes, and frowned. "She's saying 'keep calling.'"

"What does that mean?" Raoul asked.

She dabbed Shal's forehead with her shirtsleeve and whimpered. "She's stuck in a memory, and believe me, it's a fucking awful one."

Chapter Twenty-Two

The Haystack Hotel was pungent with sex and mildew—hardly an appropriate place for a honeymoon. However, it was unusual for a honeymoon to include a husband, a wife, and the wife's father, so convention was out the window anyway. Facedown on the bed, Kati screamed as Senator Danzig consummated the marriage, each sickening creak of the bedsprings enraging Shal more and more. With knife in hand, she peered into the balmy room to see her sister cut and bruised, her blood flowering across the dingy mattress.

The man cackled as he withdrew and followed who Shal assumed to be Chancellor Doa into the bathroom. Once they were gone, she slid in and crouched beside the bed.

"Kati, I'm here."

The girl turned her face to Shal and flashed a bloody, broken grin. Though she had auburn hair and a similarly shaped face, the girl on the bed was not Kati Doa.

Shal peered over the mattress into the bathroom. The men inside were Council, for sure, but they weren't Chancellor Doa or Senator Danzig—rather, Senators Hanson and Ludo. The monsters were well known for duel sport with prostitutes, but this couldn't be a chance encounter. The girl on the bed resembled Kati too closely for it to be coincidence.

She'd been tricked. After almost a year unable to communicate with Kati and teased on a monthly basis with coal renderings of her sister enduring the foulest of violations in Grace City, the first instance of Kati's voice was enough to wrench Shal out of hiding. Just like the Council knew it would.

Shal concentrated as hard as she could, through the laughter from the fiends in the bathrooms and the screams of Haystack patrons on the other side of the discolored, wafer-thin walls. Beneath it all, tucked in a dark chasm she couldn't quite see, a girl discharged her telltale whimper.

"Kati," her mind whispered. "Can you hear me?"

The whimpering stopped. Shal didn't know how, but she knew her sister lifted her head before wheezing, "Shal? Is that you?"

The hotel room shook with a metallic chorus of threats—steel from scabbards and mags into pistols—and a horde of Council soldiers leapt out from hiding with their weapons drawn. The girl on the bed screamed and wrapped the soiled bed sheet around her body as she dashed out of the room.

As the captain of the army marched to Shal, her mind continued its pleas. *Call to me, Kati. Keep calling.*

The captain chortled and wrenched the knife out of her hand.

"Where's my sister?"

He shrugged in theatrical ignorance and nodded to his men. The Council dogs swarmed at her and bound her wrists at her waist with a leather belt. Their sticky fingers found every inch of her as they tied her up and carted her from the room.

The captain shoved Shal against the corroded balcony railing, her pelvic bone slamming the metal as she groaned.

"Tell me where she is."

His body melted over her back as he whispered, "I'll tell you, baby, but I need something in return."

His hand snaked around her waist and clawed underneath her shirt. As his hands explored her ribcage and up to her breasts, Shal envisioned a violent and prolonged death for this man, including removing his manhood altogether. He squeezed her gently at first, but his fingers quickly turned violent, and he twisted Shal's tender flesh like spinning a top.

The punch of pain dropped her to the filthy concrete where the captain crouched and purred his abhorrence into her ear. "I wouldn't touch you with another man's dick, you renegade shitstain." Pressing his face to the back of her head, he added, "The Chancellor, though...He's gonna have a good ol' time with you, doll."

Shal closed her eyes as she exhaled deep and slow. Pain became no more than a jagged gasp when she jerked her head back and slammed her against the captain's nose. The ache came seconds later, but she was content with the throb as a red faucet washed the slimy smirk from the dog's face.

He fell back, knocking down a few boys like bowling pins, and Shal bolted down the hotel's precarious staircases. She had a hell of a lead on the soldiers and would've kept it if another legion of hooded men weren't waiting for her on the second level.

Faced with the subsequent wave of Council scum, Shal reeled around to retreat, but several boys latched onto her arms and ankles, and they wrestled her cheek to the cold, wet slab of a window. The Haystack Hotel's seedy occupants peeked out their rooms through squeaky doors and mildewed windows, seemingly relieved Doa's men hadn't come to apprehend them.

The drugged whelps howled in victory, hooting and high-fiving while their captain descended the stairs. He screeched for the boys to pay attention, but it was too late. Shal cocked back her foot and swung it as hard as she could at nearest pane of glass.

The broken window shredded her calf, and her brain swam with dizziness as blood rushed down her leg, but she didn't hesitate. She thrashed against her captors, wailing and throttling and spraying them with blood until the captain stopped her struggle with a rattling punch to the face.

Shal wilted to the concrete with real pain but fake unconsciousness. As the boys decided who won the honor of carrying the "Ta-whore-a" down the final flight, Shal's fingers moved covertly to the nearest shard of glass. She concealed the blade between her lashed wrists, pinning it flat to slash the leather belt as safely as possible. She rocked the fragment back and forth, thinning her bonds to threads as the boys dragged her down the steps to the van idling in the parking lot.

When the captain slid open the dented door to the van's dank, blood-spattered belly, opportunity once again revealed itself. Council boys were either forbidden improvisation or too stupid to recognize opportune moment, so when Shal ripped her bonds apart and tore a pistol from the battalion captain's holster, the hasty squaddies didn't expect it.

The captain's bullets gave their owner his last dental exam, spraying bone and enamel through the crowd. She leapt into the van and squeezed the trigger until she'd exhausted the chamber, hurled it at a Council boy's face, and slid the door shut. She locked it, pumped a mag into one of the handguns in the van, and pressed the barrel to the clammy temple of the Council boy behind the wheel.

"Don't, please! I'm just a driver," he shrieked.

Tears ran down his cheeks as Shal twisted the pistol like trying to screw death into his skull.

"Shut up and unbuckle," she said.

He whimpered as he loosened his belt buckle and opened his pants. "Please don't do this. I'm not military, I swear. Senator Danzig promised me marriage privileges if I drove tonight. I've never even been with a girl."

"By the Capesman's cock, I meant the seatbelt, you idiot."

The driver gratefully flung off his seatbelt and climbed to the passenger side. He mumbled rapidly and incoherently as he buckled up, whimpering at the wave of soldiers pummeling the side of the van.

Keep calling, Kati. Help me find you.

Shal's brain prickled with whispers as she jumped into the driver's seat, turned the key in the ignition, and pointed the gun at the sniveling man.

He squeezed his eyes shut, and she snickered.

"Please, like shutting your eyes is going to make a bullet to the brain any gentler." She waited until he opened his eyes, then bopped him on the nose with the barrel. "If I put the pistol down to drive, you're not gonna do anything idiotic, are you?"

He shook his head, and a snot bubble expanding from his left nostril popped on his top lip.

"Good. You seem like a nice guy. I don't want to hurt you."

"But you would." His wet, clumped eyelashes flicked quickly. "Wouldn't you?"

Council boys rammed the van again, and the former driver winced. The dogs gathered in front of the vehicle and howled as they beat the bonnet.

Shal tossed a look of schoolgirl innocence at the young man beside her. "I'm a cold bitch, but I'm not cold-blooded."

She grinned in hungry glee, stomped on the gas pedal, and the tires squealed out a malicious song that perfectly complemented the metallic thuds of bumper against bodies.

The former driver screamed and shielded his eyes but couldn't disregard the van's new glowing red interior. Shal flicked on the wiper blades, which swished and cut through the scarlet fluid, and she bobbed her head back and forth with the motion as she plowed over the newly bumpy road. The judders and sways dropped the visors and popped the glove compartment, shaking out napkins and various lengths of tubing.

The young man curled into a ball and wailed with each crunch and squish. A faint, sour smell wafted through the van, and Shal looked over to see he'd vomited on his pant leg.

He gripped his belly and gurgled. "Was that necessary?" he asked.

Shal certainly thought so. Plus, if those boys had survived to limp back to Skylark after allowing a dreg to steal a Council vehicle, they'd be slaughtered anyway.

She offered him a doleful smile, and he pressed his hand to his slimy lips with a shudder. When the van squealed to a stop behind an abandoned bakery, the former driver popped up and stared at Shal with tears making his eyes appear trembling in his skull.

"Get out," she said.

His hands shot to the seat belt latch plate, and a finger tapped the button. "Really?"

"I need to concentrate, and you're too loud," she said. "Unless you happen to know where Kati Doa is being held."

He shook his head, and she believed him.

"Fine. But a little advice? Go underground. You'll be better off."

"I don't have anything to offer them," he said softly.

Shal grunted and waved the gun in his face. "This myth about needing something to offer the underground, like they're running out of space, it's bullshit. Skills can be taught, and muscle can be built. Goodness can be faked and mocked, but it can never be acquired. We need people like you."

"Thank you, Ms. Shal."

"You're welcome. Now get the fuck out."

The young man fled—a little wiser, she hoped. Parked behind the building, Shal listened again to the teeming world of voices pumping through her brain as she whispered, "Keep calling, Kati."

Then, beneath the cacophony of deceiving screams, her sister's weeping blasted through Shal's brain. Her mind fixed on Kati's location, she released the emergency brake, and she peeled away from the Haystack Hotel.

The shotgun house near a collapsed mineshaft resembled a tool shed halfway through sloughing its moldy skin. Shal slowed beside the hovel, squinting at the bedroom light shining through the slats and holey curtains. She couldn't see Kati, but as a view from the other side of the slats developed in her mind, the van rumbling between, Shal knew Kati could see her.

She drove up the road and parked behind a grove of ebony trees. Jumping into the back, she searched through the assorted weaponry. The handguns and scattered mags were empty, so she pocketed a serrated dagger caked with fruit pulp—at least, Shal hoped it was fruit. She was just about to disembark when, out of the corner of her eye, something metallic winked from behind a veil of red cloth.

The chainsaw didn't look like it had been used in a decade. The teeth were dull, and patches of rust peppered the chain. She tugged the pull cord, and the chainsaw sputtered angrily before dying in her hands.

Shal grunted and then remembered the glove compartment. She crawled to the front, ripped out the tubing, and carried the supplies to the van's gas task. After feeding the tubing into the tank, she readied the chainsaw and took a deep breath.

It wasn't the first time she'd syphoned gas from a Council vehicle, and she doubted it would be the last, but it was the first time she'd sucked and spat and wincingly filled a chainsaw's oil-sludged tank. First, second, forty-fourth, it didn't matter. Syphoning wouldn't ever be a task eligible for acclimation. Her head spun as she worked, and her body churned with rank, paroxysm belches. Gasoline drool dripped from her lips as she gagged. Her eyes watered and brain buzzed from the fumes. She told Kati to "hold on and keep calling," but there was only silence. She had trouble standing, let alone breaking through the pungent fog blocking her telepathy. Gripping the pull cord handle, she spat a fresh coat of nausea from her tongue. Sickness didn't matter as long as—

The chainsaw wheezed and spluttered, and then, it whirred to life.

Hot blood rushed her veins and hardened her resolve. Shal grinned, silenced the chainsaw, and planted it against her shoulder as she careered down the road to save her sister.

The struggle was evident from outside the back door, and though it sent her gas-soaked mind into a whirling rage, she opened the door slowly. She tiptoed around the corner, her movements deliberate and silky as they could be for a furious bitch with a relic chainsaw.

Deep grunts and snorts rumbled from the only room with a closed door. Shal briefly investigated the others before standing at the closed door, a shuddering breath pelting the chapped wood. Her fingers perspired against chainsaw and slipped when she tugged the cord.

The chainsaw coughed, and the noise in the room stopped.

With a growl, Shal flung open the bedroom door, and readjusting her grip, yanking the cord again.

Senator Danzig turned to Shal slowly, his head bobbing and flabby face wearing soggy shock. He lifted his hands in surrender and stepped back from the bed, where Shal saw her half-naked sister lying motionless, terror stretching her slack, blue-tinged face.

Shal panicked. Her heart commanded her to run to her sister, but the rest of her demanded she put the chainsaw to good use. She obeyed the majority.

Her eyes were closed when she cut into him, feeling only the warm spatters and spurts of success, but she opened her eyes wide to watch his expression lose its angles and curls. Nothing so blank had ever been so beautiful, hanging frozen in air before his body succumbed to the belligerent blades. Shal tried to pull the chainsaw free, but Danzig's organs wrapped around the blades like eager children grasping for the brass ring on a carousel, so she released the chainsaw instead. It toppled with him to the floor as Shal leapt onto the bed, where her sister lay motionless.

Kati's eyes were open, bulged from her sagging eyelids, and her mouth agape, but when she bent closer and laid her hand upon her sister's chest, she felt a thin thud of life within.

Shal tilted her sister's chin, clamped her mouth to her Kati's, and pumped her breath into the precious girl's deflating lungs.

Kati didn't even flinch.

With an animalistic cry, Shal reared back, locked her hands, and slammed her fists as hard as possible against Kati's chest.

The precordial thump rattled her sister's body, and like a jack-in-the-box, the girl sprung up and gasped for breath. Her violet hue bled pink, and she fell, wheezing thin air, into Shal's arms.

She whispered against her sister's shoulder. "You found me. Thank the Capesman, you found me."

"I will always find you," Shal said, stroking her hair.

Kati abruptly pulled back. "My father. He'll be back any minute. We have to get out of here."

"Not until he's as dead as Danzig."

The front door opened and closed, and Kati quaked. "He's here. Run, Shal, before it's too late."

"I'm not going anywhere, and neither are you," she said, shutting the bedroom door. "Lie down and stay still. Stay dead. He'll be so dazed by Danzig, I can get the jump on him."

Kati whimpered as she lied back on the bed, eyes fixed on the yellow ceiling and jaw slack. Her breath was so shallow Shal barely detected the rise and fall of her chest. She looked dead again, and Shal's heart ached at the charade.

Chancellor Doa's shoes clicked on the rotted floor as he approached the bedroom, and Shal ducked into the closet. He opened the door and loosed a shuddering wail as he fell to the soggy carpet.

The world was slivers of orange light shining through the slats of the closet door. Shal watched in building rage as Rojer Doa wept over his mutilated associate before moving to his motionless daughter on the bed. Her hatred intensified so radically it incinerated all thoughts of patience or strategy, and when Rojer reached out to touch Kati, Shal burst from the closet with her knife drawn.

Doa's face was peaked, and his extended hand trembled over Kati. The one behind his back, however, was steady as he untucked his pistol and fired.

The bullet whizzed through the air, tore through the flesh of Shal's left bicep, and burrowed into the wall behind her. Shocking pain stole her strength and sent her, howling, to the sticky crimson carpet. She gritted her teeth through the pain and, launching herself at the chancellor's legs, she tackled him before he could fire again. She knocked his pistol into a coagulating puddle of Danzig's blood and screamed as she plunged her dagger into his side and gave it a good twist.

He screeched and squirmed beneath her, but his eyes remained fixed. "My boys are right behind me," he hissed. "You don't have time to play around."

"Thanks for the tip." Shal withdrew the blade roughly, and though agony echoed through her wounded arm, she raised the knife to gouge the chancellor from her life once and for all.

The heavy, brain-rattling blow of a bludgeon against Shal's skull loosened her grip on the knife and knocked her from the chancellor. On her back, the room spinning madly and her brain unable to comprehend any of it, Shal gazed up at the four Council boys crowding around her.

Several clamped rags to the chancellor's wound and helped him to his feet while others gathered, wide-eyed, beside Kati.

"Don't touch her," Shal mumbled. "I'll kill you if you touch her."

Chancellor Doa's face was glazed with greasy sweat as he glared down at his stupefied enemy. "You've done enough, darling. Killing a Senator and—" Doa choked back an unconvincing sob. "My only child."

"I didn't—I would never—" The wooziness was subsiding, and Shal tried to stand, but a Council boy planted his boot on her ribs.

Rojer gripped his side as he laughed. "Pick her up."

The dogs wrangled Shal to her feet as Kati's voice crept into her mind.

"Shal, I can't stay still much longer."

She whispered for Kati to hold on, and she snorted at the chancellor. "What are you going to do, Rojer? Kill me?"

When his laughter caused too much pain to bear, he signaled to his boys, who snickered loudly for him.

"Death is peace," he said, gagging on "peace" like it tasted of rancid meat. "And peace is one of many things a bitch like you doesn't deserve."

"Maybe you're right, but Kati does."

"Kati's dead, and so is her fertility. I don't give two shits what she deserves anymore."

His daughter's whimper came to Shal in mental resonance, which she hushed with gentle proclamations.

You deserve peace. You deserve freedom. You deserve happiness and a family who loves you. I love you, Kati. I'll get you out of here. You'll have everything you deserve.

She screwed up her face at Doa. "Then you won't mind if I take her when I leave," she said.

Chancellor Doa guffawed through his pain but turned away before she could spot his eyes filling with tears.

Shal took advantage of his pride. She slammed herself against the soldiers, pulling free of their grasp, then kicked out her leg, nailing Doa square in the tailbone.

The blow launched him at the bedroom window, and his skull bounced off the glass, cracking the pane and sending him unconscious to the floor, where his blood seeped through the rag and pooled with the late Senator Danzig's. The soldiers smacked Shal mercilessly with their batons, but she squashed her immense pain by channeling into their noses and shins and whatever tissue and bone her knuckles could find.

Though her body raged in anguish, she didn't stop swinging or kicking until every soldier was slack on the floor. She retrieved the serrated dagger and ensured the soldiers couldn't pursue her—until a hand gripped her shoulder. She swung around with a start, the knife cutting through air and stopping mere inches short of Kati's trembling face.

She looked smaller than ever, pulling a blanket tight around her body, and tears spilling down her cheeks. "We need to go."

"Not until they're all dead."

"No. Now."

"But Kati—"

Kati's face was stiff, her hands clenched to fists. "I've been with these assholes for nearly a year. You have no idea, Shal..." The resolve broke, and her knees noticeably weakened.

Shal wrapped her arm around her sister's waist, wincing, but Kati unwrapped herself and instead took on her savior's weight.

"You need medical attention," she said.

Shal whispered, "Bullshit," but an overwhelming darkness fell over her like a warm embrace. She couldn't see her surroundings, but she felt like she was moving. Kati was with her—she knew that—helping her, healing her, and Shal knew she had to help Kati next.

A cooling breath in her left bicep inspired a smile in her fevered sleep, and she said dreamily, "Go underground. Leave tonight. Leave everything behind. Including me."

Chapter Twenty-Three

A tender hand upon Shal's face roused her from unconsciousness. Her lips and chin were stiff and crusty with dried blood, and she rubbed her mouth as she sat up in bed, her gaze rolling sleepily around the steel berth and settling on Kati's rosy face.

"Thank the Capesman you're all right. You've been gone for hours," she said.

"What do you mean? Where was I?" She rubbed her head and swung her legs around to the floor.

Raoul sat beside her on the bed. "You tell us."

Kati handed her a wet cloth, which Shal used to wash away the blood. Once clean, Shal stared at the rag speckled with scabs and scarlet spots, and she gritted her teeth.

"I don't know. I think it was—" She met Kati's eyes. "The day you went underground."

Kati exhaled heavily through flared nostrils. "It was also the day you surrendered to my father, the day you got sent to Malay."

Shal pinched her sister's cheek. "I prefer to focus on you, Sis."

"So I've noticed." Kati giggled as she engaged Shal in a brief slap battle.

The leader of the Tamora flicked her sister's nose and stood, grabbing the overhead rails to steady herself as the artificial bonecruncher tunneled through the earth.

"Maybe you should take it easy," Raoul said, but Shal answered glare as she pushed past him.

"I take it the players are standing by," she said.

Greyer stepped forward. "The Tamora eagerly await your return."

"What about the King's Men?" Raoul asked.

"The remnants of the King's Men and the Tamora have unified, along with a great many others," Fleck replied. "The underground is no longer a refuge for outcasts. It is a community of great men and women, and a staging ground for revolution."

"Did you know that?" Raoul asked Shal.

"Of course. I know everything," she said smugly.

Raoul grunted in frustration. As he paced the berth, the Tempest passengers watched in confusion.

"What's he doing?" Greyer asked.

"He's cursing me out," Shal said. "He's pissed I didn't tell him about the underground. Plus, he thought he taught me how to use telepathy."

He spun on his heel and shoved himself in Shal's face. "Why did you keep it from me?"

Shal grabbed Raoul by the arms and pushed him onto to the bed. She crouched between his knees, a hand on each thigh. "Listen to me. You were solitary in Malay. You didn't talk to anyone."

He dropped his jaw and waggled his stump of a tongue.

"Smartass," she said, smirking. "Fine. I kept some shit from you, but I can't apologize for it. We both had our deceptions. Besides, my withholding gave you purpose. It opened you up to the possibility of alliance."

"Which you regret now that you remember who—*what*—I am," he said, eyes averted.

She clutched his chin and forced him to look at her. "What you are is a lost soul, someone who's been deceived, used, and mutilated. What you are is one of us."

"And we number in the thousands," Kati said. "Every quadrant but Ides has fallen to chaos and criminality, but underground, there are warriors to rival even the most skilled of Council soldiers."

"Most of the soldiers aren't as skilled as you think. They're brutish," he said, "but they're brainwashed to be that way, and unafraid to die."

A squeaky din crackled through the room, followed by a man's voice. "General Kati, we've reached the eastern bridge."

Shal raised her eyebrows at her sister. "General?"

"It's a ceremonial title. Mason's the one running the show most of the time."

Shal's expression softened to one Raoul had never seen cross her face before. Her skin flushed, and she nervously scratched under her eye patch.

"You're surprised he was chosen to lead?" Greyer asked her.

"I'm surprised he's still alive," Shal answered. "I thought he would've been the target of an assassination years ago."

"It wasn't for lack of trying," Ilana said. "After you were arrested, he staged an attack on the Violet Orchid when he knew Doa would be there having dinner. He managed to kill twenty-some soldiers and a known underground harvester, but he couldn't get close enough to take out Doa himself. Following that, every Ides battalion was after him."

"I was present for three of the assassination attempts myself," Kati said. "When he realized all of our lives were at risk because of his proximity, he disappeared for a while, but he's been back and leading for nearly three years now. Not one day has passed in all that time that he hasn't mentioned you, Shal."

Her face was blank, but she fidgeted with the shredded bottom of her tunic, and as Raoul watched her, an itchy envy rose from his belly.

He asked softly, "Who's Mason?"

Shal sighed. "Mason was my second in command for a long time. If it weren't for him—well, I don't want to think about that. Mason, Kati, and I started this whole thing. He was everything to me in the beginning."

"I suppose that will resume when we disembark," Raoul said.

"Afraid you'll be replaced?" Fleck asked with a knowing sneer.

"No one is being replaced. We need all the support we can get," Shal said.

"But," Kati started pensively, "maybe you should lay low for a while, Raoul. Stay on the Tempest for now. Some of our people are Skylark escapees, not to mention soldiers you probably fought in the past. A good deal might recognize you as a Council dog or the King's killer. We'll need time to explain it to them. Even after that, there might be some who'll refuse to trust you."

"So force them. Shal's their leader. They have to listen," he said.

"We don't force people to do what we want," she said. "That's the Council's way, not ours."

The bonecruncher transport shuddered and then squealed to a stop that threw Raoul off the bed. Shal's chuckle was thankfully swallowed by the intercom's crackle.

"Hooking up. Hold on, kids."

Raoul scrambled to his feet and grasped the overhead rails with the others. The Tempest shimmied with mechanical squeals, clicks, and whirs of machinery Raoul couldn't imagine. With one last judder, the Tempest lurched, and the intercom crackled again.

"Hooked. Door's open."

Kati led the crew to the exit, where they met Captain Banta, a mahogany skinned woman with impressive biceps and crown of loose, curly black hair framing her face. She spun the exit hatch and popped it open to the silver tunnel attached to the bonecruncher's side. At the end of the tunnel, a dim light shone like a circular haven, occasionally obstructed by inquisitive heads popping in and out to watch the passengers approach.

Though Raoul was instructed to stay, he couldn't help hiding behind the others to sneak a peek at the underground. He'd imagined it as a world in ruin, more dilapidated than Diem, and home to a rotting civilization too distraught with banishment to consider renaissance.

He'd imagined wrong.

In many ways, the underground was more magnificent than Grace City. With structures of ivory rock and steel, the metropolis was of humble but majestic construction, built by the hands of the free. It was not the work of dregs but of the divine reborn. If God were to return as the chancellor wished, this would be His kingdom, His people. Squat buildings dotted the area, along with natural bridges stretching over rushing rivers and lakes in the deep earth. Sunlight streamed down upon them from secret crevasses, spotlighting the hidden world, but Raoul's astonishment at the noble place was nothing compared to that of the people occupying it. They also did not appear as Raoul had envisioned. Their faces were clean and beaming when Shal stepped out to greet them, and they moved with a buoyancy and strength he'd never seen on the surface. They couldn't all have known Shal personally, but when they embraced her, when they bowed their hands and wept in joy, it was obvious she'd become a legend in her absence, and her return to the underground, a symbol of hope.

Chapter Twenty-Four

Raoul couldn't sleep. The Tempest's berth was fairly comfortable, but his mind raced with unwelcome thoughts. At that moment, an entire world was celebrating Shal's homecoming and waiting for the Snug to return. The second mechanical bonecruncher would deliver the surviving cons from Malay, who would be welcomed with open arms. They would be given nourishment and warmth, human contact.

Meanwhile, Raoul was stuck in a room that got colder and harder by the minute. He wanted to burst from the mechanical bonecruncher and declare himself an ally, but he feared doing so prematurely would result in violence from the underground—and from the killer Raoul fought to suppress. He could taste his chemical bloodlust now, the yearly's phantasmal surge and embrace, and worried about succumbing to those primal urges once more. As much as he'd hated doing Chancellor's Doa's bidding, the crush of knuckles against bone or enemy blood upon his lips bought beautiful satisfaction to the killer within. His enemies had changed their faces, but the hidden man didn't care. He craved death—any death.

To distract himself, he turned a golden object over and over in his hands. He'd never held his father's badge for this long while Jakob was alive. Not because it was forbidden, but because the glistening piece of prestige had intimidated him. First, because it was important to his father and represented Cartesian law and order, and second, it was the foremost reason for his family's banishment to Diem. The badge was both Jakob's pride and his downfall. Strange, Raoul thought, how something so small and bright could drag down a host of lives.

The Tempest's hatch door opened beyond the berth, and curiosity coaxed Raoul's body from the bed. He slid to the wall, his ear pressed to the cold steel and breath slowed to silence. Footsteps foretold the approach, and he backed away into the darkest corner of the berth. He wasn't afraid the underground soldiers would storm the Tempest for his blood, but it was a possibility. So, he stood on alert, the killer primed—as if he could stop it—and when the berth door unhinged and swished to welcome the corridor glow, Raoul's muscles hummed with purpose, and his father's badge stuck through his thin pocket into his thigh.

Shal's solitary eye gleamed like a searchlight scanning the dark and Raoul stepped forward, head bowed but gaze tilted upward in hope.

"Did you explain my situation to your people?"

"Yes, and most are understanding about it. Others…" She spun with a huff and sat on Raoul's bed. "They're naturally suspicious. I don't think anyone's ever come back to the light after living so long in the dark."

He nodded as he sat beside her. "What about you? How wonderful does it feel to be in the light again, free and home?"

"Freedom and light, those I'll accept gratefully. Home is another story—several, actually—and none of them end well."

Raoul chuckled. "I suppose it was stupid of me to think victory would change you."

She squinted at him. "Victory? No, Raoul. There is no victory here. Not until—"

"—until the chancellor's dead, I know."

"Until they're all dead," Shal said. She averted her eyes. "Maybe even me."

"What do you mean?"

"If this turns out well, if we destroy the Council and raise the underground, if we stand united in Cartesia to welcome the first peaceful morning in centuries, I will still be blood-drenched and broken from the soul on out. I will be an eternal symbol of these dark days and unworthy of our new world."

"Shal, no—"

She faced him again, her eyes blazing. "Stop. I didn't come here for this."

"What did you come for?"

She clamped her hand to the back of his neck and pressed her mouth to his. With their lips entwined, Raoul whispered grateful surprise to Shal's thoughts.

I didn't think this would happen again. With what I did, how I hurt you—

Shal broke the kiss, grasped his face, and said, "You can't hurt me. Now take off your fuckin' pants."

She dressed in a hurry as Raoul watched in worship from across the balmy bedroom.

"Where are you going?" he asked.

"I'm late for a meeting," Shal replied as she pulled on her boots. "Mason is going to be pissed."

"I'm not enough for you? You have to run off to your other lover?" Raoul's tone was playful, but fear trembled beneath the steadiness of the question, and Shal felt it.

She tightened her laces and marched to the bed where Raoul sat, sneering. A slight smile jumped to her lips but fled by the time she cocked back her fist. She swung hard, and her knuckles slammed against his left cheek, knocking him backward onto the mattress.

Raoul cradled his throbbing face and spat at her. "By the Capesman's cock, what the hell was that for?"

"For being jealous. You have no right to that emotion when it comes to me. Whatever you think you feel, it'll only complicate things."

"Don't tell me what I feel."

"Stop playing make-believe, and I'll be glad to. There are enough battles on the horizon, and I'm not interested in adding another feud to the list."

He stood up and shoved himself in her face, teeth gritted. "And I'm not interested in being your fucktoy."

"What did you think you were in Malay?" she hissed. When he backed away from her, she sighed and massaged her aching fist. "Admit it, Raoul. That's all I ever was to you too."

"Maybe. But sometimes a person wants more."

"Not me."

"I don't believe that."

"Then you're an idiot, and I should've let the bonecrunchers have you. I don't have time for this emotional shit."

"You don't have time for emotions whatsoever," he said. "Now I know why you don't fear death. You're already dead inside. There's nothing warm or human left of you."

"Then why would you want more from me?"

Raoul rarely opened his mouth to communicate, but his lips and teeth and breath were thrashing rage when he grabbed onto Shal and his mind screamed, "Because I fucking love you."

She shook herself out of his grasp with a grunt. "The underground has women. Warriors, beauties, prospective mothers. I'm sure one of them will make you very happy."

"I don't want one of them. I want you."

"Tough shit," Shal said.

With a disgusted scowl, she turned on her heel and trudged to the door. She tugged it open, and stepped into the hall, but Raoul's thoughts called out to her.

"I believe love will return to the people of Cartesia," he said, "I also believe it of you. You can love, Shal, and one day you'll see it as clearly as I."

She looked over her shoulder at him, her voice dripping with sorrow. "And I believed you knew me. It seems we've both been proven wrong today."

Shal kicked the door closed, and the clang echoed throughout the Tempest, but it wasn't louder than Raoul's voice still screaming through her mind.

Because I fucking love you. You're dead inside. Because I fucking love you.

She rubbed her temples as she walked the underground. Though many citizens waved and greeted her, she ignored them, focusing instead on the path to Mason's house. Her head pounded like war drums, and sweat glazed her face by the time she stood outside his window. As she wiped off the perspiration with her sleeve, she gazed in at her ex-husband sitting at his kitchen table, twirling a knife.

He looked nearly the same as the last time she saw him. New scars decorated his arms and chin, but not enough to steal his beauty. He was still that boy who'd allowed Shal to know the truth. He was the rebel who touched her, who inspired her, who made her tremble when he said, "Please don't be afraid of me."

Pain cracked through Shal's brain. Raoul's face was there. Mason's too. Then there was Kati and Doa and a man she knew better as "King" than "Father."

She cried out, and Mason turned to the window. Her vision blurred, and the blood came fast, rolling hot down her lips as his house tilted in her collapse.

Please don't be afraid of me. Because I fucking love you.

Shal's head cracked on the doorstep, hemorrhaging memories.

Chapter Twenty-Five

"Are you sure you want to do this?"

Sinking in an ocean of time, Shal flailed in helpless fury. She wished she could answer "no." She wished she could grab onto Mason and beg him to take her away from the house on Archer Avenue, back to people who cared about her, who would fight for her, but she couldn't speak for the blood clotting her throat. She couldn't move under the pressure of forced remembrance. She had to wait, half-sunk in the rocky silt of her memory, and watch as a two-eyed woman approached the house, knowing a one-eyed woman would leave.

"Are you sure you want to do this?" Mason asked again.

"Look at her," Shal said as they stared through Luai's front window. "She's nothing. Dried up Council trash. She can't hurt anyone anymore. Besides, I want my father's book. She doesn't care about Shakespeare. It belongs with me."

Luai sat hunched in her living room under the dim light of a lamp with a stained glass shade, staring blankly at a broken two-way radio as she downed her second glass of gin in less than ten minutes.

Shal hardly recognized her anymore. Luai had both lost and gained weight. She was gaunter than usual, but her face was puffy, the skin like a thick, dimpled hide hanging from her skull. She wore a dress too ritzy for a lazy Sunday and white fur gloves that made Shal crinkle her nose in disgust. People in Diem were starving, killing each other over food and shelter, and Luai was decked out in finery. She'd been moved out of Skylark two years prior, but she still called herself the chancellor's wife, no matter how much tail Rojer Doa paraded under her nose. The biggest indication that she was wife in name alone, however, was the glaring lack of guards outside her residence.

Shal and Mason crossed to the back of the house and entered through the kitchen. While he rummaged the cupboards for supplies, she shuffled into the living room where her mother munched on gin-soaked ice cubes. There were empty bottles stashed behind the furniture and blankets and pillows piled in the corner of the couch. It appeared her mother had been camping out there for a while.

"I figured you'd come sooner or later," Luai said to the bottom of her glass. "You were always too stupid to know what's good for you."

Shal stood in front of her mother with a sigh. "I expected a worse greeting than that. You're getting soft."

Luai pulled a pistol from between the couch cushions and aimed it at her daughter as steadily as she could. "Better?"

"It depends. Did anyone leave you with bullets? The Council's pretty picky about that sort of thing."

She lowered the weapon, her face screwed up into a sour knot. "I don't need them. No one would dare threaten the chancellor's wife."

"You don't have to act like nothing's changed, Mom. And you don't have to be ashamed," Shal said.

Luai growled and threw the empty gun at Shal, missing her by a sizable distance. Mason appeared in the archway between the kitchen and living room. Giving Shal a nod, he pocketed the gun and headed upstairs to give the mother and daughter some privacy.

"What would I ever have to be ashamed of? I am the most powerful woman in the world."

When Shal snorted, Luai tried to stand—perhaps to strike her daughter—but she couldn't manage a moment's balance before falling back to the couch. She discharged a furious sob, more at her empty glass than Shal, and then buried her face in her trembling hands.

"You don't have to put up with it anymore. You know that, right? All you have to do is walk away, admit that he used you like he uses everyone."

"Do you see a child toddling around here?" Luai gripped her loose belly and screeched. "Do you see one growing? I've not yet been used. I'm not done. As long as I'm fertile, I can give him what he needs."

She poured a hefty drink, and Shal sat on the coffee table.

"*Here never shines the sun,*" she said as Luai guzzled. "*Here nothing breeds, unless the nightly owl or fatal raven.* This world is an abhorred pit, Mom, with a thousand fiends and hissing snakes, swelling toads and urchins, all fearful and confused and crying themselves to madness or death."

Liquor dripped down Luai's chin, but she caught it with her middle finger and sucked up the renegade drop. "What the fuck does that mean?"

"It means it's over. Truth is, it never began, because nothing springs from a wasteland, save new ones. If you haven't conceived his heir yet, I doubt you ever will," Shal said, and added quietly, "The Capesman be praised. But," she continued, "As far as I know, it's not happening with anyone else either."

"Of course not. Rojer's a good, loyal man."

"No, he's a monster shooting blanks."

Luai slapped her daughter hard across the face and hissed. "Shame on you. He's your Chancellor."

Shal ripped the cold glass of gin from her mother's hand and pressed it to her burning cheek. "No Chancellor has ever been my Chancellor. Besides, we can't be certain the problem doesn't lie with him. Kati's mother died in childbirth, so we never got her side of the story. It's possible Kati's not even his."

Luai snorted. "Everyone is his." She slugged from the gin bottle, spilling an aromatic waterfall down her chest.

"How long has it been since he visited?'

"I'm well taken care of, if that's what you mean. I have food, water, everything I need." She patted her stomach sadly. "Almost."

Shal's hand quaked when she reached out and laid it atop Luai's glove. "You don't have to stay here. You can come with me, somewhere safe."

Luai's expression warmed for a moment, then hardened as she shook away Shal's kindness. "I would never run off with a dreg like you. I'd wind up dead, or worse, in Diem."

"I have lots of places, Mom. Many outside of Diem."

"Of course you do," she said with a bitter snarl. "Why try to find a home or build a life or God forbid commit to something of worth? Just like your father and his useless dreams."

Shal stood and glowered at her mother. "I have built more in my life than you ever have, and if my father did half as much before he died, then I am proud to be his daughter."

Her mother laughed so hard it incited a coughing fit. Pounding her chest, Luai looked even older, like her bones buckled under the force of her fist. After catching her breath, she issued one more wheeze of amusement, then pointed at the door. "Get out, or I'll call my boys."

"With what?" Shal plucked the broken radio from the table and dropped it on the floor. "You don't have any threats left, Mom. You don't have anything."

Luai scrunched her nose in disgust. "Like you do?"

"I have plenty. I have allies and people who depend on me. I have places to go when I want to be alone and when I want company. And most important, I have hope."

"You have brain damage," she spat.

"Mom, if he can't use you, he'll kill you. He's done it before."

She waved a gloved hand. "If he was going to kill me, he would've done it already. He's generous, Shal. That's what you don't understand. He gave me these," she said, flipping her hands back and forth to display her elegant fur gloves." She patted the cushion beside her, and with a sigh, Shal sat on the couch.

Gazing upon her mother, Shal searched for a glimmer of the woman who used to tuck her in at night, who used to take such pleasure in the perfect construction of her little girl's braid and read no lines but Lady Macbeth's when she and Marius recited Shakespeare. There was nothing of the sweet woman Shal thought she remembered. Lady Macbeth, however, hung cold in that gin-fat face, in her dangerously dainty timbre, in the strange, soft way she rubbed her pelt-swaddled fingers over Shal's arm.

Shal grasped Luai's hand to push it away, but three of the fingers collapsed under her grip. Her mother tried to recoil, but Shal held firm and ripped the glove from her mom's hand. The pinkie, ring, and third finger were severed at the middle knuckle, long healed to gnarled stumps.

Luai snarled as she tore the glove from Shal and stuffed her mangled hand inside.

"What the hell happened?"

"Another gift," she said, unwavering. She flexed her remaining fingers in their fur sheaths. "And a reminder." With her intact hand, she grabbed Shal's wrist and grinned. "You have hope? Big fucking deal. You have no happiness, no home, and no prospects for a normal life. With none of that, 'hope' is just a word, each letter a filthy lie you tell yourself to keep the noose slack." Luai huffed, her upper lip curled to a snarl. "Maybe you need a reminder, too."

"You don't know what you're talking about."

"I do know," she hissed, pulling her daughter close. "I know because I had the same disease once. Lucky for you there's a cure."

For a waste of a woman, her hand moved fast. It slipped into the couch again and withdrew another weapon. The silver fork was petite, a three-pronged utensil for oysters, but Shal didn't know those details until later. In the moment, all she saw was the glimmer of metal flying at her face and the tip of a filigreed handle protruding seconds later.

Shal fell to the floor, wailing and whipping the fork buried in her left eye while her mother clapped her hands in joy.

"Ah ha!" Luai warbled. "The requiem cries of hope. I know them well!"

Mason ran into the room, took one look at the woman smirking over her gouged daughter, and picked up the stained glass lamp. He swung it at Luai's shrewish face, and the shade shattered against her skull, stabbing her cheek and scalp with colorful shards. The blow knocked her to the floor, and for the first time in her life, she was incapable of complaining.

Mason held Shal still, hushing her as he pulled off his shirt to staunch the torrents pouring down the left side of her face.

"Breathe, Shal. Just breathe," he said as he gingerly closed his fingers around the fork handle.

"What are you doing?" she squealed.

"Just hold still. It's not that deep. I can get it out. Hold my hand. It'll be over in a second."

Shal felt the initial agonizing tug and then...nothing. Blood filled her nose and mouth, and she was certain the scarlet suffocation would end her. She was dying, and worse, one of the weakest people she knew had done this to her. Her brain faded to nothingness, and she waited for the Capesman.

Cold water dripped on her forehead, and she opened her eye.

Mason offered a one-sided smile as he dabbed her forehead with a wet cloth. "Just once, I'd like to avoid cleaning up gallons of your blood," he said.

Shal sat up, and dizzying pain hammered her brain. She held her head as she croaked. "Lots of people are getting that privilege lately."

He nodded. "Kati told me about the machine in Malay."

"I could've told you myself if you'd bothered to attend the meeting earlier."

"And risk running into your traitorous lover, I think not," he replied as he slipped off the side of the mattress.

Shal only then realized she was in his bedroom—in their former bed. She ran her hand over the sheets with a deep exhalation. Looking at Mason, she noticed he still wore his wedding ring.

"Don't get sentimental now, sweetheart," he said. "You wouldn't want to piss off your Council boyfriend."

She folded her body over her knees, cradling her head in her hands as she grunted, "I fucking hate men."

"Could've fooled me."

Shal glared as she scooted off the bed. Though she stood a few inches shorter than Mason, she stared him into a submissive smallness.

He said, "My apologies, General. I meant no offense."

"You did mean it, and you got it."

"Can you blame me? I've spent a decade fighting the Council with you, six more years running your show after you surrendered to Grejous, and after all they've done to us, you bring one of their most bloodthirsty dogs into our home? We promised these people safety, Shal. How safe are they now?"

"He was a kid, brainwashed, under the chancellor's complete control."

"How convenient," Mason said with a bitter rasp. "And how did he wind up under Council control? Another poor soul abducted from Cryster's, was he?"

Shal clenched her jaw and strode past him down the hall.

"No," Mason continued, chasing after her. "Way I heard it, he went looking for the Arqam Rats. He chose to go to Skylark. He chose to get dosed."

"He was an invaluable ally in Malay."

"Ah, that fixes everything then. Let's run off and tell the King about this dazzling addition to his cause. Oh wait. We can't. Do you know why?"

She turned, and Mason's eyes trembled with pain. His chin dimpled, his finger stabbed the air, and he screamed, "Because that fucking kid killed him."

Shal launched herself at Mason, pressing him against the wall, her forearm compressing his windpipe. "Listen up, asshole, because I'm only saying this once. Raoul is reformed. He's a good person who was duped into doing bad things. For fuck's sake, most of us fall into that category. He even tried to kill Doa when the dose wore off. The Council took his tongue for it, and that's why he was in Malay."

"But the King—"

"Yes, the King. It's a crime some of us may never forgive, and he knows that. But if I can set aside my anger, you can too. And I deserve mine far more."

"A general's pain is no greater than a captain's."

"A daughter's is."

Mason's lips parted, and the rage in his eyes transformed into empathetic questions.

Shal removed the pressure from his throat and stepped back. "The King was my father, Mason. I thought he was dead for most of my life, and the moment I realized I was wrong, the moment I got my father back, he died in my arms. Because of Raoul."

Mason reached out, but Shal dodged his touch.

"I don't need your sympathy, and neither does Raoul. But I do need you two to get along. If we're divided before battle, there's no way we'll defeat the Council. They twist and kill and hate each other too, and I don't ever want to be like them."

He snarled, grabbed a stone decanter from his icebox and poured out a glass of honey colored liquid. He sipped at first, then threw back the entirety. He slammed down the glass—a thudding exclamation point for the word, "Fine."

"Fine, you'll forget about it?"

He scoffed. "Never. I will never trust him. But I will do as my general commands and cooperate. Besides, how much trouble could one soldier be, right?"

"Captain," Shal corrected.

"You've got to be kidding me." This time he didn't bother with the glass. He slurped from the decanter and wiped liquor from his lips with the back of his hand.

"Even if he hadn't helped me fight off six years of Malay guards, I'd still give him the title. He's seen more of Skylark than anyone here, you included."

"And tasted every luxury, no doubt. Shaken every demon's hand—"

"He knows the layout."

"Who gives a fuck about layout when we have bonecrunchers?"

Shal lifted her chin and crossed her arms over her chest. "I do, Captain. Who the fuck is going to question me? You?"

His nostrils flared with anger and defiance, but he released both with a sigh and said, "No."

"Good." Shal trooped away from him, but she stopped at the door. "Thank you for earlier, by the way. The blood, my head—"

"Don't mention it."

She fired a smirk at him. "So noble."

"So scared," he said. Mason stood, his face fraught with desperation. "I just got you back, Shal. I can't lose you again. *We* can't lose you."

She rushed back to him and planted her lips against his. His mouth was tense at first but relaxed when she threw her arms around his neck. When she broke the kiss, Mason smiled, though suspiciously.

"What was that for? I know you don't love me."

"Not the way you've always wanted, but that doesn't mean I don't care for you, Mason. It doesn't mean I haven't missed you, or that I'm not grateful you're still alive." Shal caressed his cheek and searched his face for trust. "I love you in my way. More than any other man in Cartesia."

Her eye patch was askew, and he fixed it with a sad chuckle.

"That and a nickel, sweetheart."

He kissed her again, his mouth lingering on her bottom lip before disconnecting.

She felt nothing but smiled with genuine ease.

Mason opened the door for her with a huff. "War ring at first light. The gorge."

She stepped outside, and he whistled to catch Shal's focus.

"Bring your inside man," he said, "but don't expect the others to be as kind as me."

Chapter Twenty-Six

The gorge wailed in the early morning, a whistling moan from the underground's underground. Some citizens wrote it off as the yawns of bonecrunchers, their sleepy keening distorted by the depth and resounding walls. Others suspected the noise came from different creatures, odd, deep-earth dwellers that'd yet to emerge as boldly as the bonecrunchers had during the Shift. But as Shal and her captains stood on the precipice of the gorge, they regarded the low, almost wet moans as dirges for the dead. Before a single word was uttered, the warriors bowed their heads and remembered the good people they'd lost.

Xula's face bloomed in Raoul's mind, and so bloomed in the minds of those whose telepathy tuned to his frequency. Morchai was also a shared lament—one Shal hadn't let herself feel until that moment when the gorge howled its sympathy. Raoul sensed her pain and squeezed her shoulder, and Mason glared at the gesture from across the yawning chasm.

Kati stood on Shal's other side, next to Captains Criedo and Shiza, former members of the King's Men and Cryster stock. Captain Banta stood beside Mason, arms folded over her chest and hip popped. Flanking Mason's left were two cons Raoul recognized as Perl and Torgal from Malay, who Shal must've promoted overnight while he stewed in the Tempest. The triplets, Fleck, Grayer, and Ilana joined as well, assuming an identical pose with simultaneous flair.

After the moaning stopped and the soldiers lifted their heads, a twitchy man named Cal joined them on the gorge.

He apologized for his truancy. "My son, Kenti, had an appointment with Healer Fastel this morning. It appears I have a little telepath on my hands," he said, chuckling. He extended his hand to Shal. "I'm so pleased to see you again, General."

She shook it, her head tilted. "Have we met?"

"An era ago, it seems. You spared the life of this young idiot driver, and now he's the proud father of a telepath." He chuckled. "Apparently."

She blinked at him in shock, which quickly gave way to joy. The driver

181

from the night of Kati's rescue had taken her advice. He'd gone underground and found happiness.

He embraced her, his voice wavering with teary gratitude. "If it weren't for you, I might still be working for the Council. You saved me."

"It appears you saved yourself, Captain. And I'm so glad to have you with us," she said.

Mason cleared his throat. "I take it everyone already knows about Raoul."

Gazes jumped to Mason, who raised a combative eyebrow at one person in particular. It was as if he and Raoul were lifelong nemeses meeting for the first time. They shared a glare of revulsion that Shal cut short when she kicked up a small rock and launched it at Mason.

"Enough of that," she said. "We're here today to discuss our magnum opus. It's been a long time coming, but we've made it. We can thank the Capesman for that. But we can't thank him forever. And if we're not willing to die for this, our freedom, then what good is there in wanting better lives?"

The captains concurred. Banta also nodded, then added, "Though I can't see how we'd lose. After seeing what the bonecrunchers did to Malay, it's obvious they're one of our greatest assets."

"They're on our side, but we don't fully control them," Criedo said. "They're amiable, and the dolen root helps protect us, but we can't be positive that won't change. We still know so little about their race."

"As long as they're clear on what we need of them," Shal said.

"'Kill' translates fairly easily," Cal said. "Despite our barriers with the bonecrunchers, we have a common enemy in the Council. They will not betray us."

"We can still be cautious," Criedo said.

"Not if you want them to trust us," Banta replied. "They did well by us in Malay, exactly as they were instructed. If we show an iota of fear around them, they will think it's reasonable to fear us. And from fear comes war."

"Banta is right. We cannot fear them." Shal's gaze swept over the captains as she added, "Nor each other. We are not the same, so I won't pretend we are. Some of us come from underground stock, bred in hidden peace and terrified of the world above, that one day it would dig us out. Some have been pushed here, forced to live without the full, welcoming sun we knew, without the simple pleasures of our childhoods, when we could pretend Cartesia still had a chance. Some of us are escapees, tortured, unable to forget the sins of our pasts. We are children of a dead God, captives of the rift, meat for the Capesman, and perhaps eternally divided by our varied worship. But all those facts cannot trouble us now. We may never understand each other's paths or forgive them, but we stand here united in a common dream: whatever we choose to be, underground or above, we will live free, and in peace. Regardless of personal histories, we all agree that no one will realize that dream while the Council remains in power."

Concurrence circulated the leaders of the militia. Perl and Torgal grunted with nods, while Banta smirked and said, "Goddamn right."

Mason nodded, too, though he followed it with a sighing, "Easier said than done."

"No shit, Captain," Shal said. "It's going to be the hardest war we've ever waged on the chancellor and his cronies. Which is why I want it to be the last. No fuckups. No mercy."

"Skylark on a Sunday," Raoul said. "The Chancellor never misses his 'Sunday Service,' and neither do the others. You want to take out a shitload of Council at once, that's where you hit them."

"What about the trench?" Shiza asked. "Isn't the base of Skylark filled with their best soldiers?"

"It is, which is why you'll direct the bonecrunchers to enter there."

Shal nodded, and Mason groaned. "Translation, please," he said.

"We drive the bonecrunchers up through the trench," Kati said. "We destroy their army before they can launch it."

"And then what? There are helicopters in Skylark. If there's a commotion below, the chancellor and his men can still escape," Cal said. "Do you really want to chase them all over Cartesia? I don't want to imagine the evil they'd cook up on the run."

Mason tilted his head in thought. "We could send someone ahead of time to disable all modes of escape. Maybe someone who knows the layout?" He fired a crinkled glare in Raoul's direction but quickly looked away.

Raoul raised his hand. "I'll do it."

"No, you won't," Shal said.

"If he's volunteering, I say let him," Mason replied. "It shouldn't pose too difficult a task for a man of his experience."

"Except they're going to be on high alert because of the jailbreak," Criedo said. "There's no way Raoul's getting back in there. I doubt any of us could sneak in undetected."

"It would have to be a new face, someone born in the underground the chancellor's never seen," Torgal said.

"If you want to get close enough to the peak to disable escape vehicles, you'll have to get close to the chancellor, and in that case, you'll need someone who interests him," Raoul said.

"If you send a girl in there, you know what Rojer will do to her," Shiza said. "And the underground will hate you for it, Shal."

"Depending on Doa's mood, a boy would interest him, too," Raoul said.

Kati glared around the circle. "We're not sending in an underground citizen, and that's final."

"But maybe sending someone he knows isn't such a bad idea. Someone like me," Mason said. "I was born Council. What's to say I couldn't live a renegade life and decide it's not for me? What if I chose to be Council again?"

"He'll kill you before you get out the second lie," Shal said. "Even if he did believe you, he'd kill you just to hurt me."

Mason's face tightened, and he lifted his chin. "You think I can't handle Rojer Doa?"

"None of us have so far," Torgal said. "Shal, Raoul, lots of us have taken chunks out of the man, but he's still up there breathing free air, murdering our children, our future."

"Then let me put a stop to it," Mason said. His focus snapped to Shal. "Let me kill him for you. And if I can't do that, at least let me stop him from fleeing."

Shal exhaled heavily. "No."

"General—"

"Did you not hear what I said?"

His face reddened, and his lips disappeared in a furious clench, but he nodded in surrender.

"Good. I will think further on this issue. In the meantime, do we have enough dolen root to protect the army from the bonecrunchers?"

"Not by half," Captain Banta replied. "We've searched the outlying areas, but we haven't had much luck."

"What about the sea? That's where I found the root that helped us escape Malay."

"We understood it only grows in specific spots in the sea," Criedo said.

"So ask Loche where. He has dozens of books on Cartesian lore. That's how I knew I could find it near the prison."

Several captains looked to Kati, who nervously raked her top lip with her bottom teeth. Shal noticed and shook her head at her sister.

"What aren't you telling me?" she asked.

Kati's face twitched, and she rolled her shoulders down her back. "I was going to tell you, I swear. I had a plan."

"Forget the plan, and tell me now."

"Loche is no longer the man we knew and loved. His mind is gone. He doesn't operate the library anymore. He took what books he could and ran. He lives miles away from the community," Kati said. "I visit occasionally, but he hasn't recognized me the last few times. He refuses to believe who we are or that we need the information in those books."

Shal huffed. "Banta, Cal, prepare the Tempest and the Snug. Tune them up, sharpen the armor, do whatever needs to be done in case we can't use the bonecrunchers. Perl, Shiza, Torgal, and Criedo, gather every soldier you can. Have them fed, hydrated, and ready for training. Kati, Mason, and Raoul, you're coming with me."

"Where are we going?" Mason asked.

"To remind Loche who he is."

Shal and Kati stood beside the well, filling water bottles for the journey to Loche's.

"I didn't thank you properly for rescuing me," Shal said as Kati loaded bottles into her travel pack.

"I never expected you to," she said. "It doesn't take a genius to figure you're grateful to be out of Malay."

"But you risked your life, and I never wanted you to do that for me."

"Nor you for me, but you do it anyway, don't you?" Kati flicked water at Shal's face and chuckled. "When are you going to realize you deserve happiness and safety as much as anyone else?"

"When we prevail, of course."

Kati rolled her eyes away from Shal. "If that isn't bullshit, I don't know what is."

"What do you mean?"

She sipped from a bottle and swallowed hard. "You have no intention of embracing happiness, whether we prevail or not. You," she said, wagging her finger in her sister's face, "have no intention of surviving."

"Are you saying I'm going to fail?"

"You could never fail, Shal. But you could surrender."

Shal's face screwed up in anger, but Kati waved her hand to stop her sister's burgeoning outburst.

"Don't. You surrendered to Grejous to protect me. You lived in Malay for six torturous years for me. How can I not think you'd surrender to the Capesman if you believed that would also protect me?"

The wrath fled Shal's expression, but it still existed in her tightened fists. "I have less to lose, Kati."

"Because you refuse to build anything. Is there no love in your life? Raoul, Mason, anyone?"

Shal took Kati's hands into her hers and whispered, "You are all the love I need."

Kati smiled, but she slipped her hands free. "You're wrong. You have shown these people how to fight for the lives they want, how to stand tall against the Council's injustice, but they must know what to do when the fighting's done. The people on the surface, especially. They must be taught of love and family. They must be reminded of Cartesia's greatness."

Shal grunted. "Cartesia's greatness is something neither you or I have ever seen. No one has."

"Then we must teach them through example. We must show the quadrants what is possible when violence ends." Shal lowered her head and tried to retreat, but Kati threw her arms around her sister's neck and whispered. "You have seen it here. Knowledge, cooperation, families as there haven't been in Cartesia for decades. There is genuine love here, Shal, both utilitarian and romantic. If you can walk among these people and ignore that simple fact, I pity you."

As Raoul approached, Kati slung her pack over her shoulder and marched off to meet Mason farther down the path.

Raoul touched the general's shoulder. "Everything okay?"

She tightened the cap on her water bottle and dropped it in her pack. "We should hurry," Shal said and marched away, leaving Raoul's hand floating in air.

Beyond the majestic community of the underground lay a wasteland of ashen rock and treacherous ravines. After the last houses dwindled, the quartet strode miles in silence until Kati pointed at a misshapen structure alone in the stone desert.

As they approached the door, Mason readied his dagger.

"What are you doing?" Shal asked.

He raised his eyebrows and the knife. "You'll see."

Loche's door swung open then, and the gray man leapt out with his sword drawn and several pistols strapped to his chest.

He swung the blade at Raoul's neck but stopped an inch before opening the tender flesh. His arms steady and body tensed, Loche glared at the intruders and growled, "Who the fuck are you?"

Mason snuck up behind Loche and pressed his knife to the man's throat. "That woman," he said, staring at Shal, "is the daughter of the man whose sword you're holding."

Shal's eyes widened, and she stepped forward.

Loche trained the blade on her and demanded louder, "Who the fuck are you?"

"I am Shal, General of the Tamora and King's Men."

He cocked his head in confusion, and Shal took a giant step forward, offering her neck to his blade.

"I am a woman," she said. "Friendless, hopeless. I am fortune's fool."

It was as if Loche's lungs suddenly filled with air. He dropped the blade, clamped his hands to his face, and moaned frantic apologies.

Shal touched his wrist, and he peered at her between his fingers.

"They told me you'd come back," he whispered. "They said it, but I didn't believe it." With a shaking hand, he touched her face. "Is it really you, Shal? I've been fooled before. I swear I've seen the King, too, but he vanishes so fast. You could be like him."

"I am him," she said. "He was my father, Loche."

A smile blossomed on Loche's face, and his cheeks warmed with memory. "I know. I knew the moment Kati gave me the book."

"Book?"

Loche handed Shal the King's sword and beckoned the soldiers inside. The house was disorganized but protective of its scattered treasures. The rift gold was either swaddled in plastic or displayed upright, devoid of dust. While every wall was lined with shelving, one in particular held a surprise. Behind a false wall of shelves, Loche opened a vault and removed a double-bagged tome. He freed it gingerly, then carried it to Shal like an enchanted crown.

She received it similarly, her fingers trembling when Loche set its weight upon her palms. It felt lighter than in years past but still possessed the same heft of heart.

Shal cleared a spot at Loche's cluttered kitchen table and slowly opened *The Complete Works of William Shakespeare*. It exhaled precious breath with each page flipped, and it inhaled the worship of those bearing witness.

Raoul drew especially close. After years of knowing Shakespeare only from the facsimile in Shal's cell, he gazed upon words he knew, words she'd yet to transcribe, words from a world where God still lived and, perhaps, did here too, in these pages. Then there was the magic unwritten, living instead in Shal's face and her pulse racing in her fingertips she danced them over the ink. At that moment, she was with her father again, and Raoul couldn't help thinking of his own. Minds filled with faces and names and the memories of those first plaintive nights without.

Kati sat opposite Shal and laid her hand atop her sister's.

"You saved it for me. All these years it's been here, safe. How?"

"Before I went underground, I snuck into Luai's house and stole it."

"I told you to leave everything."

Kati smiled. "Well, I didn't. What are you going to do about it now?"

Shal stood from the table and embraced her sister. She petted her hair as she wept, speckling Kati's shoulder with tears.

Mason whistled from his spot at the bookshelf, where Loche pinned him, a pistol to the captain's head.

"Loche, no!" Kati said.

The man snarled. "What are you people doing in my house? What do you want from me?"

"Dolen root," Shal said. "Or else."

"Or else what?" Loche bent Mason's neck with a violent shove of the gun barrel to his temple.

"Kill him if you wish," Shal said. She closed the book of Shakespeare with a slam and lifted it up. "But if you do, I swear I will destroy every piece of rift gold you've squirreled away, starting with this one."

Loche glanced at the open vault in his bookshelf, then lowered the pistol. "I don't have dolen root," he growled. "But I know where you might find some." He pushed Mason away and sneered. "There's a ravine not far from here, and a shallow stream within. You could find dolen root there, but I don't see the point. They are underground allies. Root or not, they'll slurp down Council sludge like you in a second."

"We are not Council," Mason said, disgusted.

"You don't fool me. I know when something is wrong. I can hear it. My telepathy is different, sharper. I can hear the screams of my people." His face filled with recognition, and he waggled his finger at Shal. "I do know you. You have a different face, but the look in your eye is the same. I could never forget that look. Not in life, not in death. The King's gone. Shal is gone. And now you've come to take me, too. You may have gotten the rest, but I'm not going anywhere, Capesman."

Shal passed the book to Kati and advanced on Loche, her hands up in surrender. "*I* am Shal, Loche, and I mean you no harm."

"He's not the man he was. He don't understand what's going on," Mason said as he corralled the crew to the door.

"He's dying," Loche wheezed. "And his father is crying. I can hear them both."

Shal looked over her shoulder. "Who's dying?"

Mason grunted. "This is a waste of time."

A normal blink catapulted an abrupt yelp into Raoul's brain. He squeezed his eyes tighter, and the yelp became a scream. "I hear it, too," he said. "A young boy, a telepath." His mind filled with shrieks, with clashing steel, and final breaths. "I can hear them all. Listen hard."

Shal and Kati closed their eyes and quickly paled at the bloody commotion raging through their brains.

"I'm sorry," Loche whispered sadly. "I forgot again, didn't I? I get so confused these days."

"It's okay," Kati said. "Thank you for the book, but we have to go. The city is under attack, and we need to get back before it's too late."

"That's why I'm sorry," he said. "The screams started before you arrived."

Chapter Twenty-Seven

The Capesman hated going underground. He was usually able to pass places he'd lived and people he'd known without a second thought, but that day, as the ghostly hand of slaughter tugged him from the pier, dismissal wouldn't be so easy. The fresh scent of blood on stone and the echoing songs of lament came to him on otherworldly wind, reminding him that the Capesman was once the King, and the King was once just a man named Marius. He remembered himself as he materialized in the underground city, but only for a moment. The grisly scene stretching out before him obliterated all capacity for nostalgia.

While it was obvious the chancellor had ordered a squad to eradicate the underground citizens, it was also obvious the dogs had failed. There wasn't a survivor among those soldiers, and the majority of the population was unharmed. But they'd done enough damage to leave the underground limp with grief. The carnage resembled that at Malay Prison—rebels and Council boys tangled in warring demise—except the Capesman hadn't needed to collect so many children from Malay. Warriors wept over their miracle progeny, some who still gripped weapons too heavy for their small arms to lift. The Capesman wanted to comfort the mourners, to let them know he had their babies safely in tow, and he could have. He could've been corporeal enough to sympathize with their grief, but he feared the mourning rage and consequential bargaining. He feared all questions he could not answer and the pain he could not quell.

With each young body the Capesman touched, his heart roiled with the cruel desire to leave the Council soldiers, but the former heralds forced his hand. As the dead dogs looked upon their broken corpses, the Capesman delighted in their horror, but his gladness survived only moments—the time it took for him to call up the next child's soul.

The line was full. He was just about to whisk the departed to the pier when a scream turned his head.

Four people raced toward the battleground, their faces streaked with tears. The woman in the lead collapsed beside a man cradling a small, blood-drenched body. Another woman knelt beside her with a medicinal kit and pushed aside the dying boy's father. He toppled onto his side, closer to his wife who lay motionless in a scarlet pool.

The Capesman strolled over to the cluster, squinting at the one-eyed woman weeping over the boy. He sensed the child was near death and the second woman's attempts at healing him were useless, but he watched in fascination anyway.

"You have to save him," the boy's father pleaded, his voice strained from crying.

"I'm trying, Cal, but you have to give me some room," the healer replied.

The one-eyed woman escorted him away, her gaze scanning the broken landscape and falling, momentarily but poignantly, upon the Capesman.

There was something strange about her, a familiarity the herald couldn't pinpoint. Her face, her sword, the way she absorbed the pain radiating around her. His stomach prickled with the feeling that he *should* know her, that while the survivors had good reason to hate her right now, they should be grateful to know her too.

He turned to the first person in line, a stout man with a chiseled jaw and sleeves of tattooed designs. "You were a soldier, yes? For the underground?"

"Yes, sir. Name's Glau."

"Who is that woman?"

Glau exhaled sadly. "The one the dogs were looking for."

"Why?"

"She escaped Malay Prison with a bunch of other cons. She was planning to lead the underground in an attack against Skylark, but..." His sight crawled over the line behind him. "I'd say that plan's shot to shit now."

"She was your leader?"

"In a manner of speaking," Glau said. "If you want to be free, you follow Shal."

What trailed her name wasn't a sudden onslaught of memory for the Capesman, rather a drizzle that became a downpour so gradually he couldn't possibly pinpoint the beginning of the flood.

He saw her first as a baby in his arms, when he didn't know how to feel about her. She was more like a warbling toy than a person, he'd thought. But in those first months, as Luai recovered and Marius assumed Shal's care, he noticed tiny changes in his child. He noticed the moment her infantile burbles conveyed as words he used everyday. He realized when she grabbed his finger, she meant more than, "Hey, something to grab." Shal acquired personhood with her changing temperament and wonder, and oh, how Marius loved those darling evolutions.

She was on his knee then, this little girl who'd tolerate only a few bounces before insisting it was her turn to bounce him. He relived ancient legends he taught her, theatrics and tasks he performed for her, and all the while he trembled with the old fear that she'd hate how messily he plaited her hair.

She was far away as a teenager, and so was he—from each other and who they used to be. But it was best, he'd thought. Safer. He never wanted Shal to fight beside him. He never wanted her to see him die.

But she did. As he fell that day on the battlefield, she caught him and held him and begged him to stay. She risked her life to sit in her sorrow and weep over an old man as she wept now over the young. Scanning the underground carnage, Shal took on pain like gooseflesh, each innocent death a new lump to weigh her down, to armor her in grief, and to convince her she was powerless to save anyone.

The Capesman knelt beside his buckled, sobbing daughter and whispered, "But I came back."

Shal lifted her head, and tears rolled hard down her cheeks. She looked directly at the Capesman, and her chin dimpled as he opened his arms. He didn't have to choose corporeality for his daughter to see him. She knew. She *had* to know.

But when she stood for the embrace, her focus wasn't fastened to his. It shifted, and she stepped through her father's ghostly skin to embrace another man. The Capesman wasn't slighted exactly. He was glad *someone* could comfort her, but when he saw the man's face in full, rage surged from the pit of his compound soul, and with it came the flame of opportunity. It wasn't often the Capesman saw his killer standing right in front of him.

He was corporeal without willing it, not even certain he'd acquired solidity until he felt the soldier's cartilage popping and cracking under his fingers. He gritted his teeth and screamed as he constricted his killer's throat and the blood drained from his face—one squeeze from vengeance.

The Capesman's body jerked, and his belly vibrated with a hollowing sort of pressure. Looking down, seeing the tip of a sword protruding from his stomach, he released Raoul. There was no blood, no pain, no feeling of creeping death— only the blade's echoing clang when he diluted his composition and the sword dropped to the stone earth.

The Capesman whipped around with a growl, and his attacker shuddered as she stumbled backward.

With her bloodstained hands to her pallid face, Shal wheezed. "Daddy?"

Chapter Twenty-Eight

Mason knelt, his eyes watering. "The King is the Capesman?"

Ragged breath returned to Raoul's lungs, and he massaged his throat as Shal helped him stand.

"I've gone years without the old names crossing my mind, and I'd prefer to go lifetimes more," said the Capesman. "After this sight, especially." He stomped toward Raoul, who scrambled back in fear.

Shal retrieved the sword and stood between Raoul and the herald, her face rigid with resolve.

The Capesman chuckled. "You're threatening me with a sword? Were you not paying attention before? You can't kill me, you can't hurt me."

"But you would hurt an innocent person minutes after such devastation?" Kati said. "I didn't think the Capesman operated so unfairly."

"Unfair? It's *his* people who are behind this slaughter, and they laughed at you from my line over how this beast has bewitched you. You..." he said, glaring at Shal. "I haven't known you for what feels like millennia. Even as I stood before you, I did not recognize you until a ghost spoke your name. But I do now. I can once again hold you in life as you held me in death, and I find you in the arms of the man who killed me."

"He was brainwashed," Shal said. "That's not who he is anymore."

Mason sputtered as he burst out of the background. "Look around you, General. The Council hasn't attacked us here in years, and now they've destroyed all we've built in a matter of hours. Do you think it's a coincidence it happened as soon as this traitor set foot in our camp?"

"You're oversimplifying, Mason."

"And you are blind," the Capesman said to Shal.

Her remaining eye blazed with fury as she shoved herself in his face. He tried to turn from her, but she grabbed the herald by the arm and spun him around.

He hissed and pulled free. "You dare touch the Capesman?"

"I already ran him through. What's a touch after that?" she replied. "Besides, you don't control me, Capesman. I respect you, but I don't need to obey you."

"And how do you know that?" he snapped. His focus turned to the individuals gathering around him. "How do any of you know what I can and can't decree? Your legends and rift gold can't possibly decipher the complex magic that quilts my various souls, let alone the power I hold over mortals."

Several people cowered, but Shal narrowed her eyes and took a giant step forward.

"Do *you* even know your power?" she asked him.

His face dropped all expression. "Of course I do." But his voice trembled, and his nostrils flared repeatedly as a smile bloomed on Shal's face.

"I see the Capesman can lie," she said. "That's good to know."

He roared at her. His fists clenched, and his solidity flickered as he screamed. "How dare you!"

"How dare *you*!" she bellowed, her finger in his misty face. "You have no business in our affairs. Whoever you used to be doesn't matter. You corral the dead. Do it, and go."

Mason jolted forward, his arms outstretched to separate Shal and the Capesman. "Stop it now. Have some respect."

A light cough summoned their attention to a little boy, his face slick with blood, and his head cradled in his father's lap. As little Kenti's eyes fluttered and he struggled to stand, his father Cal embraced him and wailed in gratitude.

Kati Doa bent over the boy, checked his pulse and the wound in his belly. Removing a jar of salve from her knapsack, she sighed. "Take him inside and apply this to the wounds. He's very lucky."

Kenti was in too much pain to speak, but as Cal scooped him up and carried him to the house, every telepath within range heard the boy whisper, "Praise be to the Capesman."

Once they were gone, Kati ushered the group into her home. Closing the door behind the Capesman, Shal shoved herself in his face.

"Did you do that?" she asked. "Did you save him?"

His eyes wetted with sympathy, and for a glimmering moment, he truly resembled her father Marius again. "No. The girl was right. That was luck."

"But our survival wasn't," Kati said, gesturing to her companions. As she stared out the window, across the carnage, her voice shook with despair. "I don't understand why this happened. Why didn't they come after us when they saw we weren't here?"

"Because Doa didn't send them to kill us. He sent them to show us how easy it is for him to infiltrate our home. He sent them to break our hearts, and the bastard succeeded."

"Whose fault is that?" the Capesman said, his narrowed eyes fixed on Raoul.

Shal spat at him. "You were a thorn in the Council's side long before Raoul while you lived. Maybe this is all your fault."

Mason stared at Shal, aghast. "General, whatever you believe, you cannot speak that way to the Capesman."

"Why not? He was just a man once. Every Capesman was just a man. His mind isn't divine," she replied.

"He's the King, he's your father—"

"He's a fucking coward," she said. "Like every Capesman before him."

He pushed Mason aside and shoved himself in Shal's face. "I came back for you. I did this for you."

"And you haven't confronted me until now? You died over six years ago, Marius, and you come to me now, when my people have been slaughtered and I was helpless to stop it? Now you come to judge and—what—show your love? You were the fucking King. You knew who I was and chose to stay away, to keep us separated. How can you judge me for not respecting you now? What the hell did you expect?"

He blinked rapidly, each open and close eliciting a change in his face. "I wanted to come to you," he said, then looked away as he added, "I think."

"You think?"

"I can't remember," he said sadly. "I believe I wanted to see you before I took the Capesman's place. I intended to go to you straightaway, but... there are so many voices, so many people they beg to see. It's easy to get lost."

Centuries of pain creased his face, crushing all familiarity for Shal. This wasn't the scarred iron visage of the King, nor the doleful face of her indomitable father. This man was a stranger, and she owed him nothing. But her heart ached for him nonetheless.

"Would you, Marius, have ever accused me, your daughter, of corruption?" she asked. "Would the King? Can you even imagine a time when I would've let you down?"

"No."

"Then why start now?"

The Capesman dwelled on her words as if hearing her voice for the very first time. It penetrated the cluttered fog and stirred Marius's heart, and when she smiled he experienced clarity as he hadn't felt in years.

"You're right," he whispered, his eyes falling on Raoul's face. "I can see this man's mind now, and while I do not relish its contents, I know he means you no harm. Any of you. You may have done evil, son, but you are not an evil man."

A lump climbed up Raoul's throat, still sore from the Capesman's grip. It was the strangest, most beautiful of aches, however—vengeance and forgiveness in equal measure—temporarily damming his breath. He thanked the Capesman King in his mind, but his lips danced along before settling in a smile.

Mason grunted. "Very well. If we are to be allied, let's get on with it. At least we can agree to rejoice in our secret weapon."

"Secret weapon?"

He grinned. "The King has returned! And now that he has the Capesman's powers, Chancellor Doa will have no choice but to cower in surrender. Our victory is now assured."

"Yes." Cal stood in Kati Doa's doorway, his fist still drenched in his son's blood and clutched to his chest. "Let's go now. Let's show those dogs what we're made of."

The Capesman sighed as he said, "No," and Mason blinked at him in disbelief. "What do you mean 'no?'"

"This isn't my fight anymore, son. Much of my life revolved around killing, and I do not wish killing to taint my afterlife as well. But I will confess my hunger for it. Not just mine, but nearly every Capesman within chants for the Council's blood. I wish Doa could hear it, all these voices, all this desire."

"Tell him yourself," Mason said, his nostrils flared. "March straight up to the chancellor and show him once and for all that the world's hatred doesn't end with death. Show him you are still the King he feared."

The Capesman's face twitched and then melted to a smile. "But I'm not. I'm the herald of the dead. No more, no less."

"I refuse to believe a man's life and accomplishments are blinked out when he dies," Mason said.

"Good. If you didn't, man would have no need to continue accomplishing, but that time is over for me. These battles are for the young."

"I don't feel young," Mason said.

"That is also battle's doing."

"Then let it age me right now," Cal said. "Come on, Shal. Let's round up the bonecrunchers and get Doa before he can launch another attack. Let's finish this."

The captains looked to Shal, and she clenched her jaw. "No. The Capesman is right."

Mason sputtered. "Are you crazy? Look around you."

Shal's eyes snapped to Mason and she squinted in fury. "I have, and as for being crazy, you bet your ass I am. But I'm not leading an army with the rage as I feel right now. It would cloud my judgment as it's clouding yours."

"I'm as sharp as ever," Cal said. "And I want to kill the chancellor."

Shal clamped her hand to Cal's arm. "You are not alone in that lust, and I swear to you, you will be satisfied."

"When? When can I tell these people their justice will be served?" Mason asked. "They deserve swift retribution for this crime."

"And they will get it."

"When?"

"I want you with me, Mason, but not if I have to worry about you taking matters into your own hands while my back is turned."

"Then don't turn your back, General."

Shal stomped to him, her growl like a thunderstorm, but the anger on her face abruptly switched to pain. She recognized the madness rushing through her bones, but it happened so fast this time that she couldn't even feign normality. She fell like a sack of blood-drenched sack of rocks, and despite the pain, when the Capesman appeared above her, she prayed he would keep his distance.

The underground was panicked enough without seeing their fearless leader hemorrhaging. The captains carried Shal to Kati's bedroom and stood watch, but as the hours passed and the blood dried, Shal wouldn't wake. Kati begged Mason and Cal to wait for her, but fury fueled every muscle in their bodies toward disobedience. When she still hadn't woken by nightfall, the soldiers left to formulate an alternate strategy.

Raoul caught up with Mason at home, where the soldier frantically tossed rations and weaponry into a knapsack. Mason noticed Raoul's entrance, but he didn't lift his head or toss his gaze when he snarled, "Get out."

Raoul stomped his foot until the man looked up with a sigh.

"What? Why are you here? I can't hear you, and even if I could, I'd ignore you," Mason said. "There's nothing you could say to assuage, sway, or even interest me, so you might as well run back to your lover. See if she'll play this little game of yours when she wakes, because you and I will never be on the same side, kid. I ran away from the Council. You ran toward it."

Raoul dashed to the kitchen table littered with papers and pencils, and began writing.

"Don't waste the resources," Mason said as he plucked the pencil from Raoul's hand. "If Shal can't convince me to stay, you've got no chance."

Raoul crinkled his brow and pointed up at the ceiling—to the world above, more specifically.

"Am I going? You bet your ass I am." When Mason turned, Raoul latched onto his arm and was shaken away. "Don't touch me, traitor. Don't act like you care, like you know anything about me or what my life has been like underground, protecting and leading these poor people, especially when Shal was locked up with—" He glared at Raoul. "—with you."

Raoul grunted, and a smirk crawled up one side of his face.

Mason's lip curled as he hissed. "*That look* I can read, and you're wrong. I'm not jealous of you and Shal."

Raoul crossed his arms over his chest and pulled a doubtful sneer.

"You want to know why?" Mason continued. "Because there is no you and Shal, and I'm certain she's made that abundantly clear to you herself."

Raoul pointed at Mason. *And you think there's a 'you and Shal?'*

"Nope, not even me. Though I have a feeling it would be easier for me to secure that situation considering I'm the only one who's ever had it."

Raoul rolled his eyes, and Mason shoved his left hand in his rival's face, his wedding ring scuffed and dull but unmistakable.

"You think I'm lying?" he barked. "You think you're special? She's my fucking wife, asshole. You're lucky I haven't cut off your other fun bits for sticking it to her in Malay."

Raoul crossed his fingers in an "X" and pointed to Mason's ring.

"Yeah, well, you know Shal," he said. "Our marriage was an anesthetic to a lethal condition. But that doesn't mean I stopped loving her."

Raoul's eyebrows bounced, and though Mason couldn't hear him say, "We're not so different," the man recognized the expression.

"She's a bitch," he said to Raoul. "But I guess she's our bitch."

He chuckled with Mason. It would be the first and last time they shared a common amusement, but it was short-lived.

Mason sighed and said, "I take it back. She's not even ours. She's not anybody's."

Raoul grabbed the pencil and set it to paper. This time, Mason didn't stop him. He wrote clearly, boldly: "Is that why you're doing this? To hurt her?"

Mason squinted at the note and shook his head. "I'm leaving to hurt them, you idiot. It has nothing to do with her."

Again, doubt wrinkled Raoul's forehead.

"Stop," Mason said. "Yes, everything involves Shal, but this, right now, is for my people. That's something you couldn't comprehend even if I beat it into that simple brain of yours."

Raoul wrote, "They're my people too," and Mason laughed.

"You have no people, traitor. Everyone wants your blood."

"Not Shal," Raoul wrote.

"Shal's out of the equation. As much as I hate it, we can't depend on her now. We need action. We need vengeance."

Raoul dragged his finger across his neck with a creaking wheeze, and Mason slung his knapsack over his shoulder.

"You of all people should know death doesn't scare me."

Raoul wrote again. "But your death scares me, Mason."

His face softened in a way that surprised Raoul. Since meeting him, he'd seen nothing but concrete and conflict from the man.

Mason chuckled a smile onto his face. "I don't plan on dying, Raoul. Believe me, I aim to hate you for years to come."

Raoul's expression didn't break. He stared Mason square in the eyes and shook his head.

"I can't let Cal go alone," he said. "If you were a true warrior, if you wanted to be our brother, you wouldn't either."

Cal knocked on the door and entered Mason's house. "You ready?" Seeing the second man, he nodded. "Captain Raoul, are you with us?"

His voice was heavy with regret when it permeated Cal's mind. "Please don't do this. I know how hard it is to wait, but it'll be safer then. When we can all be together. When Shal can lead us."

Cal gritted his teeth. "Shal might not be in a place to lead for days, maybe weeks. I lost my wife today. I almost lost my son. I can't afford to wait. We have to take them out now."

"Do you really want to cause her more pain?"

"Of course not, but I don't want my son to be in pain either. My wife, my beautiful girl—"

His hand flew to his face, and Mason ran to comfort him.

"You see, Raoul? This has to happen now. Please, don't tell the others we're gone. If all goes well, we'll be back before Shal wakes up. If not, you can assume we're in the Capesman's care."

"You know I can't keep this from Shal," he said. "I'll tell her the moment she wakes up."

Cal wiped the tears from his eyes and gritted his teeth at Mason. "We can't allow you to do that, Raoul."

The butt of Mason's gun whistled through the air as it sailed at Raoul's head. Pain and dizziness thudded then swarmed his brain upon impact, and he collapsed to the floor at the captains' feet.

No...don't do this...

Mason snorted as he crouched beside him. "I have a feeling you were a better soldier when the chancellor had his hand up your puppet ass."

A drop of blood trickled down Raoul's neck, and Mason's eyes cleared of spite. He grabbed a towel from his table, stuffed it into Raoul's hand, and pressed the man's hand to his head to staunch the bleeding.

Chapter Twenty-Nine

Raoul was facedown on the floor when he awoke. His fingers were stiff, two digits glued together, as he held the rag to his neck. His thoughts rattled back into order as he stood and gazed about the kitchen.

Mason and Cal. The attack. Shal.

Raoul ran from the house and peered in both directions. There was no sign of the renegade captains, but the din of panic hadn't decreased since the onset of Raoul's blackout. He shouted for a telepath as he ran back toward Kati Doa's house. Many heads turned, but those citizens obviously didn't trust him enough to respond. A teenage girl finally tossed him a mental reply. Her right eye was so swollen it looked like her eyebrow was kissing her bruised cheek.

"Telepath," she said, waving her hand.

Raoul rushed to her. "Thank the Capes—" He stopped, remembering who the Capesman was.

"Who *is* he?" the girl asked, reading his thoughts.

"Never mind that. What's the commotion about?"

"Captain Cal stole the Snug," the girl said. "He and a few others left to storm Skylark."

"What about the general?"

"No one's seen her, sir. Are we off to war?"

While fear pitched her voice higher, there was a jangling excitement in the question too. Raoul exhaled and patted the girl's shoulder. "Hold steady, but prepare for the worst."

Kati opened her front door to Raoul with a somber nod. "She's not awake yet."

He followed her to the bedroom, where Shal lay sweating bullets. "Is there any change?"

"Nothing good," Kati said. Her voice stuck in her throat and she wilted to a chair.

Raoul moved to her side and touched her arm. "Hang in there, okay? Shal's going to be fine. She always is."

Kati dabbed a tear from the corner of her eye and sighed. "You really don't know her at all, do you?"

He clenched his jaw and nodded. "Maybe I don't. But I gave the brunt of my formative years to blind obedience, then more of my life to labor and penance. You'll have to excuse my lack of social skills."

Kati stood, looking down on Raoul with a sour squint. "Excuse *me* for finding your pain unremarkable. Especially when half of the underground will be burying loved ones tomorrow and the other half want to fly into open war to avenge the dead."

Raoul lifted his hands in supplication. "You're right. I can't imagine what it must be like to lose so many you care for. And that's no exaggeration, Miss Doa—"

She shuddered. "Kati. Please."

"I'm not sure I can be that intimate. After all I've done to you."

"What you've done to me is likely no worse than what the chancellor has done to us both. I can think of no greater insult than to call me 'Doa.'" She sat down again, exhaling slowly. "Please, call me Kati."

"I'm sorry, Kati."

She grunted and spun out of her chair. "I don't want it with apologies."

He chased after her as she left the room, down the hall to the kitchen. When he caught up to her, he noticed spots of blood on the left cuff of her shorts.

"Are you hurt?" he asked, gesturing to the series of slashes.

Her mouth tightened, and she nodded. "Aren't you?"

"Yes."

Kati pegged her hands to her hips and pouted. "You knew Xula, right?"

"No," he said, then corrected himself. "Yes, but not the way you did. I was a kid. I was an idiot. I was—"

"A boy," Kati said.

"My choices will shame me for the rest of my life, but shortsighted as I was, I had good intentions. I went to the Council to save Xula from worse than death."

Kati's face creased with a sad smile. "She obviously didn't need saving. You did."

Raoul lowered his head, and his eyes filled with hot tears. "I don't blame you for hating me, Kati, but I wish I could find true absolution one day." He shook his head. "Maybe I should've gone to fight with the others. I should've sacrificed myself for your people. Only in death, in the Crossroads, can I at last find forgiveness. I should've welcomed war. I should've left with Mason."

The floor creaked, and a dry voice said, "Mason left?"

Kati sprung to her feet and ran to her trembling sister, who leaned against the doorframe. She threw her arms around her and squeezed until Shal groaned in pain.

"Are you okay?"

"Where's Mason," Shal insisted.

"You know where he is, General," Raoul said. "Mason, Cal, a few others—they took the Snug, and they're headed for Skylark.

Shal's devastation shook her to the core and stole her balance. She gasped as she wilted against Kati's shoulder.

"Shal, you need to get back to bed. This is too much for you right now."

She grunted as she pressed her fingers to her throbbing forehead. "Right now and always. I think it's safe to say the Doc wasn't bluffing about the effects of the dream machine. If this shit is going to kill me, I have to deal with Doa before it's too late."

"But the army, the bonecrunchers—you said there wasn't time," Raoul said.

"There isn't, especially for Mason and the others."

The underground kept most of the guns in case of another attack. Blades boarded the Tempest with select captains while the rest brought the few motorbikes topside. The renegade captains had a few hours start on their allies, and Shal couldn't guess what they'd find upon reaching Grace City.

Children screamed. Adults tried best they could to wrangle their chaotic kids while others navigated the destructive tunnel now running through their city, collecting bits of steel the Snug left behind. Beyond those remnant citizens who dwindled by the minute, the gates of Skylark Tower were open, a rare courtesy tainted by the bodies lying limp, scattered along the path leading to the entrance.

There, in the doorway, a wobbly figure appeared. Shal ordered the Tempest to stop, and from outside the gates, she exited and stood, staring at the shadowy figure.

The man's guns were empty, and a bloody sword hung limp at his side. The dust cleared, and Mason's woozy gaze found Shal across the distance. He smiled and braced himself on the wall, then wilted to the ground.

Shal ran to him with Raoul on her heels. He stayed alert while Shal knelt beside Mason and rolled him onto his back. The captain's face was swollen and blood-slicked, peppered with too many wounds to discern the most dire.

Shal's muscles shuddered as she tried to lift him up, so Raoul also slid his arms beneath the captain and hoisted him onto his shoulder.

"Where is everyone?" Raoul asked. "Why aren't the Council soldiers attacking us?"

"Bonecrunchers," Mason said weakly.

Shal walked behind Raoul, her hands to Mason's cheeks as they returned to the Tempest. "What about them?"

The ground trembled under their feet, followed by a thunderous crash. Raoul rushed Mason into the Tempest while Shal stood on the precipice, staring at the tremors besieging the glass pillar at the heart of the Ides Quadrant. Some of the panes shook so violently the glass resembled rippling water, obscuring the flurries of activity on the other side.

Shal ducked into the Tempest, and the door closed behind her as Banta backed the mechanical bonecruncher out of the area.

"Stop. They need us," Mason wheezed. "Cal's inside. Shiza. Paget."

Shal crouched beside her husband and cleaned his face with a wet cloth. Cleanliness magnified the injuries, revealing the many slashes and bruises previously hidden beneath streaks of russet blood.

"Mason, what happened?"

He opened his mouth slowly, pained by the roots of teeth he'd recently lost. His breath was hot and smelled strongly of blood.

"The bonecrunchers came. Shiza found one before we left and convinced it to bring its people as soon as possible."

"We had trouble contacting them," Kati said.

"Because they were already with us," he said. "They came from underground like we planned. They busted through the trench."

Raoul blinked wildly. "The trench is gone?"

"Worried about your friends?" Mason coughed, spattering blood across Shal's face.

The general didn't flinch, didn't wipe it away. She drew closer to Mason, her breath heavy, and said, "Tell me everything."

As Raoul watched, his chest ached in a strange, new way. It wasn't heartbreak. This intimacy between the former spouses wasn't Shal's choice of one man over the other. She would make no choice. And if she did, her decision wouldn't favor either.

Kati drew closer to Shal and leaned over Mason, dabbing antibiotic salve on his weeping wounds.

"I killed as many Council boys as I could. I killed guards. I swear to the Capesman I slaughtered a senator or two." He smiled as he gazed up at her. "You would've been proud, sweetheart."

"That's my guy," Shal said as she caressed his face.

His eyes fell from hers, as far as they could. "Cal and I got to the seventy-third floor, to the high class whores."

"Doa's Sunday service," Kati said.

Mason grunted his concurrence. "But we didn't see him. The whores—the guards started cutting them to push us into retreat. Slashes at first, but it escalated quickly. Ears, fingers, and worse. We were ready to surrender. We couldn't bear watching those kids getting carved up in front of us."

"That's when they captured you?"

He coughed and curled his blood-speckled lips to a smile. "No. That's when the kids fought back. After what they endured, they didn't care about defensive wounds. The offensive ones were more important."

As he spoke, his strength increased. He was able to lift his head to accept water, even to roll onto his side so Kati could tend a wound along his ribcage. He grunted and tried to inspect his wound, but Shal cupped his face to capture his focus.

Mason smiled. "That bad, huh?"

Shal and Kati exchanged glances, and the healer passed the task of staunching Mason's blood to her sister. She pinched Raoul's arm and drew him away as Shal curled her body around Mason's.

"You think this is goodbye, don't you?" he whispered. "That you can finally get rid of me?"

"I think you're an asshole, and I wish you'd listened to me," she said. When blood trickled from the left side of his mouth, she sopped it up with a cloth and whispered, "Why couldn't you wait?"

"To die?" He inhaled through flared nostrils and lifted his eyebrows. "Maybe it was seeing the Capesman. Maybe it was seeing the dead, my friends, he'd come to collect. I don't know. All of a sudden, waiting for death seemed stupid, Shal."

"You don't know waiting would've killed you. You don't know it'll happen now."

"But I do. I see it—everything, really—clear and easy as that day I left the Council."

Shal sighed. "This again? I've heard it a hundred times, Mace, this story of how you left your future when you left for me."

He winced at a flush of pain, his teeth gritted, but he swallowed it. "You were the nearest buoy, Shal. The closest warmth when I was moments from freezing to death."

Raoul stood along the wall of the Tempest, his breath trapped in his lungs as he listened.

"I have loved you since the day I met you, and after everything we've done to each other, the love somehow endures. It's torturous, it's wonderful, and don't believe I don't think myself a lesser man for it, you cunt."

Shal chuckled, and Mason's pained expression transformed to one of glowing reverence.

"I have loved others since you," he continued. "I've had deeper relationships, healthier, with greater prospects, and yet—"

Shal pressed her fingers to his lips as she leaned over him. She replaced her hand with her kiss, which lingered in a shaky, gentle way that stirred no envy in Raoul.

Mason's face was blank when he whispered. "Fuck. It really *is* goodbye."

"No," Shal said. "We'll see each other again, Mason. The Crossroads will find us well rested, our burdens gone."

Mason's hand wavered as he lifted it to caress Shal's cheek. "Do what you need to do first." He gulped roughly, and Shal noticed his blood had saturated the cloth. "But don't expect me to wait for you. I hear there's some prime tail in the Crossroads."

She giggled. "Where'd you hear that?"

Mason's face relaxed. His breath rattled from his throat, and his eyes drifted slightly to the right. When he answered Shal's question, only the Capesman heard him.

Chapter Thirty

Shal didn't move, and Raoul didn't know if he should go to her. Kati's arms were soon around her sister anyway, pulling her from Mason's body and to Banta's side at the Tempest controls. There was no time to heal, not while there was more suffering to be had.

Skylark Tower looked like a glass giant hunched in smoldering defeat, but its nervous system sparked with madness. Soldiers streamed from the tilted mountain of shards, tailed by smoke and explosions. The helicopter was still atop Skylark's peak, lights on and propellers spinning to life. It lifted from the helipad, unsteady and wobbling as it took to flight. They were too late. After all this, Chancellor Doa was going to escape.

The ground juddered with ferocity, and Skylark Tower further cowered and crashed. Two bonecrunchers barreled out of the lowest levels, their bodies peppered with myriad injuries, while Council boys swarmed around them. The wind smelled of blood and oil and sounded of rattling screams fading under fire and steel, and amidst the chaos and shrapnel, the helicopter keeled and tumbled like a baby bird on its first flight. It pitched and spun as it plummeted, crashing and skidding across the ground with a shower of sparks.

The pilot stumbled out and opened the passenger side door for Doa. He wavered, his face marred by blood and debris. He spat at the earth, wiped his brow with a handkerchief, and lifted his eyes to the distance, where his enemies stood in the warring dusk.

Shal shielded her eyes and glared back for the few seconds before his boys crowded around him. Building a mobile blockade, they shielded Doa as he retreated into the skeletal remains of his beloved Skylark Tower. Shal leapt from the bonecruncher with her father's sword primed to slash the front line to ribbons while Raoul ran close behind. They were Council dogs, every last one of them killers who'd stop at nothing to defend Chancellor Doa, but only the flesh was guilty. Their muscle and bone, maybe even their doped-up brains, but not their souls. Raoul urged Shal to spare those whom he believed innocent, but her wrath deafened all cries save the final ones. Fleeing would be those boys' only survival, and few were sober enough to realize it. They charged gladly, and Raoul, with his guilt like a lake of flame, burned through them to the glassy shambles piled around his former home.

"You."

Raoul spun to face a captain among Council dogs. The man's chest pulsed with ragged breath and though his flesh was crisscrossed with oozing wounds, starvation sparked behind Josha's eyes, a desire only satiated by the blood of a traitor. He lifted his gun, pressed the barrel to Raoul's head, and grinned a shining row of crimson teeth.

The corners of his mouth fell abruptly, and a flash of steel gave way to a waterfall of blood cascading down the captain's chest. Kati ripped her dagger out of Captain Josha's throat, and he fell hard.

Senator Minsk rushed at them, flailing and screaming gibberish, a shard of glass protruding from his skull. His eyes rolled madly in his sunken sockets as he charged, but Raoul buried his blade in the man's belly, sending him moaning and leaking to the ground.

He scooped up a discarded pistol and shoved it into Kati's hands. "Take this and get back to the Tempest."

"I'm not going back. I'm never going back," she said. "I'm seeing this through to the end." She checked the chamber and exhaled. "However it ends."

"Shal would kill me if I let you follow her in there."

"You're not going to let me. You're going to try and keep up with me."

Kati fired at an oncoming soldier, clearing a path to Skylark. She, Raoul, and the underground soldiers cut through the dwindling Council army, joined by Fleck, Ilana, and Grayer who appeared in the fray, badly wounded but burning with mad survival. Cal's face was a mess of blood and meat when he met them at the tower. He had to tie a bandana around his forehead to stop the blood running into his eyes, but he was otherwise unharmed.

The Tamora panted as they stared at the off kilter entrance where clouds of pulverized glass swelled from the once great building's belly. They pushed through the haze, into the foyer were the walls between them and the stairwell stood like glassy Swiss cheese. Shal was visible on the staircase, her sword extended at Rojer Doa, who was collapsed against the banister just a few broken steps above her, his gun trained on her face.

"I'm impressed," he said, his voice wet and raspy. "You and your little scrappers inflicted more damage on me than I expected. You took a chunk out of the Council today, Shal. You might even get me in the end, but—" He hocked up a wad of phlegmy blood and smiled. "The Council is not Skylark or Grace City. The Council is Cartesia. You can't eradicate us in one day."

Shal crept up the stairs, legs quavering, while her people followed like ghostly shadows gliding up the spiraling spears of glass.

"One day? No, Doa, I'll spend weeks, years, the rest of my life taking down each and every one of your dogs." She sniffled, and the chancellor's face spread in a grimace.

"The way your brain is running out your nose, I doubt you've got much life left."

She wiped away the blood and gritted her teeth as she pushed herself up another step.

"You banished my father, you killed my mother, you've slaughtered my allies and lovers, and I'm not going to let a little nosebleed stand in the way of my vengeance."

"Me neither," Kati said, assuming the step behind her sister.

Her father shook his head, clucking softly as he ascended. "You thankless bitch. After all I gave you—"

Kati grunted as she hurled her dagger at Chancellor Doa. The blade struck his hip crease, sticking momentarily before dropping to the stairs. Pain rocketed through his arm, throwing off his aim when he squeezed the trigger. The bullet clipped Shal's right ear, and she yowled as she clamped her hand to the wound.

Doa fired again, nailing Cal's shoulder and sending him tumbling backward down the staircase. He tossed aside his empty pistol and snatched up the discarded dagger as Shal lunged at him. She slashed his right arm, and he released the dagger, blood pouring fast after the weapon. He slapped his hand to the gash and wilted in anguish.

He was distracted, drained. Shal had only to run him through, and it would be over.

Her brain went red with bad memories—of her father dying and Kati calling. She struggled to breathe through the anguish, but her nostrils were plugged with scabs and sludge, and her legs wobbled like gelatin. Her grip loosened, and the sword fell from her hand. As Shal collapsed to the stairs, Doa's face twisted into a smile, and a raspy cackle burst from his throat. Blood burbled between his fingers as he grunted at Shal.

"You came so far. You came so close. You sacrificed innocent lives for this moment, and you're a mess. I don't think your mother acted this pitiful at the end."

Shal reached dizzily for the railing, and Kati ran to her. Wrapping her arms around her waist, Kati lifted Shal to her feet. She wiped the coagulating blood from her nose, and the sisters stood shoulder to shoulder, glowering at Rojer Doa.

His eyes flashed with rage as he snarled. "Where's your respect girl? I'm your father. I'm your chancellor."

"You are obsolete," Kati said. "You're the most pitiful and reviled monster in this sea of demons."

"You think those pieces of me aren't in you, darling?" Doa sneered as he raised the King's sword. "I know about all the little scars, the little releases. I know because I planted them in you. In your mother too."

Kati's chin trembled, but she lifted it higher.

It tickled the chancellor. He snorted back blood with a chuckle. "She wasn't as strong as you, of course, and you're not as strong as Shal. I can kill you easier than anyone here because deep down, you want me to, don't you? You want all those little accidents to be intentional, to bleed out like she did."

"Shut up!" she screeched to her father's deflating laughter.

"Step aside, Kati. This is between me and Shal. That's how it's been since the beginning, and that's how it will end."

"This was never about you and me," Shal said. "It's you versus the world. Even the men who claim to love you wish you dead. Look around. You're alone in this. Is that what you wanted?"

"Fuck you. I don't need anyone, least of all your shagdead dregs."

"No, you only need God, don't you?"

"That's right. When God returns, He will see the great works I've done alone and reward me."

"And who will be there to cheer your cause, Doa? All of your friends have fled."

"Friends are aspic allies. There's too much killing to be done for caring. That will come when the days of dregs are over and done."

"And if they're never over and done?"

"Then let me live alone," he said. "Let me die alone from a long, lamentable disease."

Shal spat blood and hissed. "You will die today, Doa. Because of us."

He grunted. "Same thing."

Shal's legs were iron, and she shook with each arduous step. She ground her teeth and growled as pain surged through her skull. She felt it might burst, that the hot blood would come again, followed by horrific seizure. But instead, there was cooling light and memory.

She felt Doa's hands upon her and her fists like explosions beating him way. She felt the throttles of Malay guards and the blood of every soldier she'd slaughtered, every soul she'd sent to the pier.

Then there was Kati, a little girl with a heart-shaped face who'd saved her from a closet prison and far more fearsome. There was Mason, who'd truly loved her when they were kids and when rebuffed, redirected that love to war. There was Raoul, the silent warrior who never stopped trying to convince Shal that she was made for more than death. Then there was the Capesman, the King, her father. All she knew of him were those tender moments during her childhood, but perhaps she could know him again in the Crossroads.

As the world faded, the Capesman grew brighter. He guided her onto her back and looked down at her, his hand inches from her cheek. She wondered how would feel when he touched her, and if he would wait for her beyond the pier.

The pain peaked, and Shal gasped in agony, but when the Capesman's fingers unfolded against her face, the concept of pain became a ludicrous. Her body was at peace, her mind blank, and when her eyes fell shut, the Capesman lifted her up.

Kati crumpled atop her sister, and Raoul charged at Doa. Shots fired from the lobby, from a pair of Council boys with two eyes between them. The first bullets flew wide, but one punched a hole in Raoul's shoulder and spun him on the stair. He wilted and stumbled backward into Cal, causing several of the underground warriors to tumble down the staircase. Straggling Council soldiers stumbled in serum-first and attacked while Rojer tried to appeal to his daughter.

His face had drained of color, but his lips were crusted burgundy. He appeared a ghoulish cartoon of himself, prouder and more homicidal in the strange paint. Descending the staircase, he reveled as he surveyed the persistent battle, and the war he believed he'd already won. His greatest adversary was dead, and his fertile daughter was left alone.

"It's over, Kati. My only child, my precious girl." Rojer outstretched a blood-drenched hand and fluttered his eyes. "You have no other choice. There is only death—" He scrunched his nose. "Or Daddy."

Kati leapt to her feet and filled the tower with resounding fury as she struck. Her fist cracked Doa's jaw, and while he wavered on his heels, she latched onto his wounded wrist and dug her fingers into the gash. Pulling him close by his shredded tendons, she growled and spat hot breath at his face.

"I've spent years fearing you, fearing my own body because of you, fearing the deeper, darker hell you'd make of my life if I happened to have that natural magic you covet so. But not anymore. You took that fear when you took me from the battlefield that day. Ever since, I have eagerly anticipated watching my sister rip you apart." She fired Shal a grief-stricken look, but it was all hate when she stared into her father's eyes again. "I guess I'll have to settle for killing you myself."

"That won't be necessary," a voice interjected. It was soft, ringing through the air and staying Kati's hand. It was gentler than it had been in life, calmer, and with a summery melody in each word. The woman with the tattooed veins stood upon the topmost remaining stair, pale lips curled to one side, and two perfect eyes shining in glee.

Doa and Kati looked to Shal's corpse on the staircase, and the woman chuckled from above them, an eye patch dangling from one hooked finger.

"I believe you wanted this for your collection, Rojer. Straight to you from the herald's wearied eye." She hurled at him, but he didn't flinch.

"How is it possible?" he demanded. "Shal...you're dead..."

"Who's Shal?" she said. "You may call me the Capesman." She opened her hand, and the King's sword materialized in her grip.

Rojer Doa held up his hands in surrender as the Capesman descended the stairs, spinning the sword with casual grace. Her face flushed, and from her smile came a warning glow that tickled the length of her predecessor's blade. He protested, but his words thinned to a pained squeal when she plunged the sword through his stomach. His belly tore when she joined him on the stoop, and gore spilled thick and sloppy from the widening wound. Staccato gasps jumped from his lips as life drained from Rojer's body, but the Capesman, herald of the dead, was rosy with life.

Her teeth were clenched in a death grip, but it wasn't as cold as it had been in the past. The violence was merciful and her farewell, a vicious kiss. Her cheek was planted against his when she whispered: "You know the Capesman's mind is many, I'm sure. And let me tell you, this mind aflame with hatred for you, Rojer. As you die on our blade, know that there are dozens cheering within me. They are joyful in your demise, and very soon, the rest of Cartesia will echo them."

She withdrew the sword, and Rojer fell against the railing, his blood rushing and body frantic. His hands slipped on the banister, and in his mad panic, the rest of him followed. Doa slipped down and over the staircase railing. A yip of fright escaped his lips as he plummeted from the steps, down upon the glassy stalagmites of Skylark debris.

Kati gave her father one last look. After the last wet breath rattled from his blood-choked throat, she propelled herself up the sweaty, speckled glass to embrace her blushing sister. Shal's body accepted Kati's arms—even returned the embrace—but the woman who enfolded Kati was not her sister, not the leader of the Tamora, not a woman named Shal. Though the Capesman wore her sister's countenance, the energy was all wrong—muddled and unfocused— and Kati sobbed against the herald's chest.

"Beautiful girl, how can freedom make you cry?"

"Easy," she said. "Especially when those who fought hardest can't enjoy it."

The Capesman cradled Kati's face and smiled as she thumbed away a tear. Heat flushed through the girls' cheeks, and the herald said, "Death is also freedom."

Kati shook her head. "I don't believe that. And if it is, let her tell me herself. I want Shal to tell me she's okay."

The Capesman released her and looked down upon the hordes. The survivors gazed up from a sea of familiar faces she couldn't place, and placing them wasn't important. Nor was placating this poor mourning girl. She had a very important job to do.

She lifted the horn to her lips and the woman with the heart-shaped face latched onto her arm, tears flooding her cheeks and sorrow shaking every muscle.

"Don't go. We need you. *I* need you, Shal."

The Capesman's solidity faded, and Kati nearly fell through the herald's misty body. She vanished momentarily, giving the underground soldiers a shock when she reappeared beside Rojer Doa's corpse.

"You have the wrong person, Miss, and I have work to do."

Her fingers hovered above the former Chancellor's cheek, primed to stir his soul, but something stopped her. The strange young woman sniffled on the steps, the blood-spattered man with his tongueless mouth exposed while his words coiled around her brain.

"The dangers of the days but nearly gone," the man started, "Whose memory is written on the earth with yet appeared blood, and the examples of every minute's instance present now, hath put us in these ill-seeming arms." He stopped, his mind searching furiously for the rest of the speech. He pictured Shal writing the words in her *Henry IV* facsimile and lamented she'd never again hold the genuine tome she loved so. Grief shook his words. "Not to break peace, or any branch of it. But to...to escape...to embrace—"

"To establish," said the Capesman, looking up. "To establish here a peace indeed, concurring both in name and quality."

He smiled as he exhaled. "Shal..."

Her fingers floated away from Doa's face and curled against the other man's cheek instead. "Raoul." A whimper drew her eyes upward, and she whispered. "Kati."

It was as if Shakespeare had melted the cage of ice entombing her mind. Names quickly followed faces, tailed by the memories of a sad and strenuous life. But they did not grieve her; she was beyond that now.

She embraced Raoul, kissed both of his stained cheeks, and broke away to hold her sister, this time *as* a sister.

"It's you," Kati said, gazing into her eyes. "You came back for us. But—your father—"

"Marius came to me in the end. He took me to the pier, and as I stood among my enemies, I felt no anger toward them. But one flame raged, stronger than the Crossroads' pull, brighter than the amaranthine door."

"Killing Rojer," Kati said.

"No, Kati. It was you," she said. "Saying goodbye to you. It's all been for you."

"Then the King is finally free," Raoul said.

"And his killer forgiven," the Capesman added. "I know it personally. A part of him remains with me, with the others."

Her eyes shifted suddenly to the left, and she grunted.

"I have to go. A great many souls are waiting for me to show them to the pier." Her focus shifted again, back to Rojer Doa, and she waggled an extended finger. "Except one." The Capesman leaned over Rojer's frozen face hanging upside down, and scrunched her nose. "Find your own way, asshole. Watch your empire fall. Watch your enemies remake your halls. Alone, lost, a witness to the paradise that shall rise from your ruin."

"But you're coming back, aren't you?" Kati asked. "We'll see you when this done?"

"When you are, yes," the Capesman said. "As it will be for you all."

Raoul's forehead crinkled as he wrapped his arms around Kati. "Shal, what are you saying?"

She lifted her chin, and her gaze scanned the victorious underground. "Cartesia has a chance for a new beginning, and there is still much work to do. But I can have no part in it. I have a chance, too, my friends. I have a chance to do a different kind of good, one that doesn't require me to kill."

"But all those memories, all the Capesmen before you—won't it be maddening?"

She cupped Kati's cheek and chuckled. "Don't worry about me, sister. None of you. The fighting is not done, but for the first time in my life, I can say without reservation that love is not done, either. Neither life nor leisure nor hope is as razed as I thought before my death. The world can heal. You, Kati, my truest love, can heal."

The Capesman's solidity waned again. Despite Kati's numerous pleas and her frantic attempts to hold on, she couldn't keep Shal or the Capesman. The herald vanished, and she didn't mourn the departure as she suspected she should have—as *Shal* would have.

Back at the Crossroads, the wailing for a former life became no more than the echo of a forgotten song. She opened the door for enemies and allies, and with the last swell of Crossroads mists, she sat upon the pier and listened to the choir within. The voices merged and drowned each other out until they became a tranquil hymn that lulled into her a waking sleep. She had no want, no fear, no rage toward anything or anyone. For the first time in the warrior's life, emptiness and solitude set her free.

Chapter Thirty-One

There was love in death. Forgiveness and reverence, too. When the notion of searching for pieces of her old existence burned in her like itchy flame, the Capesman's mind dipped into pockets of remembrance. The voices snuffed the desire, however, convincing her to focus on other joys. Heralding the dead, witnessing the changes in mortal life—both well spent and greatly regretted—and most of all, watching the angelic breath of evolution. Glass cities gave way to forests, townships, to the communities that had been banished underground in the years following the rift. As the decades raced by, the dirges of war became songs of triumph and love that cleared the dark clouds over Cartesia. With the Council's drastic decline, the frequency of the Capesman's collections dwindled. She ceased visiting the mortal world for pleasure, and her soul all but forgot she'd ever been anything but the herald.

She resisted every begging request to take her place. She touched people she'd known, raised them from death, and escorted them home. And though some she'd known in life suggested she follow them, the requests were no more special than the others—nothing nobler than one lover wishing to stay with the other.

The requests themselves were extraordinary, however, because for Cartesians, love had once again grown into something to stay for. Not for lust or the sake of the human race, but for the deep, intimate agony of the partnership's absence. It was this revelation—that she'd leave the world better than she'd found it—that eventually steered the Capesman from her immortality.

That, and a recently deceased woman with a heart-shaped face.

The next corpse who begged got the gift. The Capesman transferred her powers and memories and once again found herself clad in a mortal name she'd forgotten until it slid from her sister's lips.

"It's time, Shal."

Kati slipped her hand into Shal's and, together, they opened the amaranthine door. Spent years seemed like fragments of someone else's life, and as Shal passed into the Crossroads, it felt undeniably true. Those bloody days were gone, and the battling woman was made anew.

She was free.

She was happy and loved.

At long last, she was home.

About the Author

Jessica McHugh is a novelist and internationally produced playwright running amok in the fields of horror, sci-fi, young adult, and wherever else her peculiar mind leads. She's had twenty-two books published in ten years, including her bizarro romp, *The Green Kangaroos*, her Post Mortem Press bestseller, *Rabbits in the Garden*, and her YA series, "The Darla Decker Diaries." More information on her published and forthcoming fiction can be found at JessicaMcHughBooks.com.